Oceans Apart

A Voyage of
International Adoption

Mary Mustard Reed

JKD Enterprise

Dedicated to my three wonderful children, Jenna, Kevin and Denny, my most treasured blessings; my mother Yvonne (*Thanh*), without whose love and support this book could not have been written; to all adopted children—may they be loved and cherished as the special gifts they are.

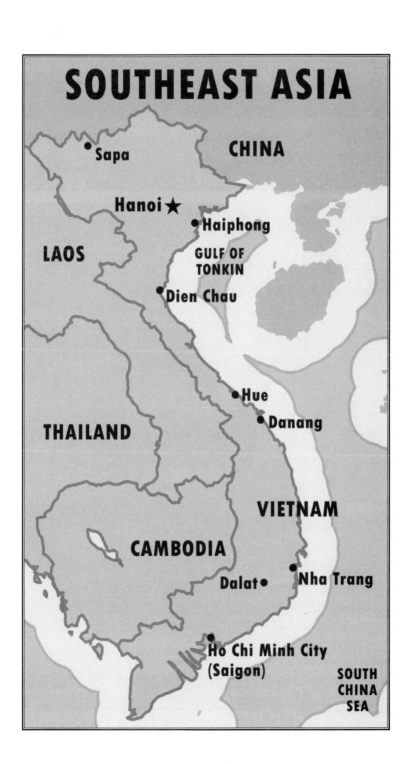

TABLE OF CONTENTS

CHANGING TIDES

A Personal Note from the Author

It is often said that to understand the future, we must understand the past. When I immigrated to the USA in 1964, I was told that I was the first Vietnamese child to be adopted by an American couple. Every Vietnamese immigrant has a story "to tell" about the hardships they endured trying to flee from Vietnam. Many of us have been traumatized in one way or another.

This book is the story of my pain and of my healing journey. I wrote it to give hope to children who have been abandoned and to enlighten parents who are considering adoption, as well as to express my gratitude to all the extraordinary people who were and are a vital part of my story.

Some of the names have been changed to protect the privacy of individuals mentioned in the book. Also, I apologize if some of the Vietnamese names and words may not be correctly written due to difficulties with the appropriate accents.

ACKNOWLEDGEMENTS

I especially wish to pay tribute to all the wonderful people who never stopped believing in me and in my mission to help adopted/abandoned children. Many have been in my life for over thirty years and continue to give me strength and encouragement.

It would have been an impossible quest for me to have completed this book without the love, support and involvement of my family and special friends.

My greatest thanks go to my sister and brother; *Phương* and *Việt Dao* for their endless hours of translations and support for my book project. As a family, we have shed many tears of sorrow and joy. *Việt's* ability to make us laugh during the difficult truth discovering moments was a phenomenal gift. He made the process less agonizing and definitely easier to pursue.

I am eternally grateful to the Eiswald family who opened their hearts and home to me, treating me as their daughter. Bettie, whose hugs and kisses were always cherished, lovingly guided me through every obstacle, never allowing me to be "down on myself."

Special *in memoriam* thanks to Fred who showed me the true meaning of a father. I will never forget his last words to Jenna, Kevin and Denny—"you are my grandchildren." They are forever embedded in my mind.

Thanks to my "sister" Karen Eiswald Klebba for always believing in me, encouraging me and standing by my side throughout my turbulent journey. To her husband, Rob and their children, Kailee and Skyler I extend thanks for the priceless holiday memories.

I am also thankful to the Agulia family for their love and support during the most trying period of my life. Thanks to Nancy Agulia Fiscus for sharing her spiritual wisdom and for being there with Candace, Christian and Chase. Together with my family we shared so many beautiful memories.

A very heartfelt thank you to Dara-lee Norris Davidson, my friend and mentor who has been exceedingly instrumental in getting me started on this project. Thank you, Dara for your enthusiasm, patience in reading the manuscript and offering pointed suggestions along the way, making sure I was not omitting important events. I should also mention my added "thanks" to Dara for keeping detailed notes, writing my story in her college years, and most of all for inspiring me to make "my story" known. To her husband, Mark and children, Jessica and Andrew—"I absolutely love being with you all."

A deep gratitude and thank you to Debbie Srery Weiss, who made sure I would be able to continue college and sorority life—if she had it her "way." I am grateful to her and her husband, Scott for their repeated generosity and unwavering faith in me. I can't forget their children, Jason and Lyndsey with whom we've shared many life experiences and fun vacations....

To my other sorority sisters, Nancy Procop Barr and Sheri Fox Weitzman, I extend my thanks for their love and support during the hard times. I am grateful to the sorority gang for keeping our "holiday traditions" alive.

I am forever thankful to the Augusta family who has been with me through thick and thin since my move to Orange County.

I wish to give special mention to Maxine for her unequivocal devotion at a "second's" notice. I have always said in addition to having my three darling children, the other amazing benefit of my marriage was inheriting Maxine, Frank, Adam and Garret as my extended family.

I would be remiss if I did not thank the Red Cross for their phenomenal role in helping me put together my life. Their persistence, loyalty and dedication to my cause were amazing. I could not have written this book without their successful intervention. The Red Cross is truly an exceptional organization.

I extend a big thank you to Nancy Genovese for her help in making my dream into a reality. Thank you for your patience, understanding and assistance in sorting out my past.

This book is to honor all of you who believe in me and in my mission! A big THANK YOU, THANK YOU, THANK YOU for giving me the encouragement I needed.

> *"We don't accomplish anything in this world*
> *alone...and whatever happens is the result*
> *of the whole tapestry of one's life and all the weavings*
> *of individual threads from one to*
> *another that creates something."*
> —Sandra Day O'Connor

The Departure:
Specter of Freedom

Tân Sơn Nhất International Airport
September 3, 1964

"Sometimes childhood ends abruptly, if not fairly for some children—so it would be for me."
—Mary Mustard Reed

The aroma of jet fuel was overpowering. It ran up my nose, burning my nostrils and throat. My eyes teared from the fumes, clouding my vision. Chaos and confusion permeated throughout *Sài Gòn's Tân Sơn Nhất* International Airport. There were crowds of men, women and children rushing to get from one gate to another in time to catch their flights. There were people joyfully welcoming family and friends and people saying emotional goodbyes to departing loved ones.

I had never seen so many people in my entire life. With my curiosity in full swing, I couldn't turn my head fast enough to catch all the action. I was confused and absolutely had to explore this new surrounding. Although I did not know why, I felt as if I had to be attentive to the turmoil, difficult as it was at the time to understand. Without even leaving the ground, I was already in a new world.

It almost seemed as if reality as I knew it was being demolished and rebuilt. Suddenly, I stepped into a strange world. It was a world of new and strikingly different sensations. There were dense clouds of smoke, odd aromas and crowds of people with their arms and legs in constant motion. Yet, everyone seemed so undisturbed by the speedy pace of the airport scene.

I did not know that this almost surrealistic scenario would mark the finality of a non-negotiable goodbye and my debut into a brand new life. Soon the curtain would rise on a very different scene. Soon my life would take on a new identity. Unaware of what the future would bring, I faced this defining moment with the fears and uncertainties of a small child thrust into an unfamiliar world. The winds were shifting, altering the direction of my journey, and I was set to sail on a very unusual course.

The sounds of airport life continued to intensify. I was holding on to my mother's hand, scared I would be lost in the bedlam if I ever let go. Feeling her hand in mine gave me a certain sense of calm, even though I was confused by the questions arising in my mind. Would I find the answers?

"We don't have far to go," Sam's voice broke through the buzzing undercurrent, interrupting my thoughts.

"I think the boarding gate is right over there," he said, pointing to a desk and a crowd of people standing in line with their tickets in hand. As we neared I felt my mother's hand tremble.

I was her first born—the innocent little girl she loved more than her life, and now she was entrusting me to Sam and

Margaret Mustard, total strangers. Her quivering hand betrayed the struggle within—the battle between letting me go for my well-being and desperately wanting to snatch me away, wrap her arms around me and take me back to her home.

Of course, at seven years of age I was incapable of understanding the depth of her inner turmoil and the intensity of her agony. I could not comprehend the heart wrenching pain that took her breath away as she came down on her knees for the final goodbye. Sadly, she knew in her heart that she would never again see the gleam in my eyes or the impish smile that brightened my tiny face.

Má gave me life. She heard me gasp for air. She listened to my cries and comforted me. She nurtured and fed me, and she loved me with the passion that belongs exclusively to a mother opening her heart to the precious infant she carried for nine months.

The overwhelming significance of the sacrifice she was about to make and the exorbitant price she was willing to pay in exchange for the chance for me to grow up in America and have a better life were unknown to my childish mind. But, feeling her extra strong grip, I realized something was not quite right. Something was about to happen that would leave me lost to myself.

Where is *Hiền*—the little Vietnamese girl with the glowing eyes?

The moment I stepped foot in *Tân Sơn Nhất* Airport *Hiền* was gone. She would not board the plane. She would not accompany us on the journey. Instead, she would remain behind, safe in my mother's mind and heart—but not with me. *Hiền* would giggle and dance again—but only in a memory.

My mother's grasp stiffened once more as she realized the separation was imminent. Each ticking second brought her closer to the moment of truth.

Sam realized what was happening and placed his hand on my shoulder. Perhaps he felt that one quick break would make the departure easier. Perhaps he was just in a hurry to get it all over and done with! His hand felt heavy on my shoulder—uncomfortable.

Suddenly, I felt a wave of sadness overcome my enthusiasm. My mother was on her knees facing me. A sophisticated woman of refined taste, as always, she looked radiant in her flowing pink *aó dài*. But this time the radiance was dimmed by the halo of sadness that encircled her head.

Sam continued walking—yet my mother would not let go. She realized every second brought us closer to the goodbye she dreaded and perhaps hoped would not happen. As the seconds passed I felt her fingers firmly clasp around my hand. I was immobilized, but more importantly, I was confused. My mother, however, knew the time had come!

"Come on, Mary," Sam said, pulling me away from my mother, "it's time to go."

My mother's face tensed and I noticed her lips slowly parted. Hearing Sam call me Mary instead of *Hiền* made it all real. I waited, but there were no words, just a few trembling movements from a woman trying desperately to protect her little child from witnessing her pain.

Moments later, gathering her forces she said, "*Hiền*, be good with Sam and Margaret. Someday I'll be coming over to join you."

The sentence ended in a long deep-mouthed sigh she never bothered to muffle. As the echo faded, I felt the force of her love.

While Sam tried to pry us apart, I resisted, turning back to my mother. He pulled harder until he disconnected us. I felt a hollow coldness as my hand slipped and hit the side of my thigh. I looked at my mom, then at my empty hand. I think she understood my thought—maybe even shared it.

"*Hai* and *Cô Cúc* are gone and now *Má*," I said to myself, "who will hold my hand?"

I fought Sam's pull and turned to look at my mom for the last time. I noticed she had slipped on a pair of dark glasses. However, just beneath the frame, I caught two crystal clear tear drops zig-zaging down along the contours of her cheeks.

"Má," I asked, "Why are you crying? You're coming to America, also. I'll be waiting for you!"

She looked at me one more time, shifted her gaze and released her sadness.

I looked down and away. But there was no comfort. This was the memory of my mother; the recollection that would keep me company through the many lonely years of my life.

As Sam was leading me towards the airplane I resisted, turning my head to catch a final glimpse of my mom. She was still on her knees, bent over, her head buried in her hands. Witnessing her pain intensified my sorrow. I wanted to run to her and put my arms around her. I could see she was trembling. Sam pulled on my hand, encouraging me to walk towards the plane. Tears flowed down my cheeks, blurring my vision.

Walking up the steps beside Sam I felt his hand, heavy and tense on my shoulder. Once again I fought the urge to turn around and run into my mother's arms. I was no longer happy—I was puzzled and I was scared.

"I'm going to live with the Mustards—*Hai, Cô Cúc* and
Má are not coming. I'm going away with strangers!"

Suddenly Sam grabbed my shoulders with both hands as if
he had intercepted my thoughts.

The entry to plane was just two steps away. Sam held me
firm. The moment we crossed the threshold into the aircraft,
I twisted away from his grip and turned my head just in time
to see my mother slowly rise to her feet. A cloud covering
the sun shifted and as she turned to leave, I saw the sadness
on her tear-stained face; a sadness that would eventually
fade—but neither in my mind nor in her heart.

The Vietnamese connection was severed—yet in the
bliss of childhood, I was totally unaware something had just
ruptured. Sometimes childhood ends abruptly, if not fairly
for some children—so it would be for me.

CHAPTER 1

The Vietnamese Connection

"Yesterday ended last night. Everyday is a new beginning.
Learn the skill of forgetting and move on."
—Norman Vincent Peale

It was mesmerizing for a seven-year-old Vietnamese girl energized with the vivacious imagination drawn from still untarnished thoughts to actually live the promise of an American experience. Although I knew I was going to live in a new country, I was not yet able to comprehend the time frame associated with 'going to live.'

Unable to grasp the concept of a 'one way ticket,' I could not imagine that my move would be forever. How could I possibly have known I would not step foot in *Sài Gòn* again? And, as a child, how could I even have imagined that I would never feel the loving embrace of my mom, or see her warm smile and glowing eyes.

As my mother, *Nguyễn Thị Thanh* slipped a beautiful pink dress over my head, I was unable to control my bubbling enthusiasm. I was unaware my journey to the United States was part of a plan without alternatives; a plan that not only would alter the course of my life, but reshape the *who* I was and the *who* I would become. In a sense it was the 'extreme makeover' that would eventually bury *Nguyễn Thị Thanh Hiền* and give birth to Mary Mustard!

During the ten months I spent at the Mustards' on *Chi Lăng* Street in *Việt Nam*, my mother *Thanh* kept a vigilant eye on me. Always attentive to my needs even though she had a six-month-old baby, *Bích Nga* to care for, she repeatedly sought reassurance I was happy in my new surroundings. And I enjoyed holding my infant sister, often rocking her to sleep at night in my little arms, as if she were my own child.

Anxious about the journey I was about to embark on, she awakened early the morning of my departure to help me dress and prepare for the trip.

"Hold still, *Hiền*," my mother said as she tried to fasten the last button. I held my breath, clenched my fists and waited until the delicate touch of her fingers behind my neck was stilled, signaling her task was completed. Pulling away, I took a big step that ended in a spinning twirl. Giggling, I ran my tiny hands down the sides of my hips. The crisp material tickled my palms from my wrist down to the tips of my outstretched fingers. It was still a new sensation—so different from the supple silk of the *aó dài* I sometimes wore on special occasions, and quite different from running around naked which was my standard way of dressing as a young child. Perhaps it was another inkling of the diverse path my life would take before the sun would set on this turning point 3rd of September in 1964.

The *aó dài* is a formal traditional Vietnamese costume consisting of a knee-length silk tunic top fitted to the natural contours of the body. Young children wear white to symbolize purity, and as they reach maturity the colors gradually deepen. The full length dress is designed with a stiff two or three inch high collar and has bilateral slits which extended to the hip line. The generously cut pants brush the soles of the feet and sweep the floor with every step.

"Come here, *Hiền*," my mother said, visibly moved to see her daughter in a brand new dress. "Let me see how pretty you look." Loving the attention and compliments, I obliged, skipping over to her and quickly turning on the tips of my toes as the bottom of my dress ballooned out.

"Do I look pretty, *Má*, Mom," I said, wanting to hear her excited voice tell me I was pretty once again. "Yes *Hiền*," she said, gazing at me with glistening eyes, careful to conceal the deep dark secret I would all too soon uncover.

"Sit down a moment," she said, "I want to slip these shoes on your feet." I ran over to where she stood, grabbed her arm to keep my balance and raised my right foot.

"*Hiền*," she said, holding on to a brand new pair of white socks, "if you don't sit down I won't be able to put these on you." I dropped my hand, looked around the room and selected a chair with my eyes. I skipped over, turned abruptly in front of the chair, jumped up and landed my *derrière* on the seat. Satisfied, I looked at my mother and said, "*Má,* I'm ready." Anticipating the joy of her attention, I extended my legs, playfully swinging them back and forth in a teasing gesture.

"Hold still, *Hiền*," my mother said, reaching for my right foot. Once firm in her grip, she gently patted it with the palm of her free hand as if she were removing a sprinkling of imaginary dust. I giggled and wiggled my toes because her dainty fingers created a tickling sensation when they traveled along the sole of my foot.

She slid my feet into a pair of cotton socks, then into the patent leather shoes. Though I had learned to wear dresses and socks during my ten-month stay at the Mustards', I was not fully accustomed to the western way of dressing. Filled with excitement, I hurriedly rotated my feet to get a better look, dropped my legs and stood up.

"Just a moment, *Hiền*," my mother whispered, "let me fasten the buckles or you will trip and hurt yourself."

I tried to control my enthusiasm, holding still until she was finished. Impatient, I sprang to my feet, staring at my shiny new shoes. My mother stood smiling; her large, dark almond eyes glistened as she shared my moment of excitement.

At the time, I did not understand that my mother's decidedly joyful mood was nothing more than a scripted role, painfully recited to convince me she also would be traveling to the United States to join me. Her enthusiasm and smile seemed so vibrant, and at such a young age I could not possibly have imagined that once I turned my back to leave, she would be in tears. The intensity of her inconsolable pain was far too complex for a seven-year-old to comprehend.

I noticed she had a pair of white sunglasses clasped in her hand. "Are those for me," I asked, extending my hand to take them from her.

"Stand still, *Hiền*," she said, smiling softly. "Let me put them on you."

I inched myself closer to my mother and raised my head to meet her glance just as she set the pair of white rimmed sunglasses around my face, making certain they were properly anchored behind my ears.

"*Hiền*," she said, turning her head from side to side to get a full view, "you look almost grown-up."

Since the lenses were cut from glass, they weighed heavily on my nose. I lifted them a couple of times, amazed by the stark contrast. Everything in the room looked dark green when I pulled the glasses over my eyes—yet when I lifted them, the softer colors returned. Thrilled with my new possession, I danced around the room.

Hiền," my mother said excitedly, "I have something else for you."

Surprised, I stopped my antics and stood at attention. "Come over here," she continued in a barely audible whisper.

"Coming, *Má*," I said, breathless with anticipation.

As she opened her slender hand, I noticed a sparkling object nestled in the center of her palm. I blinked several times in disbelief, perhaps to see if it would disappear as quickly as it had appeared.

"What is that, *Má*," I questioned, extending my hand to touch the glittering object. "It's a treble clef, *Hiền*," she responded, "and it's for you."

My mother unclasped the gold chain and fastened it around my neck. The gold metal felt cool as it brushed my skin. I looked down and lifted the treble clef—it sparkled as did my eyes in that moment. Once again, I did not yet understand the meaning of this musical sign. However, later it would have quite an interesting significance in my life. Whatever she gave me always had a very special symbol or meaning, and it was a reminder of the unconditional sentiment that bound us together.

I had my beautiful gold treble clef and the large circular gold purse my mother gave me before our departure for the airport. It was filled with my most treasured possessions. Safe inside the bag were mementos of my first years of life. There were pictures of my mother, *Hai* and *Cô Cúc* which were of great sentimental value and irreplaceable.

My mother looked at me and smiled. "How beautiful *Má* is," I thought to myself as I put my tiny hand into her inviting open hand. The stage was set—it was time to leave *Sài Gòn.*

We walked along an unpaved dirt road en route to *Tân Sơn Nhất* airport—my mother, Sam Mustard and Margaret. *Cô Cúc,* my nanny-chaperone, and *Hai,* my cook-playmate, accompanied us. It was a hot humid day, but I was much too excited to notice any discomfort.

As we walked, I was fascinated by the shimmering rays of sun reflected on my patent leather shoes and the clouds of dust I kicked up every time I shuffled my feet, trying to keep pace with my mother and the rest of the entourage. The scraping sound of the leather soles crunching the dust interrupted my thoughts about going to live in America. Not having the slightest time concept, I could not grasp the finality of this last walk with my mother.

Yes, I was going to live in America. But *Má* was coming to join us, and then we would all return to *Sài Gòn.* The thought process of a young child really has little if any bearing in time.

I kept up my playful shuffling until we reached the entry to the airport. I was having far too much fun to stop. And the memory of my dreadful bout with smallpox less than a year earlier seemed to have evaporated in midair. One moment I was living in a big house—then suddenly, I was waving goodbye.

My mother had sent me to live with Sam and Margaret Mustard about ten months prior to my actual departure. This move coincided with my smallpox contagion and the resulting deterioration of my health. With the blissful ignorance of childhood still intact, I did not know how seriously ill I was and how dangerously close I had come to losing my life. I was dangling from a thin, frayed thread that could split at any moment.

The intensity of the fever, my debilitated organism, severe malnutrition, poverty and the infection that raged through my body left me with a rather slim chance for survival. Realizing my survival was being compromised, my mother knew she had to seek immediate assistance. An uneducated, hard-working woman, she had very little options available.

Nguyễn Thị Thanh worked at *La Pagoda*, a restaurant on *Tự Do* Street frequented by GIs and other military personnel. The long hours kept her occupied until late in the evening, leaving her with little time for my care. As a result she was forced to depend upon trusted caregivers to tend to my needs and give her the reassurance I was safe and happy.

At the time, I lived in a one room, unfurnished hut with *Hoàng,* an elderly woman who survived from her livelihood of selling potatoes on the street. There were no appliances and no conveniences; not even the slightest hint of mid-Twentieth century technology. Indoors, life was lived standing, seated or reclining on the bare floor. Tight living spaces were shared with huge gray rats. They scurried about leaving claw prints and tail drags in the dirt. I remember hearing their alternating squeaks, screeches, chirps and hisses in the silent moments before I'd drift off to sleep. It was certainly not the sweet lullaby most children hear as they rest their tired heads on downy pillows at the end of the day.

Though the rats were part of daily life, "they scared the 'be-jeez' out of me," I'd say years later when describing my early life. It was an oddly 'creative' phrase, but I had developed a tendency to misquote clichés and reinvent popular American sayings; a humorous trend I never outgrew.

The inability to improve our living conditions kept us destitute and at the mercy of serious health hazards. Meningitis from rat worms was a widespread risk as well as Typhus from a contagion with rat fleas.

Outdoors, life was lived running around playing in the dirt. Sometimes during the monsoons I scurried about naked, oblivious to the danger lurking as the wind angrily ruffled my hair and blew across my bare skin. I considered it a game though often I was scared by the interaction of nature. The wind was a menacing companion, keeping me fearful of being knocked down. However, on calmer days I would enjoy the teasing breezes as I skipped and romped about laughing and chatting, often about nothing in particular as small children frequently do.

Then one day the currents shifted. Always playful and energetic, I suddenly became listless. The fidgeting stopped and the giggles were silent. I spent more time off my feet than usual, especially for a vivacious child who couldn't sit still a moment. Shortly thereafter, my mother noticed that an accumulation of shiny droplets had formed across my forehead. When she caressed my face, it felt excessively warm. My hair was damp and hung limply. A deep pallor spread across my face—it was evident I was feverish.

My hands were clammy and motionless and the constant vomiting was responsible for my exaggeratedly thin, almost wasted look.

A ruby red rash spread along the contours of my lower face, invading the delicate tissue of my mouth and tongue. It was painful to swallow and agonizing to speak. The skipping and dancing were now a memory, and the light happy chatter and tuneful chuckles were silenced. I was frail and feeble— so worrisome for a child who just days prior couldn't sit still a moment.

Frightened by the blatant appearance of ill-health, my mother ran over to *La Pagoda*. Although she did not speak English, she felt comfortable in the company of the young American service men and women who spent their free time in the restaurant, either getting something to eat and drink or just trying to relax after a grueling day. She was fascinated by the strange language they spoke and the interesting contrast of their drab military uniforms.

Quietly, she would observe their comings and goings. In return they treated her with utmost respect and courtesy—to them she was *Thanh*, the beautiful Vietnamese woman with the warm smile, colorful flowing *aó dàis* and gracious gentile manners. But they didn't know how desperately she was struggling to take care of her little child.

My mother knew I needed immediate medical attention. She also realized she could find help for her dying child among these honorable Americans.

Concerned and anxious, she sought Sam Mustard's assistance. *Liêm*, a mutual friend and high ranking military official had introduced them a few years earlier at *La Pagoda*, and a friendly relationship had developed. Actually, from Sam's perspective, it went beyond friendship. In reality, he had a very special 'fond affection' for my mother who in turn had learned to trust the older American serviceman. Convinced he would not disappoint her, the young woman felt at ease in his company. More importantly, she was confident he would do everything in his power to save my life.

Breathless, my mother ran into *La Pagoda*, certain she would find Sam enjoying a meal or a drink and chatting with the other GIs. She knew he hung out there in his spare time, and there was no reason to believe today would be any different.

The sight of a frantic young woman evidently in distress caught the interest of the soldiers. The room fell silent. The clinking of glasses hitting against the tabletops was quieted—the sudden hush, piercing as a siren, summoned everyone to attention.

Liêm was also a regular restaurant patron, spending his free time relaxing with a drink and a quick bite to eat. The men shared a common interest through their work on airplanes. Although Sam never elaborated about his professional affairs and was a rather hush-hush, close-mouthed individual, he claimed to be a mechanical engineer associated with the CIA.

Seeing my mother's frantic face, *Liêm* cut short his conversation, brusquely slammed his glass on the table, stood up and walked towards her.

"What's wrong, *Thanh?*" he asked, rubbing his hand down the sides of his khaki pants before lifting her trembling hand.

"*Liêm,*" she said, gazing up at him with the bloodshot eyes of someone who had been crying long and hard, "*Liêm,* something's wrong with *Hiền!* I need Sam's help. Do you know where he is?"

"What's the matter with *Hiền?*" he questioned, trying to understand why my mother was so upset.

Listening to her hysterical cries, he became concerned. Walking her outside, he accompanied her to find Sam.

Sam Mustard was a relatively tall man in his fifties. He stood about five feet ten inches tall when he wasn't slouching. Somewhat pudgy, his face was accentuated by oversized black rimmed glasses through which peered a set of squinty hazel eyes. His lips were exaggeratedly tapered, almost nonexistent, and hardly ever broadened to create even the vaguest trace of a smile. The only time his somber demeanor folded into a laugh was when he was in the company of his fellow parishioners from the non-denominational Church of Christ where he and his wife worshipped.

Receding at the temples, his dark hair, slightly speckled with iridescent silver strands completed the physical picture of Sam Mustard. Psychologically, he was difficult to know because of his aloof nature and lack of emotional enthusiasm. His voice was monotone and his manner rather staid and somber. Later, I understood the melancholy mood was attributed to his pitiable marital relationship with Margaret.

Because of his emotional nonchalance, Sam was such an easy person to tease and I was not one to resist the temptation, though he often seemed oblivious to my antics. Not a constant presence in my life, he was frequently away on assignment or preoccupied about his job and unavailable to spend time with me.

However, during the rare moments in which he would give me some attention, I would be encouraged to either sit on his crossed ankles or on his knees and he would rock me up and down almost smiling as my enjoyment became increasingly more evident. This was a new fun game, and it always got me giggling.

As I chuckled he would glance at me with the faraway, almost dazed expression of someone absent from the present. There was no doubt in my mind—Sam's communications skills were far below par—in fact they were practically nonexistent. Years later, I realized it was probably a profession oriented failing, the result of his alleged 'top secret' work with the CIA.

When Sam saw my agonizing little body, he lifted me from the dirt floor on which I lay twisting and turning with whatever strength I had left, unable to find a comfortable position. Realizing the gravity of my condition, he looked grim as he gathered me in his arms.

By now the rash had spread to my torso and limbs, changing from itchy, flat lesions to painful elevated sores. My face burned when the saline tears ran down my patchy cheeks. I was so frail and malnourished from the smallpox that even the slightest jarring movement caused injury. Therefore, when Sam bent over to lift me from the dirt floor, both my arms broke despite his gentle manner.

Dangling at my sides, they seemed disconnected from my body and totally limp. The pain was instantaneous and excruciating, then lingering. Furthermore, I was too weak and delirious to notice I had lost the use of my arms.

Sam put me in the car as carefully as possible to avoid any further injury to my already wasted body. Although the fever clouded my thoughts, I was never able to dismiss the impact and intensity of that agonizing ride to the hospital.

Sam's car was big and black. I remember a glass partition separated the driver from the passengers. At the time I was unaware of his supposed 'top secret' CIA work and his need for protection and security. Thinking back, I can still hear the constant shuffling footsteps of military men pacing up and down the roof during the ten months I lived with him and Margaret in *Việt Nam*. Later on this would lead to my bouts of 'ghost nightmares.' With my childish imagination, I apparently associated the footsteps on the roof with 'living in a haunted house.'

Sam rushed me over to the American Embassy Hospital where the doctors and nurses sedated me to appease my wailing and liberate me from some of the agony. I heard the echoes of several hushed voices while the doctor set my broken arms, encasing them in two rather cumbersome casts. When I tried to move, they felt like dead weights. Even the simplest tasks became a painful struggle.

It was rather unusual for a non-American, let alone an impoverished Vietnamese child to be admitted to the American Embassy Hospital. Perhaps my recovery and VIP treatment left room for serious questioning, since many other ailing children were dying in the rat infested streets, unattended to. Nobody scooped them off the damp, musty dirt floors, filled their empty stomachs with hot food and placed their sore bodies on clean sheets in warm beds.

Why was I given such preferential treatment? What set me apart from the other children running barefoot in the dirt? Why was a 'presumed' CIA agent so interested in my well-being? What was my mother's connection and relationship to Sam Mustard? Would these and other questions ever be answered? I had to wait many years before I would understand it all.

The exceptional 'event' of my recovery was certainly a curious enigma in 1960s *Sài Gòn*. Who would have dared guess, yet alone speculated about Sam's 'doting fondness' for the strikingly beautiful *Thanh:* a particular affection extending beyond friendship?

As a child I didn't waste too much time looking for answers. I was a VIP patient at the hospital and 'introduced to the marvel of a bed!" It was a wonderful experience, quite a change from reclining either on a dust-encrusted, foul-smelling straw mat or directly on the often damp dirt floor of the hut.

I was lifted and lowered onto the bed. When my thin aching bones hit the mattress I was surprised by the bouncy feeling. If it wasn't for the pain, it probably would have felt wonderful.

Meals were served three times daily, and I seemed to have a faithful wait-staff—like a princess in a palace. I was totally in awe, never having seen so much food before. This was certainly a different approach from my 'adventure' to hunt for crickets and grasshoppers if I wanted to satisfy my hunger pangs.

Growing up without any fear or repulsion for insects, when I was hungry, I would search for my little victim. Once spotted, without the slightest qualm or hand tremor, I would tiptoe barefoot and snatch it with my nimble little index finger and thumb. Satisfied with my 'treasure,' I'd pop it into my mouth and crunch down on its tiny body after pulling off the wings and severing its hind legs to enjoy the 'healthy' treat. Although I was not aware of the nutritional value of grasshoppers and crickets, years later I learned they contained more than double the protein of beef.

Once cured of the smallpox, I was dismissed from the hospital. Since my arms were still in casts, Sam decided I could not return to the hut. Instead, he invited me to stay at his house.

During this period of helplessness and dependency, I met *Hai* and *Cô Cúc;* two loving, nurturing individuals who took care of me from morning until night.

At about five foot nine or ten inches bare-foot, *Hai* was a rather tall, balding, middle-aged man of extremely slender build. Actually, he presented an almost emaciated impression of someone nourished only with bread and water. His pasty face and gaunt, hollow cheeks were dramatized by a set of badly stained, disorderly teeth. However, what he lacked in physical attributes he made up for with the goodness in his heart and soul. He was such a loving generous man, always there to satisfy my needs and wants.

In contrast, *Cô Cúc* was a young, slender, attractive girl. A head of smooth, silky dark waves severely parted down the middle, hugged the contours of her pleasant face. At only five foot two inches tall, she was a *petite* girl with bright almond eyes and voluptuous lips.

Cô Cúc dressed in loose cotton pants and pastel-colored tunic tops when she went about her daily chores. I remember squatting on the stairs and watching her serve tea to the

Mustards' guests at formal receptions. For those occasions and when she accompanied *Má* and me on outings, she always looked so beautiful dressed in her formal *aó dài*.

Although she was attentive and made certain my meals were prepared and I was bathed and dressed, *Cô Cúc's* influence in my life was not as influential as *Hai's*. Since I had a loving mom, I neither needed nor looked upon her as a substitute parental figure.

On the other hand, even though *Hai* was a part of my life for just ten months, he left a lasting mark in my heart and an equally endearing memory in my mind. He filled my need for love and affection and never demonstrated anything less than sheer joy to be able to accommodate my wishes.

When I called out to him, *"Hai,* where are you?" he would drop whatever he was doing and come immediately. The scraping sound of his short, shuffling steps always put a smile on my face. I knew he was ready and happy to grant my every request. I also knew that in just a few brief seconds, I would have a glimpse of his glowing eyes while he stood hands folded and head bowed as if he were paying homage to a deity.

My memories of *Hai* and *Cô Cúc* are vibrant, warm and endearing. *Hai* in a sense was my primary caregiver, the 'father figure' who was protective and focused entirely on his ability to please me. He was the 'doting parent' who dedicated his life to preparing my favorite foods.

Sam and Margaret Mustard's house was humongous to me—probably spacious enough to accommodate at least two hundred fifty huts. Of course, the standard of living in *Việt Nam*, the salaries and currency exchanges were not on an even par with the American; therefore, living in a 'big fancy house' according to Vietnamese standards certainly did not equate to wealth. The dollar would buy a great deal more in *Sài Gòn* than it would in Los Angeles or any other US City.

The home was a bi-level residence with an enormous staircase. Never having seen the inside of a house before, I was experiencing my first encounter with steps at six years of age. Curious and inquisitive, it did not take me long to learn and apply the step climbing process of running up and down without tripping or falling. Eventually, through endless days of 'practice,' I mastered step climbing. As my footing became more secure, I no longer held on to the railing.

The kitchen was colossal and walking around the place, I noticed there were so many different rooms—the house was divided into sections, each separated by walls of different colors!

Living in a one-room 'studio hut,' I was astounded by the maze of rooms and puzzled by the diverse pieces of furniture—chairs, tables, lamps and lights.

"What does one do with these things?" I questioned silently.

All this change was amazing to a young child. Often I would catch myself standing speechless surveying the surroundings. I'd hold my breath and wonder if I would be able to find *Hai* and *Cô Cúc*. They represented my security blanket—always there, reliable and loving. I looked forward to my daily activities—to *Hai's* desserts and his devoted attentions—I was his life.

I needed the reassurance only continual proximity could offer. But in Sam's gigantic house I sometimes felt lost in the distance separating my room from the kitchen where *Hai* and *Cô Cúc* 'lived,' as well as in the other areas of the place.

Of course, *Hai* and *Cô Cúc* spoke Vietnamese which made it easier for me to communicate with them. They were simple people, yet their familiar caring words filled a void in my life.

In front of the house, a wooden bench swing decorated and defined the entry. It was large enough to comfortably accommodate three adults. During my recovery, on days when nature was agreeable and cooperative, *Hai* would take me outside, playfully lift and set me on the swing.

Once he was certain I was secure on the bench, he would gently pull it back, then push it forward, gradually exercising a bit more pressure. Like the pendulum of a clock, I swung back and forth, calmed by the almost hypnotic movement and *Hai's* reassuring presence. I was in another world!

Often, *Hai* would call out to me excitedly, "*Hiền*! Do you want to play ball?" as he came towards me carrying a tiny red, supple object just about double the size of a golf ball. It was soft and pliable and sometimes I would take it from him and squeeze it in my hand several times before letting it drop to the ground, unattended. It would dribble in silence two or three times, then roll over and lie still.

"*Hiền*," he said as I lifted my legs to broaden the range of my swing, "are you happy? Are you hungry? Can I fix you something to eat?"

This was *Hai*, my faithful playmate and 'chef' whose mission in life was to nurture my body and heart—I had to be fed and I had to be happy. If and when those two condi-tions were met, *Hai* was satisfied.

Once again, I felt as if I had stepped into the magical role of the Princess of *Sài Gòn*. It was a 'hut to palace' fairytale. It was my story—and all because I got sick and almost died!

When my arms healed and I was finally free of my casts, *Hai* surprised me one afternoon with a special gift.

"Come here, *Hiền*," he said, almost breathless. As always the sound of his voice pronouncing my name put a big smile on my face and sent me running.

"I'm coming, *Hai*," I said, hurriedly following the direction of his echo.

"Look *Hiền*," he said, unable to stifle his excitement. "Look what I have for you."

The sight of the most beautiful red and white bicycle I had ever seen widened my gaze. I walked over to the new toy and ran my hand along the shiny chrome handlebars to see if it was real or I was just dreaming. When I moved to the rear I noticed the little black training wheels attached to the hind fender. Overcome with joy I grinned from ear to ear. Mimicking my smile, *Hai* seemed to catch my enthusiasm.

I jumped into his arms and encircled my legs around his pencil-thin waist. His large silk *aó dài* pants were slippery and I slid down a couple of times, hoisting myself up until I anchored myself firmly just above his hips. My outburst of affection was a typical father-daughter reaction. And *Hai* could not have been happier if I were truly his child.

"*Hai*," I shouted, struggling to catch my breath, "what a beautiful bike! *Hai,* I love it—I love it." The words seemed to echo in the peaceful surrounding of the early morning stillness.

"Just a minute, *Hiền*," *Hai* said, interrupting my cries of joy as he excused himself and walked away. I was just too excited to give any importance to his sudden absence.

When he returned several minutes later, a *danh từ,* a pale conical straw hat, was dangling from one of his heavily veined hands.

"Hiền," he said, walking over to me and setting the hat on my head, "the Vietnamese sun is scorching, and I don't want you riding your bicycle unless you wear this hat. The piercing sun beating down on your head will make you sick."

"OK, *Hai,*" I said, realizing the sooner I accommodated his wishes the sooner I would be able to get on my bike and just pedal around.

Sam's house was encircled by a huge, black iron fence, both locked and bolted for added security. To gain entry it was necessary to slide the bolt and insert a key to release the lock. Of course, I was not permitted to leave the property unaccompanied by an adult.

However, since the grounds of the compound were so extensive, I was able to ride the bicycle under *Hai's* watchful eye. Actually, I was quite safe considering the Mustards had a large trained-to-kill black German Shepherd, ever vigilant and at attention. I was never quite sure about his real identity, though I recall hearing the name *Niki* when he was present.

One thing was certain—if anyone tried to trespass, even with the simple gesture of extending a hand between the six-inch slots of Sam's ornamental wrought iron gate, *Niki* was trained to jump up and attack.

One day I was outside amusing myself in the garden. The dog was nowhere in sight. It was a calm, sunny morning and the only sound audible was the crunch of gravel under the wheels of my bicycle as I pedaled along the path.

Suddenly, a curious youngster approached. Perhaps tempted by the massive, confining gate, perhaps fascinated by the ability to reach in, the boy curiously stuck his arm through the bars. In a split second, *Niki* seemed to sprout from nowhere. He careened around the thick bushes and stopped short directly in front of the boy. His eyes were wide and clear, his ears straight and twitching, and his expression sinister. A set of sharply pointed teeth were exposed when his lip was drawn back.

Niki was trained to protect, guard and defend, and his intuition told him a stranger was invading. At that point he was left with no other alternative but to attack.

Before the young boy could realize what had happened, *Niki* sprang and anchored his teeth firmly in the child's arm, pulling and drawing blood from the supple flesh. The screams were ear-shattering. I jumped off the bike, shut my eyes and clasped my hands tightly over my ears.

The brusque movement caused my hat to tumble off my head. A sudden wind, like an accomplice in crime, swept it across the garden. I felt the hot rays of the sun on my bare head, but was far too scared to chase after the hat. I knew *Hai* would be close by, and I knew I was safe living in the big house with Sam and Margaret Mustard.

Sam's wife, Margaret, a woman in her early fifties, taught English at the American Embassy. She was engaged by the Government to work with the children of US military personnel stationed in *Việt Nam*. Though one would assume a teacher would be dedicated and attentive to nurturing children, Margaret was somewhat of a phantom figure in my life during the ten months I spent with the Mustards in *Việt Nam*. We rarely, if ever interacted either through conversation or displays of affection.

Actually, I recall a vague uneasiness when in her company because she had little tolerance for such an energetic child. In addition, she never made even a minimal attempt to cover it up. My exuberance and inquisitive nature drained her patience. Anxious and frustrated, she would often shake her finger at *Hai*, warning him in her shrill raspy voice not to spoil me with my favorite desserts.

"*Hai*," she would say in a scolding tone, "you'll just make her big and fat with all those sweets."

But letting Margaret's words fall on deaf ears, *Hai* continued to sneak me luscious coconut milk *chè* and other desserts, behind her back. He knew I enjoyed them too much to deprive me.

Vietnamese *chè* are not overly sweet and are frequently served between courses instead of at the conclusion of the meal. *Hai* always took pride in blending my favorite rainbow drink, *chè ba mâù,,* a multi-colored pluri-layered concoction of skinless split yellow mung beans (small circular beans enclosed in green coats originating in India), sugar, red kidney or azuki beans, coconut milk and drained longan.

Longan is a dark brown fruit similar to the lychee. The drink is garnished with strips of green gelatin. Without exception, every time *Hai* watched me sip the *chè ba mâù* he was overjoyed. He had the confirmation he had succeeded in making me happy despite Margaret's stern objections.

Margaret was much older than my mother, both chronologically in her physical appearance and mentally in her way of thinking and dressing. The deep-seated frown lines etched across her forehead accentuated the web of crow's feet around her eyes; eyes that seemed to be forever sheltered behind black arched wing-tipped spectacles. Somehow the severe look emphasized her demanding, uncompromising character.

Margaret's demeanor was in stark contrast with the youthful silkiness of my mother's sweet face, the softness of her smile and the warmth of her gaze.

Unlike my twenty-one-year-old mom with her dark, satiny, waist length hair and flowing silk tunic tops and pants that felt so pleasant on my bare skin whenever she hugged me, Margaret Mustard was a typical American woman of the fifties and sixties. Her head of rather dark, tightly curled hair cropped short was heavily lacquered to keep it from frizzing in the heat and humidity.

A *petite* woman with a well endowed *derrière,* Margaret usually wore mid-calf length solid white, pink or blue Dacron polyester or cotton shirt-waist dresses that swelled over the stiff bouffant net petticoats which were an essential part of the era's fashion trend. The tucked and starched bodices seemed severely constrained behind three-inch-wide belts.

I often wondered how she was able to breathe. Somehow the stiffness of her hair and clothing were in harmony with the harshness of her character and demeanor—such a striking difference from my mother's docile nature and affectionate manner. But the dissimilarity did not end here. And eventually I would discover just how radically different the two women really were.

ROOTS: PART I

CHAPTER 2

Flashback: The Family
1940-1957

"Strength does not come from physical capacity.
It comes from an indomitable will."
—Mahatma Gandhi

When tracing ancestral roots, it is interesting to discover the similarities and differences pertaining to the circumstances affecting the lives of family members, often hailing from different generations. Learning about my mother's life, I noticed there were a series of striking parallels between certain facets of her life and mine.

Similar to mine, my mom's story begins around the age of six. Born to *Nguyễn Thi Tài* and *Trần Văn Chất* on July 2, 1940, in the port city of *Hải Phòng,* she was given the name *Thanh.* This was the beginning of a happy time for my mother, even though many experiences and events of her first five years cannot be relived through memory.

At six, *Thanh* lived with her parents on a sprawling farm in North *Việt Nam.* A carefree child, she frolicked outdoors under blue skies and warm sunny rays that during the summer months would give her little face a golden-bronze glow.

My mother's family owned and operated a successful business which permitted a comfortable, affluent lifestyle. They produced salt and *nước mắm,* a pungent, salty juice made from fermented anchovies and other sea or fresh water fish. The finest sauce is made from the anchovy recipe and has *Cá Cơm* printed on the label to differentiate it from other less expensive varieties.

Nước mắm is a primary ingredient in Vietnamese cuisine, comparable to salt in Western cooking, *soy* in Chinese dishes and *shottsuru* in Japanese specialties. It is clear amber in color, has a distinctive heady penetrating aroma, and takes several months for the decanting of digestible enzymes to be completed.

The fish selected are generously sprinkled with salt, layered in wooden barrels, and left standing until a liquid drains from the spigots. The first dripping is considered *nhi,* which means the most refined quality and is usually utilized as a table condiment to enhance flavoring. A second or third dripping in which the liquid is poured back into the barrels produces a lower priced, inferior grade seasoning. This product is commonly used in the actual preparation of dishes to add zest.

In addition to the business, my grandparents also had about twenty-five pigs and twenty *cyclos* tricycle taxis, which they rented, adding more income to the already lucrative *nước mắm* business. Although the farm house was rather large, my grandmother, *Nguyễn Thị Tài* was in a financial position to afford domestic assistance—a driver and a housekeeper. This staff permitted her a certain luxury while my grandfather,

Trần Văn Chất, busied himself with the daily routine of managing the different aspects of his agricultural affairs.

Thanh's story begins with the *Nạn đói Ất Dậu,* the Vietnamese Famine of 1945, which occurred from October 1944 to May 1945 during the years of the Monkey and Rooster. According to the Vietnamese calendar, the *Tết Nguyên Đán,* Lunar New Year falls between the last ten days of January and mid February, placing the 1945 Famine between the year of the Monkey (January 25, 1944 to February 12, 1945) and the year of the Rooster (February 13, 1945 to February 1, 1946.)

Unlike the '*blight,*' potato fungus, responsible for the Great Irish Famine a century earlier, the *Nạn đói Ất Dậu* which occurred during the Japanese occupation of *Việt Nam* was a consequence of the aftereffects of World War II on French Indochina. This 'capitalist' intrusion resulted in a disadvantageous outcome, leading to the collapse of the Vietnamese economic structure. The military felt the impact when forced into a wartime spending cutback. Consequently, the northern region of the country, already unstable in sustaining provisions, was plummeted into a devastating famine.

The Japanese invasion put an end to French rule in Indochina, establishing an independent *Việt Nam* under the governance of Emperor *Bảo Đại.* However, the bombings destroyed roads, disrupting the transportation of rice from South *Việt Nam.* The peasants were exploited—their livelihoods destroyed.

Once the demand for provisions outweighed the supply, the French and Japanese prioritized their own needs and using force, gathered rice from the local farmers to nourish their troops. The meager remnants after the military had depleted the supply left the Vietnamese population with little if any resources for survival.

The devastating situation was not solely a consequence of the military's hoarding of food and the instability of a weakened government. Instead, many issues contributed to the disasters, among which was the destruction of the winter-spring harvest of '44 by an oppressive drought coupled with a swarm of fungus-infecting pests.

Whenever one crop dominates, there is the risk of an epidemic contagion, since different pests infect different plants. Therefore, once the rice was contaminated the infection spread, wiping out most of the harvest. As a result, prices soared beyond means, and people were left deprived of nourishment.

Although accurate statistics are nonexistent, it is estimated that the Famine of 1945 depleted the population, taking the lives of between four hundred thousand to almost two million people. Many starved to death, and countless individuals and children perished from the untreatable disease. The *Việt Minh* headed a relief expedition with the intent to bring supplies to the northern area and at least try to prevent death from illness and starvation.

While the peasants were cursed with the certainty of not satisfying their dietary needs, my grandparents were privileged to cultivate rice on their land and to be able to keep it free from infestation. This left the family with plenty of food in a country of starvation and scarcity.

However, kind and courageous by nature, my grandmother, *Nguyễni Thị Tài,* jeopardizing her safety and that of her family, asked the servants to prepare pots of *cháo,* a soupy rice dish, and distribute them to the malnourished peasants. She was fully aware that if the French caught anyone assisting the needy, they would be mercilessly executed. Nevertheless, her noble conscience not only calmed her fear, but outweighed the potentially threatening consequences of her actions.

Although my mother was just a small child at the time, she was greatly influenced by her mother's nurturing nature. Through young naive eyes, she observed and learned from the examples set before her. Today, she can still envision my grandmother's petite silhouette as she stood cradling a pot of *cháo* in her silk-sleeved arms.

"*Thanh*," she would say, gazing down into her daughter's dark gleaming eyes, "there are so many unfortunate people living along our countryside. We are blessed with all that we have and must give to those who are hungry. Always be good to people, *Thanh*—if you have, you must give."

Reared in this self-less, altruistic environment, my mother matured into a caring, benevolent woman. If she chances upon a beggar or a destitute homeless individual, she doesn't think twice about opening her purse to lend a helping hand. Feeling as if it is almost a responsibility to assist the less fortunate, she is never reluctant to give.

Thanh's memories of her father, *Trần Văn Chất,* are not as vibrant as the recollections of her mother, since he had joined the French Foreign Legion while she was still a very young child. And although she was unaware at the time, today she likes to think his efforts were heroic.

According to tradition, life in *La Légion Étrangère*, the French Legion's foreign section begins at the *Fort De Nogent* recruitment center in Paris. After extensive physical and psychological testing and a stringent security clearance, my grandfather had to face two interviews. These question and answer sessions are designed to determine the recruits' intentions and expectations. If all goes well, the candidate is asked to sign the two page, five year contract with the Foreign Legion. He signed the contract and pledged to serve "*avec honneur et fidélité*—with honour and fidelity," together with Algerians, Vietnamese, Madagascans, Spaniards as well as men from Taiwan, Mexico and ninety other nations of the world.

At this point my grandfather was indoctrinated with the military mindset and a comprehension of the discipline concept, which included a working knowledge of "The Legion way of doing things." Orders were followed without contention, contradiction or discussion, boots were shined sometimes as often as five times a day, and uniforms were hand washed with a block of thick, coarse soap.

Although most of my grandfather's 'brothers-at-arms' had enlisted to escape either a political upheaval in their native countries or personal financial adversity, many embraced life in the Legion as an escape from the past—and a chance at a new beginning in service for an honorable cause.

After pronouncing the solemn oath of fidelity, *Trấn Văn Chất* became involved in the *Cách mạng tháng Tám,* the "August Revolution of 1945" after *Hồ Chí Minh* led the Vietnamese Communist forces into action. Although it was called a revolution, the conflict reflected neither a high-causality revolt nor a wave of sweeping change.

On the second of September, 1945, just a few days prior to the Chinese occupation of *Việt Nam* north of the sixteenth parallel, *Hồ Chí Minh* formed the *Việt Nam Dân Chủ Cộng Hòa,* Democratic Republic of *Việt Nam.* A couple of months later, together with the Communist dominated *Việt Minh,* he initiated negotiations with the French

By now my grandfather had attained the rank of Major in the French Foreign Legion and was off to the battlefield. The last memory my mother has of her father dates back to 1948. Shortly thereafter, Major *Trần Văn Chất* was declared MIA.

After seven years of grueling battle in Indochina in which endless lives were lost, in 1954, the French Air Force and Foreign Legion forces under the command of General *Võ Nguyễn Giáp,* suffered defeat at the battle of *Điện Biên Phủ.*

For my mother, little *Thanh,* there would be no more kisses and hugs and no more delighted giggles as *Trần Văn Chất* would swing his daughter off her feet, twirling her around in a wide circle. She always enjoyed her father's undivided attentions. *Thanh* would never again see that special gleam in her mother's eyes whenever her husband walked through the heavy wood farmhouse door.

Thanh still recalls how he would stomp his feet several times before entering, mimicking his marching pace to shake loose the remnants of mud encrusted under the soles of his sturdy black uniform boots. The steady pounding sound, though quick and brief, signaled his arrival.

My grandmother was devastated by the loss of her husband. Suddenly and unexpectedly she was the sole proprietor of the salt and *nước mắm* business. Not wanting to disappoint *Trần Văn Chất,* she tried her best to assume his role hoping he would return to assume his responsibility. Despite her yearnings and hopes, this was an unlikely event. And as the days and months passed without the familiar sounds of his homecoming, my grandmother was forced to come to terms with reality—her husband was not returning. She was widowed and little *Thanh* was fatherless.

Though her memories are somewhat fuzzy, she clearly recalls my grandmother, *Nguyễn Thị Tài*'s incredible love and passion for music. Together, mother and daughter frequented a theater company group and would delight in listening to the lighthearted songs while they watched the agile-footed dancers swing and sway to the beat of the spirited music.

This musical outing became a ritual, and after delivering the pots of *cháo* to the impoverished peasants, *Thanh* and her mother would head for the theater. Actually, it was more than a ritual—it was a way of life and the source of some wonderful memories for the small child.

Eventually, my grandmother's health deteriorated to the point in which her life was compromised beyond survival. And after a brief illness, *Nguyễn Thị Tài* passed away, leaving *Thanh* an orphan—bereft of both parents.

The nature of the illness as well as the events leading up to and immediately following my grandmother's death remain unknown. This scarcity of facts continued to be a source of great frustration and sadness for my mother. It seemed as if parts of her life had just been deleted, leaving neither traces nor clues of any experiences. And yet, certain flash backs still remained somewhat vivid.

Thanh remembers riding to her mother's funeral in an auto traveling at a slow, steady pace, tailing the black hearse in which her mother's body was being transported. It was 1948, and throughout the years the impressionable eight-year-old girl was unable to misplace in her mind the stark vision of a long, dark wood coffin decorated with a house constructed of votive papers. The funeral scenario had a profound impact on her, even though at the time she was unaware this procession was part of the Vietnamese funeral practice.

Family members were dressed in traditional, oversized white crepe garments, their heads entwined in matching turbans. In lieu of black, white is the official mourning color in *Việt Nam*. Sobs, cries and laments penetrated the stillness to the accompaniment of wind and string instruments. The effect was dramatic.

Despite the rituals and somber procession, *Thanh* was unaware her mother had passed on. Her tender age left her unable to comprehend the meaning of death until she realized her mother was no longer a presence in her life. Recognizing the loss, she broke into tears understanding she would never again see her mother.

However, traditionally, it is common for Vietnamese, like most children to be initially un-accepting of the death of a parent. The dearly departed is laid out for viewing, and a chopstick is slid between the teeth to coerce him/her into a return to life as the children watch.

Following this procedure, the first-born child collects a garment from the parent's wardrobe, raises it in the air and waves it overhead, summoning the deceased soul to re-take possession of the body. This ritual precedes the ceremonial bathing of the body to rid it of the earthly soot accumulated throughout life. Once cleansed, the corpse is swaddled in a white gauze cloth.

In affluent families, the mouth of the deceased is stuffed with money, gold and rice as a testimonial the departed traveled on to the afterlife without suffering need, starvation or deprivation. Succeeding this 'statement,' the body is buried, freeing the immortal soul to enjoy eternal rest in the spirit world with the Supreme Being.

"Funeral rites represent a traditional way of life to the Vietnamese people. They are based on the concept of the indestructible soul and the close relationship between members of the same blood line. By assuming this responsibility, generation after generation retains the strong fabric of our society."
—Lê Văn Siê, *Vietnamese writer*

Several weeks had passed before Thanh realized the absence of her mother's presence. Recollections at this point in time dim once again, however, she remembers the sudden and unexpected arrival of six unknown individuals who moved in and took over the house.

The details of this 'invasion' remain a mystery. However, judging from the fact that when asked, my mother was able to name each person, I believe the individuals in question were, most likely, distant maternal family members. Her list includes *Thông, Thùy, Thanh, Thài, Tạo and Thục*—six people who drastically altered the course of her life.

Once enjoying the privacy of her own room, my mother was now forced to share her quarters with *Tạo and Thục*. In just a couple of weeks, her former comfortable way of life was transformed into an existence of privation and hardship. Stripped of her silk *aó dài*, she was forced into a position of servitude, at the beck and call of the 'invading individuals.'

As a small child, my mother was given the task of feeding and caring for the pigs. No longer the farm princess, she was treated like a servant girl. Feeling lost and abandoned, every waking moment of every day she lived in fear of the six heartless strangers who took over her life, replacing her loving parents. Fearful of disobeying her guardians, my mother struggled to complete her daily chores, taking care of twenty pigs.

The hardship of *Thanh's* new life wore heavily on the young child. Soon the neighbors, *Bà Phán* and *Bà Đối*, observing this daily scene and witnessing the signs of suffering on her unnaturally furrowed face, questioned why the little girl was forced into servitude. Answers were unavailable, and the situation persisted.

A stranger in her own home, mistreated, exhausted and far too young to understand the sudden life change, *Thanh* sought refuge with the same theater group she often frequented with her mother. Among these artistic souls she felt comfort, acceptance and the camaraderie missing since her mother's death just a few weeks earlier. Music and the stage always filled her with a certain calmness.

One afternoon during rehearsals, *Bích Hợp,* an actor and opera singer in the theater group approached the young girl. The singing stopped, the music was quieted and a voice penetrated the stillness—"rich girl," a woman said, pointing her index finger in the child's direction, "she's a rich girl—send her home!"

Bích Hợp leaned over and looked into little *Thanh's* scared eyes. "Where is your Mom?" she asked, puzzled at the sight of the girl unaccompanied by her mother.

"My mom is dead," *Thanh* responded in a barely audible whisper. "Can I stay here—I have nowhere to go and no place to sleep. My dad died in the war and I am alone."

The words turned into a desperate plea for help as the anxious child realized this was her only hope for survival.

Bích Hợp, moved by Mother's emotional request, agreed to allow the child to remain with the theater company.

Impressed by the girl's love for music she took *Thanh* under her wing.

In return, my mother bonded with the players, finding peace and solace. The songs and dances were engaging and compelling self-expressions that nurtured her artistic soul. Emotionally invested, *Thanh* was able to lower the curtain on her doleful memories.

The theater company traveled in four large trucks that to the eyes of a child were as massive and powerful as the HET, Heavy Equipment Trucks employed by the military. Two served as transport vehicles for the fifty members of the group. Besides actors and actresses, there were the production crew, stage hands and lighting/prop technicians.

Touring from city to city, the theater group entertained Vietnamese people in *Nha Trang*, the city of endless balmy sea beaches, in *Huế,* the underpinning of *Việt Nam*'s two rice baskets and in *Đà Nẵng*. Although the evenings were spent in small town hotels, *Thanh* felt safe, looking upon *Bích Hợp* as a surrogate mother. The two became emotionally attached, and my mother became totally immersed in the theater culture, enthralled by the music, singing and dancing.

Thanh blossomed under the influence of *Bích Hợp*. Eventually she joined the theater cast as a dancer. Now in her early teens and without any formal training, she had become quite an accomplished entertainer—enjoying every minute of it.

Loving the music and passion of the theater she was always ready and willing to perform at the least encouragement. I have seen many photos of the stage with microphones that hang down attached to wires that seem to be scattered everywhere. Much to the amusement of the other entertainers, when on stage, my mother who was more of a dancer than singer would sometimes catch her foot in the mass of microphone wires, and come crashing down with a vibrating thud. Though thankfully not injuring herself, she was lovingly teased for her clumsy performance.

Life was turning into a different experience. *Thanh* no longer lived in terror—the icy feelings of abandonment and loneliness were gone. But she realized, despite the newfound companionship with the theater group, she had to accept the responsibility of working to maintain herself.

At the age of fifteen, *Thanh* fell in love with *Tống Ngọc*, a thirty-three-year-old actor with *Bích Hợp's* theater group. He was a dashingly handsome 'older' man, a *baryton noble*, noble baritone whose powerful voice sent chills racing up and down her spine whenever he performed. She looked at him with admiration, totally captivate by his artistic charm.

Tống Ngọc was well aware of the tantalizing effect of his '*Don Juan*' persona, enhanced by a striking demeanor and gallant manner. There was no doubt he was a womanizer.

Smitten with his good looks and chivalrous manners, my mother fell prey to *Tống Ngọc's* winsome charm. In his company *Thanh* felt the protection and attention she lost when her parents passed away. Fantasizing about *Tống Ngọc*, she cast him the role of provider, certain the charismatic older man would attend to her needs, filling the emptiness in her life.

The couple lived together in a small run-down hotel in *Thành phố Hồ Chí Minh* near the *An Đông* Market in District Five. This was a tri-level market, selling everything from food, jewelry, clothing and furniture and neither as antiquated in architecture nor as populated by natives and tourists as today's *Bình Tây* markets.

Discovering she was pregnant my mother was overjoyed—a joy that would soon turn into sorrow. *Thanh* and *Tống Ngọc* spent five months in the hotel, until one evening when the charming baritone disappeared, leaving behind an unpaid hotel bill and the young beautiful girl, carrying his unborn child.

Thanh learned that her beloved *Tống Ngọc* was a married man who had returned to his wife and family. Shocked and saddened by his betrayal and abandonment, she faced the prospect of bringing her child into the world alone. Soon confronted with a demand for payment by the hotel proprietor, scared and without resources, she fled in the night having neither a destination nor a means of support.

Thanh was pregnant, alone, deserted, terrified and sixteen years old. She feared the hotel proprietor would contact the theater group to collect the money owed. Embarrassed and unwilling to disappoint *Bích Hợp* and the theater group who had welcomed her for the past eight years, she left, took to the street and lived the life of a poor peasant girl desperate to fend for herself.

Seeking employment as a servant, she cleaned cafes and private homes, and wherever she worked in restaurants she would remain and sleep, unbeknown to her employer. Sometimes people would feel sorry for the homeless pregnant teen, take her in and offer her a hot meal.

To supplement her meager wages, *Thanh* sold corn and potatoes on the street. Life was challenging and often the young girl spent the night curled on the floor. The rain penetrated her flimsy clothing. Saturated to the bone, she would roam aimlessly in search of shelter, especially during the dangerous monsoon season.

She persisted, however, for courageous and tenacious even as a teen-ager, she stood as firm as she could even towards the final weeks of her pregnancy. Determined not only to survive, but thrive, *Thanh* refused to accept defeat. Her strength was an unfaltering ally, always faithful, never abandoning her, not even during the darkest moments of her life.

ROOTS: PART II

CHAPTER 3

The Early Years
1957-1964

"Where there is no struggle, there is no strength."
—Oprah Winfrey

Reliving in words the thoughts, feelings and actions of my past, will, I hope, lead me to a better self-understanding. The early years are the 'who I am' that I had to confront once again if I wanted to come to terms with my identity. And in returning to my beginning, I was able to make the same journey.

It was nearing the conclusion of the final quarter of 1956. After several months of struggling to find work, food and shelter, my mother, heading to South *Việt Nam,* found refuge with a family in *Hóc Môn,* a little suburban district just fifteen miles on the outskirts of *Sài Gòn.* Swollen, tired and uncomfortable, *Thanh* experienced the kindness as a relief in her time of need. In return, to demonstrate her gratitude and earn her keep, she took on domestic chores.

As the days passed, however, *Thanh's* discomfort increased. Her breathing was labored and the least bit of exertion drained her. By now, my mother was in the ninth month of her pregnancy, and meeting even simple daily responsibilities became a difficult task.

Although the Lamaze method of natural childbirth had been popular in parts of Europe since the forties, it was not utilized in the United States until 1959. Therefore, in a country such as *Việt Nam*, seven years into the second half of the Twentieth century, it was decades away. Consequently, my mother faced childbirth without the reassurance of either spousal partnership or the support of a caring friend or family member. Epidurals were not in vogue; consequently throbbing, pounding, 'pull and squeeze' dilating contractions were faced without any pain deadening IV hookups to lessen the agony.

As a teenager and soon to be novice parent, my mother was totally ignorant about the birth process. She went about her day unconcerned, clueless about what to expect. However, one afternoon, nearing her due date, she was frightened when the amniotic sac ruptured, sending a trickle of warm water running down her legs. Unaware this was part of the process, she thought the final rush of gushing liquid equated with the loss of her baby—a child conceived in love with a man she adored.

A terrifying moment, the stress of her surging emotional state caused her to suffer severe, excruciating labor pains. Witnessing *Thanh's* distress, the woman with whom she lived summoned help.

It was January of 1957, and at only sixteen years of age with the assistance of a *mụ đê,* mid-wife, my mother brought me into the world. She named her tiny infant *Nguyễn Thị Thanh Hiền* which in Vietnamese means sweet, nice and tender. Although there was no official recording of the birth, years later my mother selected the date of January 24, using the prevailing weather conditions as criteria.

Emotionally, I never accepted my 1957 birth date, convinced I am at least two years younger. Now, decades later I certainly welcome any possibility of error that would make me younger. As the years pass I try to get around the truth by repeating that my birth date was not officially recorded. Jokingly, I tell my friends I am a few years younger than they are. And who can say my mother did not unintentionally make me older than I really am! Naturally, my school friends do not 'buy into' this theory.

I had first seen the light of day in early winter on the bustling *Phan Đình Phùng* Street; a street that would eventually play an important, yet uncanny role in the phenomenal unraveling of my life.

While gently rocking me in her arms, my mother overheard the *mụ đẻ* asking the family to pay for her birthing services. Fearing the midwife would take me in retribution, she bundled me up in whatever she had available to safeguard me against the humid night air and fled in the darkness. Thus began the first lap of my life's intricate journey.

To support herself and her newborn child, the teenaged *Thanh* continued to assume menial cleaning jobs, seeking refuge either in the homes in which she worked, or remaining after the customers had departed in the darkened restaurants in which she was hired.

My mother worked a full day and sometimes late into the evenings. Afterwards, when the last patrons had paid for their meals and left, she would put me under her arm and settle down to sleep on the cold, dirty restaurant floors, rolled in a ball.

Sometimes I find it hard to believe that a vulnerable young teen and a newborn baby were able to survive a 'life on the streets' in *Sài Gòn* during the late fifties. My mother had no adult supervision, no formal education, and no financial security—penniless, unskilled and illiterate, she was left with little if any possibilities.

Thanh was a 'child' alone with a child in a country and an era in which the rigors of single parenting were not eased by state or government assisted programs. Survival was entirely up to her street smarts and courage.

Life was certainly oppressive for my mother. Awakening each morning with a thorn in her side, and by day's end, after having made it through another twenty-four hours, she repeatedly questioned if she would be able to brace the fear of tomorrow's unknown. Would she be able to care for herself and baby *Hiền*?

Eventually, my mother met *Tư*, a woman who befriended her in a moment of dire necessity. Initially, *Tư* presented herself as a person of integrity. In the eyes of an inexperienced, naive girl, she seemed honest and trustworthy. Perhaps the teen-mother urgently needed to have faith in someone. Perhaps she was just a desperate soul at the crossroads with hope as her only option.

Tư represented a solution. Since my mother did not have many options at the time, it was tempting for her to entrust her new friend with my care. Not having to worry about me would certainly make her day less cumbersome and maybe even more fruitful. Thus, *Tư* took on the role of my caregiver.

One day after many long hours on the streets peddling corn and potatoes under the pelting rain, my mother returned home exhausted and famished. With barely enough strength left in her frail body, she pulled open the door and slid her delicate body through the narrow opening. The uncomfortable stillness of emptiness startled her. Standing in the cold vacant dwelling, my mother suddenly realized both *Tu* and I were gone!

The distraught girl cried whenever she had the strength. She found it difficult to sleep at night, not knowing where her child was. And upon awakening every morning she wept again feeling the loneliness. Desperate and heartbroken she searched days and nights for her baby girl. Exhaustion was her only refuge from the agonizing sorrow, even if momentarily.

My mother had no photos of me, and it was almost ridiculous to attempt to find a tiny child in an overpopulated city in which physical similarities among people were more the norm than differences. The only identifying element promising a ray of hope was the large brown birthmark situated on the lower portion of my right hip. But would this be of any assistance? To *Thanh* it seemed as if I was lost forever.

Frantic, my mother searched for *Tu*, fully aware that if she found the 'baby-snatcher,' she would likewise find me. It really wouldn't be that difficult—all she had to do was undress me and uncover the distinguishing birthmark, to verify my identity.

Unyielding in her search my mother walked miles, through run down and dangerous streets, stopping people passing to inquire if they had seen a woman carrying a small child in her arms. Determined to find her daughter, she searched throughout the village with the tenacity of a detective. She observed vacant houses hoping to catch a glimpse of someone entering and exiting with a baby in their arms. With bloody toes and tired achy legs, she returned home only to resume her search the following day.

I guess the Lord rewards persistence. Days later, my mother spotted *Tu* hurriedly leaving one of the vacant homes. Assuming she was off on a shopping errand, *Thanh* entered the house. The surroundings had a musky aroma of mildew mixed with refried peanut oil. In a remote corner, resting in a heavily chipped wooden crib was a tiny child, wrapped in layers of white gauze. Running over, not daring to hope, my mother reached out for the infant.

Trembling, but careful not to disturb the child's serenity, she unwound the first layer of garments. Gently pulling down the wet, soiled diaper, her eyes spotted the dark birthmark. My mother's prayer had been answered—I was back in the sanctuary of her arms and heart.

However, from that day forward *Thanh* was mistrusting of every individual, until about three years later while working at a café, she met *Tho,* a *cyclo* driver, and husband of *Hoang*, the street potato 'merchant' who later took care of me in the hut.

What inspired my mother about *Tho* and *Hoàng* was the fact that they lived near the *Tân Kiên Buddhist* temple. My mother, a devout Buddhist, interpreted this 'coincidence' as a sign attesting to their good and righteous natures. *Thanh* had learned to trust again.

About a year previous to my birth, my mother went to meet my father, *Tống Ngọc,* while he was on tour with the theater group. He had some free time and was lonely for his young, beautiful girlfriend.

In order to reach him and the theater group she had to take a small wooden paddle boat from *Bến Tàu* Port to *Thư Thiên* Port. Excited about seeing her *Tống Ngọc*, my mother never questioned the increasing waves that rocked the craft as she boarded along with about twelve other passengers. They sat squashed together in a tiny space. Despite the turbulence and overcrowding, the boat left the port. Midway through the voyage, it capsized.

The waves hit against the side of the boat causing it to rock incessantly. Everybody was crying and screaming. Most of the passengers dropped to the bottom of the boat. Many like my mother scraped their knees and elbows when they fell. The waves spilled over the side of the boat as the oarsmen tried to steady it unsuccessfully. It seemed as if it would split in half. Eventually, it tripped, emptying everyone into the water.

Rain was pouring down, making visibility extremely poor. Drenched, my mother felt her body tremble as the wind aggravated the coldness of the sea. Slipping under the raging waves, she swallowed large amounts of salty water which burned her nose and throat.

Fearing for her life, she tried to climb back into the boat. She dug her fingers into the side in a desperate attempt to keep her head above the water. Ignoring the pain of her splitting nails she held on until the water numbed her fingers, bringing relief from the agonizing discomfort.

It was harrowing tale for a young girl. What bravery she demonstrated. Yet, there was another facet to this remarkable story. *Thanh* was able to find the amazing strength within to fight for her life; a special strength she drew from her faith in *Phật Bà,* the Goddess of Mercy.

Begging the goddess to save her life *Thanh* promised that if she did, she would pray to her for the rest of her life. *Phật Bà* heard my mother's prayer—when the rescuers arrived they told her she was the only survivor.

This was a spine-tingling experience bearing testimony to the extraordinary faith and bravery my mother demonstrated so early on. What an exceptional and phenomenal woman she is. I really did not need proof—but somehow her life repeatedly confirmed the power of her exceptional survival spirit.

Spirituality is a major force in *Việt Nam*, a country of diverse cultures; a country which despite its communist politics has a constitutional clause guaranteeing religious freedom, as long as it doesn't threaten or infringe upon national security. In 1989, the restrictions were lifted. Scholars claim that *Mau Bac*, born around 165 A.C. in *Wu-chou* south China, introduced Buddhism to *Việt Nam* about twenty-five years thereafter.

Although, today Christianity, in particular Roman Catholicism, has risen to second place among Vietnamese worshippers, *Buddhism* still remains the dominant religion.

Like most of the prominent faiths, Buddhism has distinctive traditions which revolve around worship, meditation and a series of essential beliefs among which is the theory of rebirth and reincarnation. Life cycles are many and a devout Buddhist makes clear distinctions between rebirth and reincarnation.

The doctrine of reincarnation teaches that a person has the ability to reappear repeatedly in different body forms. However, rebirth is a reoccurrence of an individual's consciousness. It does not necessarily signify a return to Earth as the same being of a former life.

After many such cycles, if a person is able to relinquish their connection to desire and the self, they can attain *Niết bàn*, Nirvana. According to Buddha, Nirvana is "highest happiness." It is a state of perfect serenity where mental-physical constraints, suffering, yearnings and death are nonexistent and rebirths no longer occur. Although Buddhists believe in the reality of suffering, they also strive and pray for the end of agony and the onset of serenity.

Besides her prayers and faith, *Thanh* tried to improve the quality of her life by working two jobs. She felt the burden of her missing education and sought learning wherever she could—even among the American GIs.

One of her jobs was at *La Pagoda* bakery. The other was at the café-restaurant frequented by US military personnel. Since her hours were long, often from sunrise to way past sunset, she left me with *Hoàng* in the hut while she struggled to make a living to support her little family of two and be able to offer the 'potato lady' some additional money for having assumed my care.

During these years, my mother lived part-time with me and *Hoàng* and part-time in the restaurants in which she worked, finding spare rooms to accommodate her needs. I remember visiting her before work one afternoon. I was always so excited to see her and loved all the kisses and caresses she so generously gave me every time I was in her company.

She came to the hut to pick me up, and together we went to the restaurant. I was in my silk pajamas, all smiles and couldn't keep still. Hand in hand we walked over to the restaurant and climbed up the narrow wooden staircase. Each step I took resulted in a series of eerie creaks that echoed in the stillness. If I walked on my toes the steps creaked, and if

I climbed stepping with my foot flat, they still creaked. I
didn't know how to move without the echo of those scary
sounds haunting me.

I remember shuddering as my imagination associated the
presence of ghosts with the crackles and creaks. As an
impressionable child I believed in ghosts and always slept
with my head buried under the covers. Somehow, I thought if
I hid my face, I would be safe from the spirits roaming about
in the darkness of night. This fear resulted in sleepless,
restless nights, and my preference to return to *Hoàng* and
Thọ's. Even though I loved sleeping in a bed huddled together
with my mother, I felt calmer in the silence of the hut. At least
I didn't have to deal with eerie creaks and prowling ghosts.

Whenever I was scared, my mother tried to calm me
down. She would gently stroke my hair and sing a *hát ru*, a
tuneful Vietnamese lullaby, with her sweet melodious voice.
She cradled me in her arms when I was an infant, and as I
grew older she sat beside me, leaned over, playfully tickled
my back, and caressed my face ever so softly with her warm
hand. Then taking a deep breath, she would break into song.

"Con ơi, con ngủ cho lành,
Để mẹ gánh nước rửa bành cho voi
Muốn coi lên núi mà coi,
Có bà Trưng, Triệu cưỡi voi bành vàng."

"My child sleep well,
So mom can carry water to wash the elephant's back,
If anyone wants to see, go up the mountain
To see Mesdames *Trưng, Triệu* riding the elephant's
golden back."

In Southern *Việt Nam*, mothers begin their lullabies with the words *ví dầu,* which translates into 'imagine.' As a carryover from her theater days, my mother loved to sing. After she ran through her mellow *hát ru* repertoire, I would drift off to sleep, feeling loved, protected and serene. However, my 'ghost-phobia' was never really 'cured,' and even today the darkness has an uncanny effect on me. Somehow, I always get the creepy feeling spirits are floating about spying on me.

Life with the 'potato lady' was far from ideal. Although my mother paid for my up-keep, I couldn't help feeling *Hoàng* and *Thọ,* although nice gentle people were somewhat selfish with the daily rations, especially since I was always hungry. They never seemed to give me enough to eat. Whenever I expressed my desire for food *Thọ* would say, "*Hiền,* if you're hungry go out and catch some crickets for *Hoàng* to cook."

I was handed a tan cardboard box and told to fill it with crickets. I grabbed the box with both hands, trying to protect it from falling into the mud. In tears I ran from the house, desperately looking for my only friend in the village, a little boy named *Nhàn.* Although poor, his mother and father, *Ông Bà Ri,* often befriended my mom and were a comfort to me in moments of distress. Eventually, they opened their hearts and home to me, and I visited them often.

After listening to my cries, *Nhàn* and I went out, totally naked in the scorching heat of summer in search of crickets. As small children we never wore clothes because the theory was that they would only get wet and soiled anyway, so why even bother.

It was a fun time for *Nhàn* and me, and we ran about, knee deep in the slushy mud giggling, shouting and whispering at different intervals, as we looked for crickets. When we spotted them, we reached out with our tiny slender arms to trap them between our little fingers and quickly drop them into *Thọ's* box. Later *Hoàng* would throw them into a pan of hot, sizzling peanut oil and fry them to a crisp. Then we would savor their brittle bodies, pulverized between our teeth. The crackling echo following each bite made the 'cricket delicacy' even more delectable.

Nhàn and I spent hours together, and it was always fun to play our fantasy games. Attracted by the exciting sounds of the trains passing, we loved to run over to the railroad tracks and invent an amusing pastime. Leaving his side, I would skip across the wide steel tracks. *"Hiền,* you are now in North *Việt Nam,"* he would shout wildly, waving at me.

Despite our childish imaginations and the fun we had running about stark naked, life in the village was below the poverty level, especially according to modern day standards. Since there was neither electricity nor plumbing, many of the comforts we take for granted were missing. For instance— adhering to the call of nature was a novel process in itself. My 'potty training' ritual certainly was not devised by Dr. Spock and did not appear in any child rearing manuals. Even the concept of a Spartan 'port-a-potty' or old fashioned 'outhouse' was nonexistent.

I was trained to squat over two rectangular bricks about a foot long. They were large enough to accommodate the length and width of an adult foot, and strategically placed at what I assume was a 'tested for success' distance. Between the two brick 'guideposts' a hole had been dug. To correctly imple-ment this system, each foot had to rest flat on the hard surface. This game of balance kept the squatter from tumbling head over heels and falling face down in the dirt. Once I was able to squat with my feet on the brick, I was able to 'do my business' without difficulty. At this point the ordeal was virtually painless, although I did have an awful episode. One morning, while squatting over the bricks, I felt a sharp gnawing sting on my *derrière*. It seemed as if something had snacked on my flesh. To my surprise when I gazed down I caught the culprit flying off.

The pain, however, was dreadful, not to mention the stomach-turning stench from the accumulation of waste materials—a magnet for rodents, mosquitoes and other swarming insects. Several buckets of clouded water containing the carcasses of deceased insects and a rusted ladle stood beside the 'squatting station.' This was the plumbing system. The user would dip the ladle into the water and pour it over the mess—rather gross to say the least!

In pain from the bite, I stood up and ran screaming back to the hut, leaving behind a messy trail of 'unfinished business.' And although for a long time I suffered from PTSS—'POST TRAUMATIC SQUAT SYNDROME,' whenever I felt the urge to relieve myself, I would squat—it was almost a reflex action.

While living in the hut this did not represent a problem, but when I went to live with the Mustards in *Sài Gòn* and squatted in the center of the living room, in front of guests at a dinner party, it was a comical scene. Rushed out of the room, I was saved from a very embarrassing moment. However, it was obvious I had to be 'potty-trained' all over again.

Life moved forward. I was living in the one room hut with *Thọ* and *Hoàng,* sleeping on a hard mat on the dirt floor.

Meanwhile, my mother continued her grueling work shifts in the bakery and restaurant. One day while serving in the GI café, she met Bill Neal, Sam Mustard's best friend and colleague. The men had worked together on many military projects since the Second World War.

Bill was a good looking, all American guy with cropped sandy blonde hair and a witty sense of humor. Standing at six feet tall, his slender athletic build was eye-catching. Although he was an imposing figure to a small child, he was a gentle and charming man.

Bill and Sam, though long-time friends, had very diverse characters. Sam was a somber, phlegmatic type, full of himself and noticeably quiet. It seemed as if he weighed every word before he spoke. Bill on the other hand was gracious, extroverted and loved an engaging conversation. The contrast was striking. Perhaps they complimented each other in an odd sort of way.

When Bill spotted my mother, he was immediately enchanted with the young, beautiful Vietnamese girl whose dark, shiny locks extended down her back and never seemed to come to an end. Noticing she was different from the other employees in the café, he was intrigued by her class and refined mannerisms. My mother's well-bred initial upbringing was more than evident even though as a result of unforeseen circumstances, she was forced to live the life of a peasant.

In return, my mother found Bill's open personality appealing. She felt comfortable in his company and appreciated his lighthearted, simple, few word comments which were easy for her to understand. In return, admiring her tenacious persistence, determination and commitment to work for meager money, he offered his assistance.

By now it was 1963, and *Thanh* was no longer a street merchant. She was relieved when she realized her restaurant jobs gave her a more stable income. Recently cured from my bout with the debilitating, life-threatening smallpox, I was now six years old. *Liêm* had introduced my mother to Sam Mustard the previous year while she was working at the GI café.

Sam had stopped in at the day's end for a bite to eat and a cool, refreshing beer. From across the bar his eyes focused on my mom as she busied herself tending to the needs of her customers.

"*Liêm*," Sam said, trying to swallow the piece of bread he was munching on, "who is that gorgeous girl serving drinks to those GIs? I want to meet her."

With a quick wave of his hand, *Liêm* summoned my mother. Quickly she walked over to the bar. Her tiny, graceful steps made her even more endearing. There was a short exchange of Vietnamese words before *Liêm* introduced her to Sam. It was a 'destiny unraveling moment.' This meeting would be the beginning of a new life; a life that would redesign who I was and am.

Thanh looked up at the tall stranger and smiled coyly. Her large almond eyes glistened in the dim restaurant. Immediately, Sam was smitten by my mom's exotic beauty. "I hear *Liêm* calls you Yvonne," Sam said, leaning towards *Thanh*. He wanted to be certain she heard what he had to say since the sounds of rowdy laughter, bungled conversations and clinking glasses often made it difficult to make sense out of any words.

"Yes," she said, "you call me Yvonne, too—*Liêm* think too many *Thanh* in café." Yvonne was a unique name, and *Liêm* felt it was perfect for my mother.

"OK," Sam responded, "I'll call you Yvonne." And from that day onward my mother had two personnas—she was *Thanh* to the Vietnamese writers and authors at *La Pagoda* and though proud of her heritage, switched to her non-Vietnamese 'identity' when she worked among the American servicemen at the GI café to make it easier for them. It was the beginning of an important new chapter, although my mother did not have the slightest inkling how one American would spin her life around. My mother kept her private life a secret, and neither the Vietnamese nor Americans knew she had a child until my smallpox contagion and her need for immediate help.

Although not many troops had been deployed to *Việt Nam* in the early sixties, sounds of exploding bombs were a daily background for a life already filled with hardships and deprivation. One evening, after I had gone to live with the Mustards in their big house on *Chi Lang* Street, Sam and Margaret attended a reception at the Continental Hotel Saigon located on 132-134 *Đồng Khởi , Quận 1, Hồ Chí Minh* across the street from the Opera House in a bustling part of the city. Trying to sleep that evening, I was terrified by the graveling echoes of armed soldiers: their heavy footsteps on the roof terrified me.

While the Mustards dined, a bomb detonated. Panic struck. As the hotel foundation shook and started to splinter, frightened people poured onto the streets, desperate to get as far away as possible. War is never easy to accept, and although the country was in turmoil, living with the echoes of bombs blasting, whenever an explosion occurs, is cause for alarm and apprehension.

I remember several occasions on which Sam would speak about the war. He would repeatedly emphasize his consternation over the fact that the South Vietnamese were forced to adapt the American military mindset in fighting battles. However, pressured by the *Việt Cộng* from the North, they were confused and misguided, and like double-edged swords the *Quon Doi Nhan Dan,* People's Army from the South would turn in the evening and slaughter the same Americans with whom they were allied in the daytime. Although I was too young to understand the politics of the era, it was difficult to forget the few, but tumultuous opinions Sam did express on rare occasions.

Not long after, the Mustards met the Halls who were missionaries at the non-denominational Church of Christ. A friendship soon developed and Sam and Margaret were invited to attend Sunday service.

When I moved in with the Mustards, I was enrolled in the American Embassy School where Margaret taught, along with the other American children and included in their weekly worship. Later on when I began to understand a little English, I remember learning about Jesus and listening to the inspiring homilies based on the New Testament readings. I found a special comfort in the church and its Christian beliefs.

Musical instruments were prohibited based on the opinion that our voices were a sufficient medium to pay homage to the Lord. The congregation was small, but interestingly mixed. Though the parishioners were predominately Vietnamese, some American GIs and government personnel did attend, as well as a sprinkling of Embassy people.

I loved the beautiful hymns and the Halls encouraged me to sing, believing it was a great way to learn English. My favorite was "Jesus Loves Me," and I made certain I would memorize the Vietnamese words. It became my mantra. I sang it repeatedly—fearful I would forget the beautiful words.

"Jesus loves me! This I know,
For the Bible tells me so.
Little ones to Him belong;
They are weak, but He is strong."

Refrain
Yes Jesus loves me!
Yes Jesus loves me!
Yes Jesus loves me!
The Bible tells me so!

This was my daily chant—my prayer. However, sadly with the passage of time, I began to mispronounce the words, forgetting the Vietnamese dialects and different accents. Feeling alone and abandoned, the encouraging words reassured me Jesus loved me even if no one else did. I knew God would be looking out for me all my life—I knew that even in my loneliness, I was not alone.

One day, *Hai* woke me excitedly. *"Hiền,"* he said, his eyes twinkling, "we're going to *Đà Lạt* with your mother, the Mustards and *Cô Cúc.*" I jumped out of bed, thrilled to be going on a fun outing with my mother.

Situated fifteen hundred meters above sea level in the *Lang Bài Highlands* of Central *Việt Nam, Đà Lạt* is an evergreen resort of serene lakes and rushing waterfalls. It is about two hundred miles northeast of *Hồ Chí Minh City*, populated with predominately French colonialists and elaborate architectural villas.

Walking between Sam and my mother, I felt happy and serene. Several minutes into the stroll, Sam pulled on my hand. *"Hiền,"* he said, "Margaret and I are going home to America, and you will be coming to live with us."

"America," I repeated, with nonchalance as if it were just down the street. Not realizing the meaning of this life-altering event, I accepted the news with the resignation of a child unable to control the circumstances of her life. "OK, Sam," I said, dismissing the idea. I broke into a skip, tugging at both Sam and my mother's hands to get free.

I had to have documents in order to accompany the Mustards to America. However, my mother did not receive a birth certificate from the *mụ đẻ* who delivered me. When asked about my birth she smiled and replied, *"Hiền,* was born during the nice season."

In *Việt Nam*, the good weather season is between November and January. My mother remembered it was near the *Tết Nguyên Đán* Lunar New Year which occurs in January. It was important to have a date of birth to apply for adoption papers—and my mother quickly responded, *"Hiền* was born on January 24, 1957."

Margaret approached me as I slowed my sprightly skip to a walk, kicking up some granules of sand. *"Hiền"* she said, in a dry almost monotone voice, "come with me. Let's take a walk along the beach." I nodded my approval and followed her, my feet sinking into the soft mounds of sand.

"Hiền," she said, "when you come to live with us in America, you will have to have a new name—something like Mary Ann or Kim Anh. Choose the one you like best. You can keep *Hiền* if you want, but it will be difficult for Americans to understand."

I was excited about getting a new name. Ever since I had begun studying English and learned the nursery rhyme,

One, two, buckle my shoe

Three, four, knock at the door
Five, six, pick up sticks
Seven, eight, lay them straight
Nine, ten, a big fat **hen!**

I was delighted to have my name in the rhyme. But when Margaret explained the meaning of big fat hen by turning and slapping her big *derrière,* I no longer liked being called *Hiền,* because I resented being associated with a big fat chicken. Consequently, that day in *Đà Lạt, Hiền* was re-named.

"I want to be called Mary Ann," I said, thrilled to have a new American name. I refused Kim Anh—it sounded like people shouting 'come on' at me.

"OK," Margaret said, "you are now Mary Ann." And with the 'birth' of Mary Ann, *Hiền* was slowly pushed aside— buried behind memories, soon forgotten—even if not forever.

Soon I would bid her a tearful farewell at *Tân Sơn Nhất* International Airport, minutes before crossing the threshold separating *Việt Nam* from the United States, and begin a new life; a life like my mother's redesigned by one American— Sam Mustard.

CHAPTER 4

The Destination: America on the Horizon

"With the new day comes new strength and new thoughts."
—Eleanor Roosevelt

The PAN AM jet that would transport me to another life loomed ahead. It was massive, almost intimidating. The sun reflected on the large silver wing casting a glowing beam that hit me directly in the eye. I blinked several times as Sam held my hand while we crossed the threshold into the airplane, walking away from the life I had known for seven years.

Nothing would ever recapture this moment. Like the fading splendor of a dying sunset, all that remains of yesterday is its memory. *Việt Nam* was my yesterday and it would live only through my thoughts. Today was my reality and I would live it moment by moment.

The interior of the plane was huge. In the center of the first class seating area was a spiral staircase leading to the dining section. I stood for an instant, motionless. Always curious, I circled the plane with my eyes, eager to see it all. My gaze stopped on what looked like a big screen TV.

"Mary," the flight attendant said, bending down to meet my eyes, "we are going to show a film in a little while."

She was so tall, and once she stood up I had to force my neck into an uncomfortable position to see her round face and the cascade of golden curls dangling beneath her hat. Different from the *petite* black silken-haired Vietnamese women in flowing *aó dài* and the American servicewomen in their drab cord suits and matching green garrison hats I had been accustomed to seeing until now.

The flight attendants were all gorgeous—tall slender women dressed to the hilt in stylish pale blue uniforms, accessorized with crisp pearl-white blouses, starched for perfection. The flawlessly pressed skirts had a slight flair beginning mid-calf and extending to about an inch below the knees. The look was enhanced with matching hats and fitted, long-sleeved blazers decorated with gold buttons that shimmered when the girls walked up and down the aisles.

I was just finishing lunch. The menu selections were mouth-watering and more appetizingly presented than the hospital food. Unable to resist, I wanted to taste it all. However, with the limited appetite of a small child, I did the best I could, taking tiny bites of everything that was put in front of me.

"Look over there, Mary," the flight attendant said, pointing to the large drop-down screen, as I was reaching for dessert. "*Voyage to the Bottom of the Sea* will be playing shortly." I smiled coyly, nodded my head as if I knew what she was talking about and sat staring at the screen waiting to see what would eventually happen.

Suddenly, the screen came to life. I saw images of people; people talking and moving. There was an Admiral Nelson and a Captain Crane—and both men were under water! I didn't understand what I was seeing. The two men were riding in a submarine between schools of colorful fish and other strange floating objects.

I couldn't take my eyes off the screen. This was exciting. I had never before seen anything like it. Even though I was unable to understand all the dialogue, the distinctive sounds and bright darting images held my attention. I had stepped into a fantasy world and was curious to see what it was all about.

I sat following Admiral Nelson and Captain Crane for over two hours, until one of the girls with the golden curls approached.

"Mary," she said in the softest hint of a whisper, "would you like some milk?"

Before I could respond, a smiling girl handed me a cool glass of milk, interrupting my thoughts.

The crew was attentive, and I remember how delighted I was to see the large seat they had prepared for me. Since the flight was long and exhausting, it gave me a chance to take a nap when I became too tired to keep my eyes open, or two restless to behave properly.

I couldn't control my enthusiasm, had a difficult time sitting still and kept walking and skipping up and down the aisle, pestering the other passengers. I had to see it all. I had to hear it all, and I absolutely had to stick my nose everywhere. Distracted but still confused, I had so many questions, but not one single answer—at least not yet.

"Be good, Mary," Sam repeated over and over, intruding on my thoughts. It almost seemed as if those were the only words in the English language he knew how to say! Perhaps he believed if I heard them often enough I would eventually obey.

I had studied English for several months prior to my departure, and although I was far from fluent, I knew enough to be interested in eavesdropping on the other passengers. Undoubtedly, I was a pesky annoyance and I guess the fact that the flight attendants would smile, gently take my hand and escort me back to my seat, confirmed this theory. But I just wanted to talk. With *Hai* I would chatter all the time. Somehow, there was always something to say.

I knew that if I spoke I would not have to think, and if I did not have to think I would feel neither the sadness nor the confusion that took possession of my once happy spirit the moment I bid farewell to my mom.

Exhausted from the day's emotions and events, I stretched out on the soft warm seat after the flight attendant had lowered the back to assure more comfort. I dozed off for awhile, happily leaving behind all the unanswered questions and unfamiliar events of the day.

Instead, I dreamt of *Má* and my 'yesterday' in *Việt Nam*. Safe in my dream, I felt at peace until a "put on your seat belts" command awakened me.

"Mary, let me fasten your belt," Sam said, leaning over to buckle me in. "We are ready to land," he continued, "and you must sit still until the captain gives the OK to stand up. Do you understand?" I nodded and he seemed satisfied.

We were flying over Hawaii, and the captain was preparing to land the plane at Honolulu International Airport. I noticed the passengers in the window seats had their heads turned. "I wonder what they are all looking at," I said to myself, thinking it was far more exciting inside the plane.

Children like to imitate, and I guess I was no different. Following the others, I turned my head towards the window. From where I sat all I could see were patches of the most intense blue I had ever seen. In the middle were big white fluffy mounds of strange 'things' that seemed to be chasing each other at a steady pace.

"What are those big white things?" I said aloud to no one in particular.

"Mary," Sam said, assuming the question was addressed to him, "those are clouds. Don't you remember how the sky looks on a hazy day?"

Were these the same clouds I saw in *Việt Nam* when I gazed up at the sky on a misty day? How could that be, I questioned. They look so much bigger—and so close. It seemed as if I could extend my hand and touch them if the window were opened.

"Mary, the landing will be a bit bumpy and noisy," the flight attendant said, leaning over to check my belt. "When the wheels hit the runway the plane will shake—but if you remain still and keep the seat belt buckled, everything will be OK. It'll be over in a few minutes."

I sat up straight in my seat and waited for the jolt and scraping sound of the wheels skimming the ground, to announce my arrival in Hawaii.

It all happened as the flight attendant had promised. I shut my eyes when I felt the plane veer downward. Although I felt a bit queasy for a brief moment, it was more or less as she said it would be. We vibrated and swayed from side to side, bounced a couple of times and came to a screeching halt.

The page had been turned to a new chapter: Mary was in the United States.

This time I expected the chaos and confusion that greeted me at the airport. The scene was similar—people hurrying about, loud voices and lots of baggage. After we passed through customs we walked to the domestic terminal to catch the connecting flight to California.

"Sit here," Sam said, pointing to an empty seat in a crowded area. "I don't think we have much time to wait." I sat and placed my gold purse on the floor beside my feet— too fascinated by my surroundings to be concerned with its safety. I was tired and restless, but the constant movement held my attention. Unable to sit for any lengthy period of time, I would stand and wander off. Sam would immediately beckon me back to my seat.

"Stay close by, Mary," he'd repeat, every time I tried to roam about. "It's easy to get lost here. Anyway, it won't be long. We'll be boarding soon."

I'd sit still awhile, until my restless childish nature would get me jumping to my feet.

"OK Mary," Sam said, rising and turning his head to see if Margaret was ready, "get your things—it's time to go."

When I bent over and extended my hand under the seat to get my purse, I felt the coolness of nothing. I tried again, wildly moving my arm from left to right in wide circles—still nothing. I jumped off the seat, got down on my hands and knees and peered under the seat. It was gone!

"My purse—my purse," I cried, "it's missing! My purse is gone." I was breathless and sobbing, realizing my treasured possessions were in the bag. Now, even my memories of *Má, Hai and Cô Cúc* were taken from me.

"Where did you leave the purse?" Sam questioned, trying to find a clue that would help us find it.

"I put it right here under the seat," I stammered in Vietnamese mixed with the sparse English words in my vocabulary. I pointed my shaking finger to the exact spot in which I had placed the purse.

"There! Over there!" I said. Sam looked down and immediately understood what had happened. However, he went to the authorities and requested an announcement be made over the loud speaker, asking to have it returned should someone find it.

"Mary," Sam said after several minutes had passed, "what was in the bag?"

"Photos—*Má, Hai, Cô Cúc,* photos—photos—*Má's* photo," I muttered between the sobs, too upset to speak a full sentence in any language.

Although there was nothing of monetary value, for me it was a devastating loss. The pictures of my mom were gone as well as those of *Hai* and *Cô Cúc* .

It was almost as if I was brutally awakened from a beautiful dream and thrown into a dark, gloomy reality.

"*Má* will be furious with me," I thought to myself, sobbing, "when she comes here and finds out I lost the purse. How could I be such a stupid little girl? How could I loose something *Má* gave me?"

The more I blamed myself for being so careless, the faster the tears rolled down my cheeks. Sam tried his best to calm me until we boarded the plane en route to San Francisco.

Although the second aircraft was smaller, not as elaborately decorated as the first and did not offer the same comforts, I was far too tired and upset to dwell on the differences. Instead, I withdrew into a silent world. My outgoing personality was quieted. My smile faded and my childish curiosity as well as my appetite seemed lost.

Though I did not know I was already in the United States, the excitement of my 'going to live in America' was gone. My happy, up-beat thoughts were suddenly laced with sad undertones. I questioned why I had to leave behind a perfect life in *Sài Gòn*.

I was cured of the smallpox. I was healthy and strong. I was happy living at the Mustards' with *Hai* and *Cô Cúc*. And above all, I was excited to see my mother every day when she came to visit before going to work.

Why did I have to go to another country—and for what? Why me and not my little half-sister?

These were the 'ten million dollar questions;' the puzzling unknowns that would haunt me well into adulthood; questions that would remain unanswered for decades.

Sam fastened my seat belt, once again cutting through my confusing thoughts. This time I did not turn my head to look at the big white clouds. Instead, I shut my eyes and waited for the jolt and the swishing sound of the wheels slapping the runway.

By the time we landed at SFO, San Francisco International Airport, my head was throbbing from the tears and from my stubborn refusal to eat. I was restless and missed *Hai, Cô Cúc* and my mom.

Sam went to collect the luggage and told us to meet him at the entry. Margaret extended her arm and reached for my hand. "Come Mary," she said, "hold tight so you won't get lost." Without verbally acknowledging her comment, I wrapped my tiny fingers around her fleshy hand.

Although Margaret's grip represented safety and security, it lacked the emotional intensity of my mom's warm, passionate grasp. It was, however, a convenient support. I clung to her and quickened my steps to keep pace.

Actually, my memories of Margaret during the trip were and are hazy and vague. I know she was present, but her role and intervention were not as defined or intense in my mind as Sam's. He was undoubtedly the major player—at least at this point in time. And my affection was predominately for him.

Margaret and I walked over to where Sam was waiting. The sudden vision of my big yellow Samsonite luggage put a faint smile on my face.

"At least I did not lose my bag," I said to myself, thankful I had not put all my personal mementos in the gold purse. At the last minute I had stashed some additional photos in the suitcase. I now realized this 'important' piece of luggage contained more of my treasures—among which was the one and only photo of my mom and me standing together.

Gazing at the bag, I recalled how *Má* had taken a last long look at the picture, smiled and gently slid it into a tri-fold wallet sized folder between her photo and a photo of myself.

Once outside the crisp wind tossed my hair and seemed to reinvigorate my spirit. It felt good to be able to fill my lungs with some fresh air after the endless hours spent in flight and roaming through stuffy airports. It felt refreshing to be outdoors and standing on my feet.

My recently repressed curiosity inflated. I twisted my head to catch a look at the new surroundings. Although I had already landed at the Honolulu Airport, it was just the first part of the journey to my final destination. But, now I was seeing America for the first time.

I had not seen my mom in over twenty-four hours. I missed the warmth and security of her reassuring hand holding me tight. I missed her big, dark, glowing eyes, savoring my every move. I missed her attentions, her caresses and her love. I felt so alone in this labyrinthine maze of odd faces, strange sounds and unfamiliar things. Here I was a defenseless Asian girl in a totally different society.

Today I was an outsider, but would I ever feel at home? Would I ever 'belong' to someone or someplace—and if so what price would I have to pay to become Mary Mustard?

The sounds of horns tooting and tires skimming the pavement were startling—likewise the fast pace of the cars traveling up and down the highway. They looked so big and scary.

In *Việt Nam* people travel either on foot, bicycle or the *xích lô* cyclo, a type of 'taxi vehicle' pedaled for speed. The driver sits up front. Behind him there is a wooden bench wide enough to accommodate two adults. A rectangular roof protects the passengers from the scorching sun. Apart from Sam's black car, this was the only vehicle of transportation I knew.

Margaret Mustard took my hand. "Let's go, Mary," she said, "Bob is waiting for us."

Hand in hand we walked towards a 1959 white Chevrolet. I saw Bob, a tall, slender, handsome young man, nineteen years my senior, jump out.

"Hi Mom," he said, greeting Margaret and giving me a big hug. We had met during the ten months in which I lived with the Mustards in *Việt Nam*. Bob seemed happy to see me. He was a familiar face in a world of strangers. Already an adult, he no longer lived with the Mustards. Although he was not a constant in my life, his presence was reassuring. However, at his parents' request, he had come to the airport to help with the luggage and drive us home.

Bob shut the front door just as I was inspecting the car. It was huge—so huge it looked like the submarine I had seen in *Voyage to the Bottom of the Sea*. The Chevrolet was a six window model, typical of the era, with glistening chrome trim. Since I had lost my pretty white sunglasses when my bag was stolen, I was thankful the dusk had softened the sun's glare into an almost shadowy darkness.

We followed Bob to the back of the car. Two gigantic bat wings seemed to sprout from both sides of the trunk. Beneath each wing was an oblong red light that looked like a pair of glistening cat eyes. I had never before seen anything like this, and felt somewhat overpowered by it all. I kept my gaze focused on the dazzling red lights, still puzzled by it all.

When Sam arrived with the luggage, Bob helped him slide the bags into the trunk.

"Come over here, Mary," Sam said, opening the rear door. I peered in—everything was red; the seats, the carpet and the ceiling. I climbed in, slid along the cool leather seat and settled down beside the window. Sam jumped in, shut the door and we took off.

The drive on the freeway was terrorizing. The incessant procession of speeding cars with their blinding red and white lights racing up and down, one behind the other, petrified me.

"Would they be able to stay in a straight line without hitting us?" I said to myself. Every time a car passed I would duck down, as if I were dodging a dangerous flying object coming directly at me.

My stomach somersaulted. Not having the protection of a seat belt, I caught myself sliding forward in my seat. Grabbing on to the back of the driver's seat, I jumped up and sat Indian style on the floor, burying my face in my hands.

"At least now I don't have to see the cars racing towards me," I thought.

The blinding headlights no longer represented a threat. If I couldn't see them they would not collide with us: the reasoning of a small child, in a strange new world, scared to death by so many unknowns.

I wanted Sam to stop the car. I wanted to get out. I wanted to walk. I wanted to see *Hai's* smile and hear his lightedhearted, almost musical voice. I wanted one of his delicious *chè*. I even wanted to see *Niki* again, with his wagging, bushy tail. And above all, I wanted to run back into my mother's arms. I missed her so much—it hurt.

Sam's window was open midway. I turned my head to catch the swiftness of the wind on my face. For a brief moment, the impact took my breath away. The evening air smelled of fuel bringing me back to yesterday's journey from Sam's house to *Tân Sơn Nhất* Airport. Once again, there was that familiar scent.

I sat down, almost listless. Weary from the travel, lack of sleep and the late hour, I felt totally drained. My emotions had spun around on a carousel and come to an abrupt halt. The tears stopped, and I seemed almost unresponsive. From an energetic, alert and spirited child, I turned into a lethargic, apathetic little girl, resigned to just go with the flow and do as I was told.

"Are we there yet, Sam?" I asked, anxious to just lie down and drift off to sleep without any interruptions. I just wanted a reprieve from the discomfort of the endless journey.

"Not yet, Mary," Sam responded, "but it won't be long now."

I waited all of three seconds and called out again, "Sam, are we there yet?" My fussing and insistence shortened his patience. I was becoming a nuisance. Sam, on the other hand, was too tired to keep me appeased.

The tears rolled down my cheeks as if they were in competition with the speeding cars passing us by. Again, I clapped my palms over my ears and shut my eyes in a childish attempt to block out my surroundings. However, unable to lower the curtain on this scary scene, I behaved like small, terrified child and shouted in my native Vietnamese, above the noise of the San Francisco traffic.

"Where is my mom? I want to go home. I want to go to *Sài Gòn—Sài Gòn!*"

The horns quieted and the sounds of speeding cars were silenced. I untwined my legs, stood up and peered out the window. We had exited the freeway and were cruising down a two lane road in San Jose. The onrush of traffic had ceased, and one or two other vehicles were passing from the opposite direction.

"We're here," Sam announced, pulling into a circular driveway. My curiosity returned. The house stood humbly in the evening darkness. It was much smaller than Sam's house in *Sài Gòn.* There were no huge wrought iron gates, no swing swaying in the entry and no *Niki* to greet us with his excited bark and wagging tail.

Sam jumped out, darted over to the other side of the car and opened the door. When Margaret was on her feet, he reached in and pulled me out. The cooling late summer breeze felt refreshing on my tired face. As I took a deep breath, I welcomed the fresh aroma of the clean, crisp air. Above all, I was so happy to be able to freely walk around after the long, confining trip.

The house, at *2159 Casa Mia Drive*, my first in the United States, unlike the one in *Việt Nam* was built on one level. There were three bedrooms, a living room, dining area, kitchen and two baths. It was modestly and sparsely decorated and quite a striking contrast to the Mustards' Vietnamese 'mansion.'

When I walked into the front door my eyes immediately focused on a large TV set into a wood cabinet. The screen looked a bit like the one on the airplane except it was smaller. I wondered if I would be able to see Admiral Nelson and Captain Crane in their submarine.

Turning right, I noticed the kitchen. There was a tiny window situated just above the sink offering a view of the circular driveway and the street. This window eventually became a beacon of light in my life, because it permitted me to observe the comings and goings of our neighbors, the Brown Family.

Since the window was built close to the ceiling, I had to drag a stool over to the sink, climb up and kneel on the counter top in order to peek out. However, it was worth the effort as it afforded me the opportunity to spy on the neighbors. Whenever I noticed their car pull into the driveway or spotted one of them in the yard, I would run over for a visit.

I was in America with Sam and Margaret Mustard. They were my family now. If I was to be nurtured, loved and tended to—if my needs were to be satisfied, it would have to be the responsibility of my new American parents.

My life was in their hands. As a young, vulnerable child, I was totally and unconditionally dependent on them.

I was exhausted, but as I watched Sam and Margaret pull their luggage into the living room I thought how dramatically my life had changed in one year. I moved from a one room, unfurnished grass hut into a huge guarded 'mansion' with *Hai* and *Cô Cúc* to take care of my every wish and need.

Now, I was in a new country where no one spoke Vietnamese. The people were diverse. The sounds and smells were different. I felt so uneasy and apprehensive. It seemed as if in just a few hours I was stripped of everything familiar and secure.

As soon as my head hit the pillow I was snatched from the confusion and uncertainty. I was safe in my world of deep sleep—at least for a few short hours.

When I awoke the following morning, I found the silence disturbing. The familiar sounds of Vietnamese chatter enhanced by *Hai's* melodious voice were missing. I sat upright in my little bed slowly realizing the spicy aroma of egg rolls was substituted by the stale, musky odor of a house that had been uninhabited for quite some time.

I looked towards the door, remembering how excited I always felt counting the seconds until a smiling *Hai* would appear in the doorway to walk me downstairs to the kitchen. Many times I would just bolt from my bed, dash down the stairs and extend my arms for *Hai* or *Cô Cúc* to lift me to my seat and serve me breakfast.

This morning no one greeted me. The shuffling of *Hai's* rubber scandals had sound and movement only in my imagination. A sudden melancholy interrupted my memories as I realized the joy and happiness I lived in *Việt Nam* were gone.

I got out of bed and went to the kitchen. The smell of fresh brewed coffee was not a fair substitute for the appetizing fragrance of Vietnamese specialties. But there would be new aromas and different customs to learn.

Margaret was standing in front of the stove looking rather pensive and somber. I wondered why she always looked so forlorn. Her forsaken demeanor puzzled me. However, during the ten months we spent together in *Việt Nam*, I had seen her interact with Bob and realized her cool, emotionally secluded manner was just part of her character. She was neither a warm nor passionate person, but a woman unable to physically demonstrate her affections and feelings.

Although Margaret would try to behave like a loving, doting mother, all the resentment she harbored within prohibited her from succeeding. There was no warm smile and little if any outward enthusiasm for my presence.

"When can I go home, Margaret? When is *Má* coming?" I asked, reaching for a glass of milk.

There was a moment of silence. Margaret turned and gazing at the cup of coffee she had just poured for herself, said, "Mary you are an American now. Your life is here. You are in America. You are home. You must focus on other things, like learning English, attending school and eating like an American. There will be no more Vietnamese food, including rice. We don't eat rice here."

It was decided that I had to face, accept and adapt to a major life adjustment without any accommodating interventions on the part of the Mustards. There would be no smooth transitions and no gradual easing into the radically diverse lifestyle. Instead, there would be just a 'cold turkey' withdrawal from my Vietnamese culture and traditions and a dive into the American way!

The TV was constantly blaring because Sam and Margaret agreed it was one of the best ways for me to learn English. One evening, *Voyage to the Bottom of the Sea* was playing and I remember thinking, "Admiral Nelson and Captain Crane were on the airplane—how did they get here?"

I was convinced they were actual people who lived behind the TV. They did, however, remind me of the tall, beautiful blonde PAN AM flight attendants. Those kind and caring girls were the only Americans I had met besides the Mustards since leaving *Sài Gòn*.

During my first week in California Sam was an excellent guide, taking me around town, showing me where I would be attending school and trying to get me grounded with my surroundings. On one of our drives, we stopped at Dairy Queen.

Sam pulled up to the entrance and drove around to a vacant parking space. "Let's go get some 'Dilly Bars,'" he suggested, opening the car door. "This is one of my favorite places and I have to take you here."

I had no idea what he was suggesting, but it sounded like it could be a fun adventure. "OK Sam," I said, "let's get Dilly Bars."

I skipped alongside Sam, trying to keep pace with his wide steps. When we arrived at the entrance, I looked up at the large blue sign. Bright white letters sprawled across the darker surface spelled Dairy Queen.

Sam ordered two Dilly Bars and soon I would have my first taste of ice cream.

"Ok, Mary," he said, smiling, handing me a flat wooden stick on which sat a slab of dark chocolate. "Eat it slowly because it's ice cold."

I extended my tongue and slammed the tip over the edge of the bar. Sam was right—it was cold! I repeated the gesture several times and realized it tasted good. Then I rested it flat on my tongue and chomped down, biting off the top. My front teeth burned for a brief fleeting instant, but not enough to discourage me from trying again. I persisted, biting more deeply. Much to my surprise there was a layer of delicious creamy vanilla ice cream beneath the crunchy chocolate coating.

"Mary, do you like the Dilly Bar?" Sam asked, already sure of my answer. My smiling face, licking tongue and chomping teeth answered his question. I loved it! In fact, I devoured it with such enthusiasm that I was left branded with chocolate stains on my face, hands and clothing. However, despite the mess I made of myself, it was such a delicious finger-licking experience.

I rotated between the sadness of missing my mom and the excitement of discovery. Every day in America gave rise to a new experience. I was beginning to look forward to every sunrise, eager to see what the new day would bring.

One morning after breakfast, Sam placed his knife and fork on his plate, joined his hands and looked up. He seemed more reflective than usual. From his slow, studied movements it seemed as if he had something on his mind he needed to share with me.

He looked at me and I noticed a flash of sadness. Though brief and fleeting, I felt it zap through me like a bolt of lightening.

"Mary," he said, "I have been offered a new job. I will have to move away for awhile. We will see each over the weekends. Sometimes you and Margaret will come to see me, and other times I will drive back to visit you. We will alternate."

I listened to his words, uncertain I understood the full meaning behind what was actually happening. However,

I was certain I did not like what he was telling me. If I understood correctly, I was being abandoned again.

Catching my sadness, he reassured me everything was OK and things would eventually work out. "It has to be this way, Mary," he said. He slid his chair away from the table, stood and walked over to his desk, picking up a map. Returning, he said, "Mary this is where I am going." He pointed to a spot which on paper did not seem too distant from where we lived. However, in reality it was a seven hour car ride from our house at *2159 Casa Mia Drive* to where Sam was being transferred in the San Fernando Valley.

The following morning with his luggage packed Sam headed for the front door. I raced after him, tears rolling down my cheeks. He heard my footsteps and the echoes of my sobs, paused in the driveway and turned to face me.

I ran up to him, reached to grab his trouser pocket and tugged on it.

"Sam," I begged, "please don't go—Sam, don't leave me."

My heart was racing. I was breathless. But the pain of losing Sam was unbearable. Another person was leaving me!

"Mary," Sam said, kneeling to meet my gaze, "don't cry, I'll see you on the weekends."

He leaned forward and I felt his cool lips brush against my flushed cheeks. Then he rose, encircled my trembling body with his long steady arms and gave me a big hug.

"Be good Mary," he whispered, patting me on the shoulder.

I nodded. "Goodbye, Sam!" I murmured. I shut my eyes, lowered my head and broke into uncontrollable sobs.

CHAPTER 5

Christened Mustard: Growing Up Mary Ann

*"Loneliness and the feeling of being unwanted
is the most terrible poverty."*
—Mother Teresa

There are many different stages in a child's life with many rites of passage to complete before a young girl begins her life's journey as an adult. However, although the process is often intricate and seldom painless, the challenge can be a timeless learning experience with benefits lasting a lifetime. Character and personality are developed during these formative years.

Elementary school is the start of the official learning process. Like every other child about to let go of a parent's hand and take those first major steps into the first grade classroom, my enthusiasm and excitement were seasoned with a bit of apprehension. I was frightened, because not attending kindergarten with the other children in my class, I did not know anyone.

Living in San Jose with my adopted mom, Margaret Mustard, I was busy adjusting to life as a seven-year-old Vietnamese girl in a diverse world.

Even life at home was different. Margaret did not fuss over me the way my mom did. There were no sweet songs, signs of affection or devoted attentions. In fact, she seemed almost motorized and emotionless. Dressing me involved handing me an outfit and giving an instruction, "Put this on, Mary, it's time for school."

Sharp contrasting moments like this lured my mind into flash back, replaying various scenes from my life in *Sài Gòn*. During the gloomy melancholy periods these endearing memories filled the void of loneliness and calmed my nostalgia, even if temporarily.

It was mid-September and although the days were still rather warm, the stifling discomfort of a prolonged Indian summer had come to an abrupt end. And with the cooler, refreshing breezes came the beautiful autumn days with crisp, burnt-orange leaves carpeting the sidewalks.

Most of the others had playmates and little clicks had formed as early as kindergarten. Furthermore, because of my poor English I was at a disadvantage and unable to speak with and understand what the children were saying.

Margaret was an elementary school teacher, and although she was trained to deal with small children, she did not offer me much support. She graded papers and completed her lesson plans for the following day, at school, postponing her return home to later in the evening. This left me alone and without direction. I did my homework alone even with my limited English skills.

After my classes with Mrs. Gillham, my first grade teacher, I came home to a vacant house. There was neither a nanny, nor a domestic housekeeper or baby sitter to secure my safety and tend to my needs in the absence of a parent. Instead, I was alone and unsupervised, a child who had to stoop down and pick up a key hidden under the doormat in order to enter the house.

Sadly, Margaret chose to indulge her selfish desire for solitude, instead of fulfilling her maternal obligation. Maybe she had no idea how badly the dark scared me—it was terrifying to be so little and feel so alone. Painful as it was, I learned how to cope and survive by surroundings myself with friends and caring individuals.

Every day was the same. After school I slid my key into the lock and walked into the emptiness as my pulse quickened with each cautious step I took, looking into every room for signs of intruders. Since the possibility of ghosts lurking around was still a constant thought in my mind, I dreaded the idea of entering the house.

Quickly I darted over to the TV and switched it on both for light and company. The voices were momentarily reassuring in the creepy stillness. After several minutes, hesitant and apprehensive, I would slowly inch my way around the back and try to catch the 'little people' I thought lived behind the TV, waiting to pounce on me. I was certain that when my eyes moved away from the screen, these 'little people' would jump out, run, hide and eventually ambush me.

Terrified of the imaginary scenario I created in my mind, I limited myself to the part of the house I could reach without having to walk through the dark hallway to the bedroom. I'd stay in the family room in front of the TV, then head for the kitchen to make myself a snack. Surprisingly, I soon discovered the kitchen was an ideal place, not only for finding food, but for amusement.

One afternoon on my way home from school, I spotted some neighbor children playfully chasing another child outside a house. They were laughing, playing and just seemed to be having fun—something I had lost when I left *Việt Nam*. But I wanted it back. I wanted to laugh again and I wanted to play. "I'm sick and tired of being alone," I whispered aloud. I think I'll go over and ask if I can play, also." Instead of heading for my driveway I took a detour, stepped off the curb, and ran across the street.

"Hi, I'm Mary Ann," I said, trying to catch my breath. "Can I play with you?"

"Sure, Mary Ann," Mrs. Brown responded for her daughter. "You can come over whenever you like and play with Eileen."

I enjoyed going over to the Browns' because they always had a house buzzing with children, and I just wanted to be in the company of others. For a moment I thought about *Việt Nam* and my little playmate, *Nhàn*. How different it all was.

In America I had to wear clothes and shoes. There was no carefree running around barefoot and naked—no soft soothing mud to step into or to stick between my toes. This was another world—another life.

As time passed, I acquired a fluency in the English language, adjusted to my life as a student, and made friends at school. I desperately wanted to belong—to fit in—to be one of the kids.

The seasons turned from spring and summer to fall, and soon I was in second grade. Life with was still less than endearing, though I was learning about the American way of life and adapting accordingly.

In school I was teased about my name since Margaret had taught me to pronounce Mustard as if it was a French name. She would say with a snooty look on her face, "Mary—your name is Mus-*TARRRD*," and made me repeat it over and over again with an emphatic and exaggeratedly drawn out inflection on the second syllable.

When the teacher called my name she would pronounce it Mary Mustard. "No, no, no, no," I would say in my heavily accented English. "It's Mary Mus-*TARRRD*."

"Well," she would respond, "how do you spell it?"

"M-u-s-t-a-r-d," I responded, slowly, clearly enunciating while exaggeratedly emphasizing each letter to be certain she understood how to write my name. Again, she would repeat, "Mary that spells Mustard." And again, I'd correct her saying, "No, it's Mus-*TARRRD*—it's French!"

This little dialogue always produced snickers and giggles from the other children who would correct me. "No, Mary," they would say, laughing, "your name is Mustard—mustard like the seasoning on hot dogs and burgers! You are Mary Mustard!" Having a sense of humor, I would smile and walk way.

That evening, when I heard the click of Margaret's key flick open the lock, I ran to the entry. "Margaret," I asked, "what's mustard?"

In silence Margaret walked to the pantry, her heavy, determined steps echoing under her weight. I skipped along, following her trail. When she reached her destination, she raised her arm slightly above her head, enclosed her hand around a jar, pulled it from the shelf and unscrewed the cap.

"Mary," she said, sticking the jar under my nose, "this is mustard." Curiously, I inhaled. The pungent aroma reminded me of the Vietnamese fish based *nước mắm* sauce for a brief moment, though the mustard was decidedly sweeter. I inhaled again and felt a tickle in my nose.

"What is mustard?" I asked, raising my eyes to meet Margaret's gaze.

"Mary," she said, screwing the cap back on the jar, "it's a relish—a seasoning we put on hot dogs and burgers to make them taste better."

"That's what the children said," I responded, now with an awareness of the purpose of mustard.

My name became a joke on the playground. By the time I was in second grade the kids would tease me ruthlessly. "I'm Mary Mustard," I'd say, giggling, "and when I marry Harry Hot Dog, I'll name my first daughter Kathy Ketchup!"

Once again, blessed with a sense of humor, I took the playful badgering good naturedly, actually turning the 'name game' into a comedy routine.

Thanks to my sense of humor or ignorance, as some would say, and my playful personality, I made many friends in a short period of time. The children seemed to delight in my antics and my entertaining way of expressing myself. I was different—I made them laugh, and they were happy to be in my company and have me as a playmate.

Inheriting a passion and talent for music from my mom, *Thanh,* who answered to the name Yvonne she received from the American servicemen at *La Pagoda,* I loved to perform in front of an audience—even if just for two other children.

With so many new friends in my life, I felt encouraged to entertain. Not only was I excited about giving a 'performance'—but I soon discovered the perfect stage setting.

The Mustards' house on *Casa Mia* Drive had an 's'-shaped brick path leading to the rear patio. With my imagination in full bloom, I pretended the red brick road was a walkway leading to the stage, which was the gray slate patio. Once the stage was set, I was ready to perform. I soon discovered it would be more fun to have a larger audience with different types of people to applaud me.

Often times, as most kids do, I would set up a lemonade stand directly in front of my house. In my mind this would attract a crowd. I would make some lemonade and sell it for five cents a glass to draw an audience for my performances. It was an ingenious plan—and best of all, it worked!

Singing and dancing were therapeutic, a comfort filling the loneliness in my life. Since Margaret Mustard was an almost 'absent' mother, I was forced to fend for myself if I wanted to survive. And being a non-defeatist, I resolved earlier on that like my mom, I too would overcome.

My nutritional needs were not Margaret's concern, therefore in order to avoid hunger pangs, I acquired a proficiency in making PBJs *aka* peanut butter and jelly sandwiches. Although a basic staple in my diet, this menu selection did not provide a complete range of healthy nutrients for a growing child. When I did have a hot meal, it was usually Kentucky Fried Chicken, burgers, a Jack in the Box specialty and tacos—all fast food.

Sometimes I would have scrambled eggs, toast and cold cereal. We never had fresh fruit or vegetables. Instead, our main dietary elements came from cans and packages. Life at the Mustards was so unlike the situation comedies of the era, *Leave it to Beaver*, *Father Knows Best* and the *Donna Reed Show*, projecting stay-at-home moms like June Cleaver, Margaret Anderson and Donna Stone dedicated to caring for and attending to their families.

As a substitute for nourishing early morning breakfasts and prepared from scratch hot dinners served to a united family seated around a table, Margaret depended on 'take out.' In a way she 'pioneered' this type of quick dining before it became a 'trendy' resource for busy working moms looking for time and energy saving strategies.

At first, I didn't know any better and thought it was the American way. Later on, as a frequent dinner guest in my friends' homes, I was suddenly made aware of Margaret's parental failings.

The months passed quickly and I was learning much about my new country and its inhabitants. I was good in school, and my teachers noticed I had an excellent aptitude for math. In fact, I was able to calculate the multiplication tables up to the double digits without even pausing to take a breath. I enjoyed studying and soon discovered learning was a necessity if I wanted to get promoted to the next grade.

Sam was slowly fading into a memory because his absence far outweighed his presence in my life. However, during his sporadic visits he would continually encourage me to improve my English and write to my mom, Yvonne, in *Việt Nam*.

"Mary," he would say, "you should write to your mom after school every day and tell her all about your life here in America. I think she would enjoy hearing from you."

"What should I tell her, Sam?" I asked, tearing a blank page from my notebook and digging for a pencil that still had a point.

"I don't know, Mary," he replied, fussing with his dark-rimmed glasses, "just tell her about school and your friends. Tell her you are learning English and explain what you are studying."

"How will she get my letter?" I questioned, not under-standing the postal system's delivery process.

"After you finish writing, we'll take it to the post office and get a stamp for it. Then, it will be sent to her in *Việt Nam*," Sam responded. He made it seem so simple.

"Will she write to me?" I asked, excited about the possibility of receiving news from my mom in *Sài Gòn*.

"Yes, Mary," Sam answered. "That's why I want you to write. When she receives your letter, she'll send you one back in return. Then we will know how she is and what she's doing."

"How long does it take for a letter to get to *Việt Nam*?" I asked, intrigued by the letter writing and receiving mystery.

"Oh, I don't know the exact time," Sam responded, "but when it arrives the mailman will deliver it right to the house."

I was so excited by the thought of receiving a letter from my mom. I wrote her faithfully, mentioning my school and friends. Margaret took the letters to the post office as soon as I handed the sealed envelopes to her.

Every Saturday I stood outside, rain or shine, anxiously waiting for the mail truck to pull up. I would watch the postman climb out, walk to the back and grab a handful of mail. As soon as he turned to begin his delivery journey, I'd run over to meet him midway.

"I'm waiting for some letters from my mom in *Việt Nam*," I'd blurt out in one breath. "Do you have anything for me today?"

Most Saturdays he'd walk up the driveway, shaking his head "no," as I continued to inquire if I had mail from *Việt Nam*.

"You know," he'd say, smiling, "a letter from *Việt Nam* could take weeks, even months to arrive. *Việt Nam* is a long way from here. You just have to be patient and it will arrive." Several months had passed and one morning before school I approached Margaret as she was dressing for work.

"Margaret," I asked excitedly, "isn't it time for me to go home? When am I going back to *Sài Gòn*? I want to see my mom."

Still a young child, I was unable to understand the concept of time. Days, weeks and months meant little if anything. I often wondered why my mom never came to visit as she promised when we hugged and kissed goodbye at *Tân Sơn Nhất* airport—so many questions and unknowns and so few answers and certainties.

"Mary," Margaret said, "you *are* home—America is your home."

I listened to her words and felt a deep sadness—did this mean I would not be going back to *Việt Nam* ever? Did it mean I would never see *Hai* or *Cô Cúc* again?

The tears spilled down my cheeks as I began to understand that the Mustards were my family and that school and my friends were all part of my new life. It was a moment of truth—even if in a child's world. I realized I had to stop my delightful daydreams in which my mom, Yvonne stood smiling in front of me. Her warm, tender caresses and sweet kisses were mine only in a recollection. But, as a consolation I would have her letters to keep me company during the lonely periods in which my thoughts were my only companion.

Then my prayers were answered. One Saturday morning the mailman shouted my name from the curb. "Mary," he said, breathless, "I have a letter for you from *Việt Nam!*"

I sprinted down the driveway and jumped up to snatch it from his hand. My hair tumbled forward covering my eyes. Quickly, I brushed it back so I could see the fancy envelope with the colorful stamp. Then protecting my newly acquired treasure, I clutched it with both hands, locking it in a tight hug.

"I got a letter from Mom," I sang repeatedly, inventing my own melody, as I skipped, zigzagging along the path back to the house. I couldn't wait to show it to Sam.

He had driven up for a visit that weekend. "I got a letter from my mom," I shouted loud enough for him to hear. Excited, I ran through the front door and repeated, "Sam I got a letter from *Việt Nam!*"

"OK, Mary," he said, lifting his gaze from the newspaper he was reading. He folded the page and extended his hand to take the letter from me. "Let's read it Mary!"

For a brief moment Sam's face softened. I handed my treasure to Sam. His eyes lit up when he saw my mom's handwriting on the envelope. He walked over to the desk, took a long slender shiny object, slipped it under the top part on the back side of the envelope and sliced it open with one quick flick of the wrist.

Excited, I clapped my hands and repeated in a barely audible whisper, "*Má* wrote to me."

Sam unfolded the letter—from where I stood I saw it was one sheet, handwritten. My pulse was racing. I couldn't wait to hear what my mom had to say!

He cleared his throat and began:

"Dear Baby,
I'm very sad because you are gone. I miss you
very much. I had a letter from you one month ago."

"*Má* got my letter," I blurted out, interrupting Sam.

"Mary, be still and let me finish the letter," he said without removing his eyes from the page he was reading. I could see the letter fluttering—years later I realized his hand was trembling from emotion.

"Let me continue to read, Mary," he muttered, showing his impatience.

Sam started again from where he was abruptly interrupted.

"I'm very happy you have a lot of friends in school.
I've kept your Vietnamese dress and the phonograph.
Please write me a letter. Be happy. Do what Mr. and
Mrs. Mustard say. Study hard. You are now not a
Vietnamese. I'm happy for you. You're a big girl, very
pretty. I hope some day to come to California to see you.
                                                    Love,
                                                    Mother
                          I live at 346/A Phan Đình Phùng"

I cried myself to sleep that night with my mother's letter clutched in my hand. But despite the tears, for the first time in months I went to bed happy, entertaining childish thoughts of a return to *Sài Gòn*. But morning came soon enough, and with it the start of another new day and my daily routine.

After school on Fridays Margaret and I would get into the 1959 white Chevrolet with the prominent rear batwings and glowing red cat eyes and make the trip south to visit Sam.

The drive from San Jose to Northridge took almost seven hours depending on the traffic. Suffering from motion sickness, I'd be nauseous every time.

"Mom," I'd say, sometimes calling her Mom and other times, Margaret, "I don't feel so good. I think I'm going to throw up."

Margaret would sigh.

"Mary, don't dirty the car," she'd shout without even turning her head to look at me. I could have turned purple or stopped breathing and she would have continued driving, oblivious to it all. I could never understand where I was supposed to 'throw up.' She refused to pull over and stop driving, yet at the same time she kept yelling at me not to soil the car.

My own personal memories of Margaret are that of a cold, almost indifferent woman, incapable of caring for or loving anyone. I never once received a kiss or hug—not even as a lonely, vulnerable child abruptly separated from her mother. Every evening was the same—I ate alone, cleaned up, and waited for Margaret to come home. Irritated and exhausted, she would slump through the door, drop her brief case, and stagger to the kitchen.

She neither inquired about my day nor if I had eaten. Her apathy was straightforward and consistent. There was not even a minimal attempt on her part to cover up the emotional indifference.

"Mary," she would say after eating a quick bite, "it's getting late—shouldn't you be getting ready for bed?"

Without a word, I turned on my heels and left the room. Reaching my bedroom, I undressed myself, brushed my teeth, crawled into bed and cried myself to sleep—all alone.

I kept my mom, Yvonne's letters in my big yellow suitcase, and whenever I was lonely I would run to the bag, unlock it with the tiny key I carefully hid in my room and *'voila'* I was immediately transported back to my Vietnamese world. Among my secret treasures were letters and pictures of Mom and me, *Hai* and *Cô Cúc* as well as gifts she sent me through Bill Neal. These were my most precious possessions.

Our only link with *Việt Nam* was Sam's friend, Bill Neal who acted as a *liaison* between my mom and me. He spent six months of the year in *Việt Nam* and six in the United States. Every time he returned from abroad he visited the Mustards.

I was amused whenever Bill came to the house because sometimes he seemed so comical. With his arms crammed full with packages and gifts from my mom, he would bend over, lift his arm and knock on the door with his elbow, attentive not to drop any of the parcels and letters he was carrying. This was certainly not an easy feat, but always brought a smile to my face at his contortions.

Of course the letters made me the happiest girl in the world. And I loved it when my mom would ask me what I wanted her to send me. Actually, I liked everything she wrote and treated every letter as a special treat.

In one letter she wrote:

"See where Sam mails his letter & mail me some—am waiting for your letter. How is Sam treating you? Are they talking to you about me?"

In another she said:

"I'm going to record music for you (an old traditional folk song). When you're in America do you like the

food or do you remember nược mắm? Tell me what
you want…I buy."

I was not shy in expressing my wishes and wrote back telling
my mom exactly what I wanted. She would try to satisfy all
my requests and send the goodies back with Bill, her personal
courier. Although I didn't have my mom with me, I was
happy to at least have her correspondences and thoughtful
gifts. It made me feel loved—she was so unlike my American
parents. What a striking contrast!

Both Sam and Margaret lived their lives as bigots,
unashamed of their ignorant, racist mentality. In the sixties,
cultural diversity was neither pronounced nor looked upon as
the distinctive trait that made and makes America such a
special and culturally rich nation in the world.

In this era, Asians were a rarity and usually stigmatized by
a population that drew second hand facts and information
from the daily coverage of the media's recountal of the *Việt*
Nam War. It was a conflict that left Americans politically
divided with respect to US participation. Consequently, I was
hesitant to admit my Vietnamese origins. Of course, it was the
main topic of conversation at dinner tables and among my
friends' parents and always made me feel somewhat uneasy
and embarrassed of who I was.

The awful images and continual tabulations of American
lives lost were a daily event, causing dissension and pulling
the country apart. The repeated coverage was sufficient to
influence the thoughts and actions of many individuals who
made biased judgments based on political decisions and
actions.

I remember Sam would often degrade individuals from
other races by resorting to racial slurs and demeaning name-

calling. His use of the "n" word when referring to African Americans would make me cringe. Often after being present during one of his name-calling tirades, I couldn't understand how such an uncouth and prejudiced man could have adopted an Asian child! His two-faced hypocritical personality was both confusing and disturbing—especially when he tried to impose his biased views on me.

Not only was I prohibited from speaking to or bringing home culturally diverse people, but Margaret also forbade any and all references to *Việt Nam*. Absolutely no one knew about my *Sài Gòn* connection with the exception of Bill and the postman who delivered my mom's letters from *Việt Nam*.

I had to depend on Bill for any news from my native land. On one of his visits when Sam was in San Jose, he walked through the door and handed me several packages. Excited, I picked up the smaller box, ripped off the wrapping and noticed two glittering bracelets. One was a child's eighteen karat gold link ID bracelet engraved with my birth name, *Thanh Hiền,* and the second was a larger bracelet with Chinese lettering for when I outgrew the little one. I put them in the palm of my hand to get a better look. They were so beautiful my eyes lit up.

Curious to see what was in the larger box, I put the bracelets on the table, moved the package in front of me and lifted the lid. Much to my delight I uncovered a beautiful Asian doll with long black hair dressed in a dark purple *aó dài*. Sitting on her head was a *danh từ*, the traditional conical palm hat.

"The hat looks exactly like the one *Hai* made me wear when I got the bicycle!" I said all in one breath. It was obvious my mother did not want me to forget my Vietnamese roots, and this was her way to insure the memories would be kept alive.

I named my little doll *Bích Nga* after my baby sister. I thought of her often and didn't yet understand why she could stay in *Việt Nam* with *Má,* whereas I had to move with strange people to a new country.

I pictured *Bích Nga's* smooth, silky skin and the mass of short, thick hair that would sometimes fall over her eyes when she rolled on her side. I saw her tiny fingers and the miniature feet my mom and I would kiss and tickle. I missed her so much and would break into endless sobs at the thought of her so far away. But the tears did nothing to ease the agonizing ache in my heart.

I was still in second grade and progressing quite well with my studies. However, not having anyone to speak with, I noticed I started forgetting my Vietnamese. On weekends I played with my friends after cleaning the house and taking care of my nutritional needs. Margaret was continually irritated with me for watching too much TV, not 'properly' cleaning the house according to her standards or because I expressed a desire to play with my friends.

When angry she would scowl and her complexion would redden. On several occasions when I would disobey her by not taking all the baths she required from morning to night, she would chase me around the house shouting disturbing insults, making puzzling references to my mom and the fact that I knew nothing about the motives behind my adoption.

"Mary," she'd shriek, "you don't know the whole story about *Việt Nam*! One day you will grow up to be a *tramp* like your mother!"

I listened to her angry words, unable to understand what she was talking about. The following day, confused by Margaret's words, I approached my second grade teacher.

"What's a tramp?" I asked, with the innocent candor of a young child.

"What do you mean, Mary?" she responded, rather shocked by my question.

"Well, Margaret told me I was going to grow up to be a *tramp* like my mom in *Việt Nam*," I blurted, looking up into her startled eyes.

"Margaret is not my real mom!" I continued.

Taking a deep breath after that mouthful, I told her I had looked in the dictionary but couldn't find the meaning of *tramp*! She gazed down at me with a stunned expression, unable to believe what she was witnessing from such a young child.

Mrs. Gillham pulled me toward her, giving me a big, reassuring hug. Eventually, I received a lot of special attention. My empathetic teacher would dedicate extra time to me after school to encourage me to speak and improve my English. I guess it was her way of helping me deal with the emotional abuse I was receiving from Margaret. In her own special way she compensated for my lack of parental love and caring.

On one of his visits to the Mustards', Bill Neal was accompanied by his wife Flo, who today is a charming ninety-year-old lady living in Oregon. Her memory is clear and precise, and she told me about one incident that remains engraved in her mind.

During a visit with her husband, Flo had strolled past my bedroom. Noticing a faint glimmer of light in the pitch darkness, she peeked in. I had the covers over my head and was reading using a flashlight to see the words.

"Mary," she said, "what are you doing? Why don't you turn on the light?"

"I'm scared," I said, dropping the covers to my neck, so I could see her.

"What are you scared of?" she responded, crinkling her brow in a puzzled frown.

"Well," I whispered, "if Margaret finds out I'm reading, she will get mad and spank me—so I have to hide and do it under the covers. I love to read, and with the flashlight she will not see a light under the door when she walks down the hall." I feared her wrath and tried not to cross her when possible.

Margaret was not timid about showing her disapproval with me for not scrubbing the bathrooms, or kitchen and not behaving as she saw fit. She would scream and swat my bottom or face with the open palm of her hand shouting, "Do it over again, Mary—this is not clean. Can't you do anything right!"

Holding back the tears at least momentarily, I would cringe, obeying her command. Later in the quiet of my room, I would break into uncontrollable sobs. But all the tears in the world could neither wash away the mean streak that ran straight through Margaret nor the pain she caused me.

At school I received an 'N' (needs to improve) on my report card because I talked incessantly in class. My teacher wanted me to stop the chattering and my constant jumping up from my seat and walking around. She said it was distracting to everyone and interrupted the lessons. However, for me it was a way of learning English. The more I spoke the better I became. The words began to flow easily and I gained fluency.

When Margaret saw the 'N' grade, she yelled at me seconds before she raised her arm, swung it around and gave me a quick hard slap across the face. My cheeks were red and puffy for hours afterwards from the force of her hand hitting against my skin.

"You have to do better," she shouted. "I don't want to see this poor grade ever again on your report card. Do you understand, Mary?" Of course, she never expected, wanted or waited for a reply, but stormed out of the room leaving me alone, humiliated and in tears.

What Margaret failed to understand was the why behind my being so talkative in school. She never realized I was growing up in a communication challenged house. There was absolutely no personal interaction or exchange of dialogue. No questions were asked about my day; therefore no answers were sought or given.

Basically, I lived alone. No one spoke to me—and likewise I had no one to speak to. In a sense I was living in solitary confinement and starved for attention and the opportunity to speak and learn the language.

By now, the first two years of schooling were completed. My English was fluent and I had made many new friends. At home, however, my cultural background was painfully fading into extinction. Since my life pre-Mustard was taboo, in a sense I had lost my identity as an Asian child.

Looking back, I now realize how seriously wrong it was for the Mustards to try to erase my heritage. Repeatedly taught that being Vietnamese was nothing to be proud of, I was forbidden to even discuss my native land at home. It seemed as if it was something shameful!

However after many decades of frustration and anxiety, I was able to embrace the Vietnamese Culture. Consequently, I feel very strongly about the importance of encouraging adopted children to live and fully experience the culture, history, language and traditions of their native countries. An integral part of 'who' they are, it is what allows them to grow up comfortable in their own skin and proud of the persons they are.

I was forced to abandon *'Hiền,'* the little Vietnamese girl who had been a part of me for seven years because Margaret led me to believe people would neither like nor accept me if they knew I was from *Sài Gòn!* I had to conceal my roots as if it was a crime to be an Asian child, often telling everyone I was from Hawaii.

Bill Neal in a sense was my savior—the link to the world the Mustards tried to destroy. Happily, he would visit from time to time bringing news from *Việt Nam* and stirring up my fading memories.

One afternoon he came to the house to talk to Sam and Margaret. Bill had phoned Sam in Northridge and asked him to drive up to San Jose because he had something important to discuss.

I was in the next room, but inquisitive as I was, I found it impossible to concentrate on anything less than eavesdropping on the conversation taking place in the living room.

Bill seemed distracted, extremely somber and of sparse words as he followed Sam's slow steady steps and seated himself on the sofa. Even the volume of his voice was not as exuberant as usual. Believing something was in the air, I stood trying to listen to what was about to be said.

I tiptoed closer and quietly put my ear to the wall, just in time to hear Bill's voice. "Sam, I went back to the village where Yvonne lives."

"Yvonne," I whispered to myself, that's my mom. Once again, I was careful not make any noise, fearful I would be dismissed or reprimanded.

"Well," Bill continued, nervously clearing his throat, "the village was heavily bombed—there were no survivors! Sam, I'm afraid Yvonne is dead!"

He paused before speaking again. There was a dreadful silence—the quiet of emptiness. "Sam," Bill continued, "I looked everywhere. I had Yvonne's picture in my hand as I went through the whole village over and over every day for endless days. I walked through the rubble and dead bodies scattered about. The smell of decayed flesh nauseated me. Sam—women and children were just torn apart. The bombs had destroyed most of their faces and many were beyond recognition. It was ghastly—a terrifying bloody mess."

I leaned over and peeked into the room. Sam was ashen—his body paralyzed from the shock. With rigid, almost mechanical movements he removed his dark-rimmed glasses and rubbed his eyes.

"Sam," Bill said, after a few minutes, "how are you going to tell Mary?"

The question remained unacknowledged and unanswered. It was as if he was never asked.

That weekend Sam sat around, listless. His eyes were swollen and bloodshot—evidence of the tears he had shed for the death of my mother. Once he pulled himself together he realized I had to be told.

There were no more discussions either between Sam and Bill or with Margaret. It seemed as if not talking about the tragedy would make it nonexistent. Then while I was doing my homework, Sam stepped into my room. Since he rarely stopped by to talk or show any interest in my school events or homework, I suspected something big was up.

Sam sat on the edge of my bed. His head was bowed, giving him a rather forlorn look. He appeared tense and kept staring down at his shoes for what seemed like an endless amount of time.

"Mary," he said, abruptly breaking the silence, "I received some bad news from *Sài Gòn.*" I froze. "Mary, your mother has been killed in the war." I trembled and shook. "Mary, Bill looked all over for your mom. The village was bombed—and everything was destroyed."

Something shattered within. It felt as if someone had cut through my chest. I felt a burning heat rush to my face accompanied by the most excruciating pain imaginable.

"*Má* is dead," I repeated over and over in my mind. "I will never see *Má* again."

I felt the tears roll down my cheeks as I buried my head in my still trembling hands.

The bitter cold of loss made me shudder. I felt completely alone.

That evening the tears continued. I pushed the pillow down over my head to be certain Margaret would not hear my sobs. I didn't want to get a nasty slap for crying because my mother had died—I couldn't bear any more pain.

In between the moans, gasps and tears I sang one of my favorite hymns, *Chua Yeu Em – Jesus loves me this I know,* over and over in Vietnamese. By now, they were the only Vietnamese words I remembered apart from my name and my mother's. I recited them fearing they would be lost forever like all the other words of my native tongue.

However, deep down I felt a rising doubt—possibly even a hope. Perhaps it was a mistake—maybe my mom had been able to escape. Somewhere in my subconscious that seed was planted, and I held on to the tiniest of hopes it promised.

The consoling words of *Jesus Loves Me* were my only link to *Hiền*, my mom *Thanh*, and my roots. But they were as fragile as an old piece of frayed thread; a delicate thread that had been pulled far too many times.

CHAPTER 6

The Path to Maturity: A Legacy of Torment Part I

"Every trial endured and weathered in the right spirit makes a soul nobler and stronger than it was before."
—James Buckham

It was autumn of 1966, and I was enrolled in the third grade. After two years of driving endless hours to visit Sam in Northridge, the Mustards decided it would be better for us to move from San Jose, to join him. This would eliminate the tiring ordeal of the bi-monthly commute.

Margaret was offered a teaching position in the Newhall School District. Apart from the ten months I spent in *Việt Nam* with Sam, Margaret, *Hai* and *Cô Cúc,* this was the first time the three of us would be living united under one roof for a lengthy period of time.

The trip from San Jose to Northridge was long, tedious and tiring. I remained silent throughout, allowing my thoughts to be my only company. I was moving again—another life-changing moment. I wondered what it would bring this time.

Just like all children who are uprooted from their familiar surroundings, this change of address was a major adjustment. There would be a new school, different teachers and nameless children who would eventually befriend me. However, despite my apprehensions, I was thrilled to be living with Sam again and felt certain his proximity would offer me support and encouragement during this challenging transition. I truly missed him when Margaret and I lived in San Jose.

Sam continued driving through the maze of congested traffic, although the heat was stifling. The warm dry breezes of the Santa Ana winds invaded through the open windows making the ride even more uncomfortable. Finally, he exited off the freeway and slowed down. About fifteen minutes later, he pulled into a condo complex on Dearborn Street.

The buildings were three stories tall, square in contour and rather nondescript. There were no tall trees framing the structures like in San Jose. Instead, patches of thick, freshly mowed grass tinted a deep blue-green decorated the entrance.

Sam stopped in front of one of the buildings, stepped out of the car and headed for the rear of the vehicle. I heard a snap, turned my head to monitor his actions, and noticed he was about to unload the trunk.

I opened the door eager to see my yellow suitcase settled on the ground beside Margaret's bags and various boxes. When I spotted it sitting among the others, I breathed a sigh of relief. My bag was safe—at least I had my mom's letters, gifts and photos to ease me out of the strange unfamiliarity.

"Mary," Margaret said, interrupting my thoughts, "Sam will take care of the bags. Let's go inside. Without responding I followed in her footsteps like an obedient child.

Our condo was on the second floor. When we entered the door squeaked. Immediately, I thought of ghosts. I gasped as a series of goose bumps popped up on my arms. Fear of ghostly apparitions troubled me well into my high school years when I eventually came to the realization that such eerie creatures did not exist except as a figment of my own imagination.

Once inside, I was surprised to see how small the interior of the condo was. There was a combination living-dining room, sparsely decorated with drab furniture. In a corner in front of the TV were several chairs and a sofa, upholstered in muted gold and green tones.

After breezing through the kitchen, I moved forward to survey the sleeping quarters. There were just two bedrooms—one with two twin beds and the other with a full size bed. The atmosphere was rather cold and stark as the décor was so exaggeratedly somber.

Since the Mustards were a married couple I was surprised to learn I was expected to share a bedroom with Margaret. Apparently they lived as husband and wife in name only, without any physical intimacy.

When we entered the room, I was assigned a bed rather brusquely—not by voice, but with a pointed finger waved in the air. Walking over, I sat on the edge of the bed and dangled my feet. I sank into the mattress. It seemed much softer than my bed in San Jose.

By this time I felt detached and indifferent towards Margaret. She was everything my birth mother wasn't—uncaring, selfish, paternally negligent, inattentive, harsh and demeaning.

Life in the new 'mini' house was tight. I couldn't escape seeing Margaret, especially in the evenings when we said our 'good nights' before switching off the lights. Several days later, I discovered there was a little girl living in the apartment beneath ours, on the first floor. Since she seemed to be about my age, I decided it would be fun to meet her and maybe have her as a playmate.

Leaving the condo, I went downstairs and introduced myself. She was agreeable, smiled enthusiastically when I told her my name, and responded with a cheerful, "My name is Candy."

Candy and I soon became best friends—we were inseparable. She told me her parents were divorced, but usually spent the weekends together taking her on outings.

It all sounded like fun to me. I imagined the times I went with my mother, *Hai* and *Cô Cúc* to the beautiful Vietnamese resort, *Đà Lạt*—the City of Eternal Spring, on the *Langbian* highland. Overwhelmed with nostalgia and deprived of any 'family life' with Sam and Margaret, I told Candy about my own day trips before I moved to America.

Candy's broad smile narrowed, then faded into a puzzled frown. "Mary," she asked, "don't your parents take you out on the weekends?"

"No, Candy," I responded, "the Mustards never take me anywhere."

Soon after, Candy and her parents asked me if I would like to join them on an outing. Thrilled to receive such a fun invitation, I quickly accepted. Eventually, it became a pattern. Noticing how happy I was, they continued to include me in their weekend activities.

Family life *a la* Mustard was best characterized by repeated and persistent conflicts, which often ended in explosive battles. Between Sam and Margaret there was neither mental compatibility nor sentimental harmony. Observing, the two of them united under one roof presented evidence of a definite separation of hearts, minds and souls—certainly not the qualities of a successful and thriving relationship. In fact, their life together seemed like a tumultuous hurricane worsened by the intrusion of tornados and cyclones. I felt as if I lived in a field of eternal strife and quarreling. The bickering was loud and frequent with interludes of jostling, sarcastic comments.

I never knew what to expect from the Mustards, but realized I dreaded returning home after school. When Sam and Margaret were in 'truce mode,' it was bearable, otherwise it was a nightmare. Undoubtedly, it was far from a serene atmosphere for a young child to grow up in. In order to escape the infernal environment in which I found myself, I reached out to friends.

Several months had passed since our move to Northridge. I had friends and was doing well in school. We were nearing the Christmas Season, and one evening Sam called out to me while I was playing in my room. "Mary," he said, come into the living room. Come watch the Bob Hope Special. He's in *Việt Nam* entertaining the troops."

I didn't need a second invitation. At the sound of the word *Việt Nam*, I darted into the living room and threw myself on the carpet next to Sam's chair.

"Sam," I asked without removing my gaze from the TV images flashing in front of me, "what's so important about the Bob Hope Special?"

"Mary," he responded, pointing his finger at a laughing Bob Hope teasing one of his guests, "Bob Hope is a famous man. He's an actor, a comedian and an entertainer. Furthermore, he is an incredible person who has been organizing and putting on shows for the military since the Second World War. Bob Hope tours with a group of actors, singers, dancers and comics. Furthermore, he invites Miss America and other beautiful girls."

I sat with my eyes glued to the TV while pictures of my beloved *Sài Gòn* and *Đà Lạt* came on the screen. In between the scenic tours of *Việt Nam,* Bob Hope featured an impressive roster of world renowned celebrities. Red Skelton and John Wayne entertained with comic skits whereas Bing Crosby, Ann Margaret, Dean Martin and Frank Sinatra crooned medleys of their hit songs. Then there was the beautiful Raquel Welch with her endless legs, stark white boots, colorfully patriotic red, white and blue costume and the enormous mound of hair that fascinated me.

When interviewed, Bob Hope was always asked why he hosted the USO Christmas Shows in *Việt Nam.* His response was always the same: "It's a reminder of what they were fighting for." In fact, it was a wonderful treat for the service men fighting a war and certainly a pleasant diversion from life on the bloody battlefields.

At the conclusion of the show I turned to Sam, "Will Bob Hope come on again?" I asked, hoping the answer would be yes. Sam was silent. It was the special quiet of a man wrapped in his own thoughts. From the distant look in his eyes I knew he was miles away—lost in another world.

Sam's response was barely a whisper. "Yes," he said, sighing, "Bob Hope will be back next Christmas." When he turned his head slightly in my direction, I noticed he was teary-eyed, and imagined he missed my mother, Yvonne. 'Maybe he is a lonely man' flashed across my mind, especially since Margaret never honored us with her presence. She would never pay any attention to any news about *Việt Nam.* It was as if she wiped the entire country off the face of the earth with one swift sweep of her hand.

My life continued to unravel between school, my friends and practically living alone in the presence of the Mustards.

The year passed, and in 1967 I entered the fourth grade, Lyndel Cash's class. My memories of Mr. Cash are so vivid because he was the focus of my first major crush.

As a radically bald mature gentleman in an era in which 'shaved heads' were neither in vogue nor the fashion trend, Mr. Cash had a rather unique appearance. Moreover, almost to accentuate his distinctive look, he wore dark-rimmed glasses. It was not his physical appearance, but his whimsical sense of humor that attracted me, mainly because it was in stark contrast to the somber stoicism *a la* Mustard.

The year 1967 brought new, life changing experiences. More importantly, it was the year in which I became an American citizen. To say it was an exciting time would truly not do justice.

Sam told me that in order to qualify for naturalization, I had to memorize, recite and write the "Preamble to the Constitution," the "Star Spangled Banner" and the "Pledge of Allegiance." Furthermore, he informed me I would be questioned about the US Government and be expected to have a basic knowledge of some significant American History events.

I studied hard and felt ready. The following morning I awoke early barely able to stay in bed. I dressed myself and Sam accompanied me to the US Citizenship and Immigration Services. Hyper and delirious with joy, I could only skip instead of walk through the long halls. In contrast to my childish exuberance, Sam remained composed and silent.

Gazing around the room, I noticed I was the only child among the many people waiting to be 'tested and sworn in." I sang the anthem, recited the Pledge and Preamble without stumbling or stuttering and correctly answered the civics and history questions.

It was the 8th of December, 1967, a date that remains forever imprinted in my mind and heart. The little girl from *Sài Gòn* was now an American! Today, thanks to the CCA, Child Citizen Act of 2000, all foreign born children adopted by Americans are granted US citizenship upon immigrating to the United States.

I was so happy that day, and upon my return to school I was thrilled to see Mr. Cash had organized a big celebration in my honor. When I entered the classroom, everyone stood at attention. Mr. Cash called my name, motioned for me to come to the front of the classroom, and handed me an American flag. Smiling, he said, "Mary, here is your new country's flag—can you sing the "Star Spangled Banner" for us?"

Being a bit of a ham with a love and talent for 'center stage,' I belted out the famous words, trying to hit all the high pitched notes.

The "Star Spangled Banner" is not an easy piece to sing at any age and the vocal range required is attainable only by extremely talented or professionally trained singers. Therefore, I did not exactly give a Grammy winning performance. However, although my voice cracked and I lost the melody, I was too exhilarated about becoming an American to let anything ruin my moment. Unruffled by my rather sour, off-key finale, I pretended my performance was spectacular and perfect.

The children looked at me with admiration, ignored my exaggeratedly jarring and discordant screeches and awarded me an ear-shattering round of applause. It was exhilarating. In a sense it was my moment of glory.

Excited and surprised by the applause and whistles of approval, I thought to myself, *Heavens to Betsy, Mary, you better take a big bow.*

A minute into the applause, I took a full body *prima donna* curtsy, holding my bowed position for what seemed like an endless period of time. Meanwhile, the clapping intensified. I was over-confident about my achievement and loving every second I was experiencing.

When I returned home that evening, I couldn't wait to tell Sam about my exciting day at school. However, Sam had other things on his mind. He was seated in front of the TV, listening to *The Huntley-Brinkley Report*.

Sam slipped a cigarette between his lips, lit it with a flick of his lighter and motioned for me to come over. As I walked towards him, I heard David Brinkley discussing the latest events and casualties of the *Việt Nam* War.

He was summarizing the week's events and reporting on the loss of Communist troops. "However," Brinkley said, "not yielding to this setback, the *Việt Cộng* persisted and raged some of their bloodiest battles in a continual, almost non-stop wave of attacks."

I didn't quite understand the impact of what Brinkley was reporting and asked Sam to explain. Taking a long drag on his Marlboro and exhaling several puffs of smoke,

Sam, aware that I was studying the Civil War in school, took the opportunity to correlate this with the *Việt Nam* conflict—the North at odds with the South. In essence, it was their own civil war. He told me the situation was grave and consequently, the US felt terrorized by the threat of a Communist takeover since communism was spreading in the Soviet Union and edging its way into Eastern Europe, as well as Korea and Cuba.

Sam rarely, if ever, took the time to explain or answer any of my questions about *Việt Nam*. This was undoubtedly one of the few moments in which he shared any feelings, thoughts or comments about the war. Consequently, I listened to his every word, paying attention not to miss anything.

It was at this point in the discussion that Sam, an 'alleged' undercover agent for the CIA, told me he completed numerous assignments flying in the C-130 four-engine turbo prop cargo planes.

"Mary," he explained, "since these planes were easy to land on short runways and on the grounds of old plantations, they were utilized to drop supplies to survivors in the various war zones who were left devastated after the bombings."

Sam also mentioned he sometimes was part of a medical evacuation team that transported severely wounded soldiers to hospitals for emergency treatments.

At the time *Việt Nam* was divided basically in two classes: the well educated with origins from the French aristocracy and the impoverished peasants.

Sam told me that the Communist *Việt Cộng* put heavy pressure on the peasant families to win them over as allies. I still remember his repeated comments and the sadness in his gaze as he announced, "It was a no win situation for the Americans and the South Vietnamese." "Mary," he said, puffing on his cigarette, "during the daytime the South Vietnamese soldiers were your friends and by night, your enemies."

Pausing just long enough to light another Marlboro, he continued sighing. "These poor South Vietnamese soldiers endured a devastating internal conflict."

I noticed his anger was laced with melancholy as he shifted his glance towards me. "Mary," he said, "so many lives have been lost, even your mom. Yvonne was a good woman."

I couldn't control my surprise. This was the first time I heard any positive comment or consideration regarding my mom. As Sam spoke, I envisioned her in my mind. For a brief moment it seemed as if she was standing in front of me.

I felt a rush of sadness mixed within my joy. Sam had stirred all the beautiful memories I had of my mom during my early life in *Sài Gòn.* Now she was gone and it all seemed so far away. It was my yesterday. Today, I had become and American citizen—now I was Vietnamese in skin only!

It was a brief explanation, but that was Sam's technique. In keeping with his style, he spent a few words discussing, then shut down in silence for days on end. I, on the other hand, was grateful for any kind of interaction or communication.

However, Sam lived in his own world; a world that did not permit any intrusions. Frustrated by his prolonged bouts of silence, Margaret oftentimes would try to rile him out of his stupor. "If you had never gone to *Việt Nam,*" she'd shout in a shrill voice, "you never would have met *that* woman and never brought *this* girl over."

Margaret pronounced those demeaning words repeatedly, using them like a weapon to verbally attack whenever she was upset either with Sam or me. Consequently the hurtful comment was cemented in my mind. Though still a young child, I knew Margaret was referring to my mother and me.

Sam never responded to her tirades. However, his apathy in her regard only infuriated her more. "I never wanted to adopt her," she ranted, breathless, her face taking on the color of a scalded lobster. "You were the one who wanted to take her back to the United States. You threatened to leave me if I didn't agree to the adoption. Sam, I always knew you were in love with Mary's mother. Everything you did for this child was because of her!"

Sam was emotionally detached, and Margaret aggressively ruled by her jealousy for my mother. With tears streaming down my face, I walked away. Now I was beginning to understand the motive behind my adoption. And it was neither comforting nor enlightening.

During this period my brother and sister-in-law, Bob and Helen began to have a stronger influence in my life. Helen was an incredible cook and quite accomplished in domestic skills. She taught me everything Margaret didn't—how to sew, knit and cook. Always accommodating, Helen was graciously available whenever possible to fill in for some of Margaret's deficiencies.

One of my sewing lessons focused on making potholders. I was excited to be able to create something all my own and already had a recipient for my first pair—Mr. Lyndel Cash.

The potholders were bright orange, canary yellow and brown. Actually, thinking back, I'd say they were rather hideous. However, they were a labor of love. I made each one, putting my heart and soul into it, and decided they would be a more than worthy gift for my Mr. Cash.

Upon completion, I placed them side by side in a square cardboard box I had stumbled upon in Margaret's closet. I thought I had prepared a beautiful present and was proud of myself. Knowing I would hand my gift to my 'special' teacher in the morning kept me sleepless with excitement.

The following day bubbling with enthusiasm, I marched to the front of the class. Smiling coyly, I presented the package to my teacher. Graciously, like the gentleman he was, Mr. Cash accepted the gift. Smiling, he tore off the paper, lifted the cover and pulled out the garish pot holders. He flipped them over to get a better look, then held them up for the whole class to see.

The children snickered and giggled, whispering among themselves through barely parted lips. Realizing I was being laughed at, I lived one of my first 'most embarrassing moments!' However, I was determined not to allow this awkward experience to trump my creativity. It was an important part of who I was becoming, broadened my outlook and gave me a different flair, separating me from my dull, narrow-minded adoptive parents.

The Mustards rarely hosted any celebrations, and I always felt embarrassed about accepting the many invitations I received to other children's birthday parties. I knew I would never be able to reciprocate the kindness they demonstrated by having them over to my house. This made me sad because as a people person, I loved to be in the company of others.

I also have few memories of either festive family dinners or other important moments that occur in the life of a child growing to maturity. There were never any pictures taken on my birthdays or to commemorate my graduations or piano recitals.

Furthermore, there were never any pictures taken of me in the company of the Mustards. In fact, I would not have had any 'souvenirs' of my early school years if it wasn't for my yearly class photos. And unlike the other children's parents, the Mustards never purchased any class photos.

But, thank God for Helen! She was sweet and endearing. We would have many conversations in which she would say, "Mary I wish Bob and I could adopt you and take you away from that awful house. I don't know if it's any consolation, but your brother's life was just as gloomy as yours. Sam and Margaret were equally critical of him, scolding him for every insignificant or petty thing he did or didn't do. He grew up to a chorus of incessant name-calling and downright degrading remarks and accusations.

You found comfort reaching out to teachers, friends and their families for love and support. They filled and continue to fill the big dark voids in your life! Bob was unable to resolve his situation, so he just walked out, slammed the door and said goodbye."

As an adult looking back, I realized my role in the Mustard family was as Margaret's 'trophy daughter.' It was her goal to have me always looking like a fashion trend setter. Therefore, my outfits were always hand picked and of excellent quality. In a sense I was a statement of who she either pretended to be, or who she wanted to be. This part of Margaret's character actually pleased me since I loved to wear beautiful and fashionable clothes.

I also loved music and when I discovered Mr. Cash played the piano, I wanted to imitate him. Sam answered my pleas for a piano with little protest. Within a short period of time, a beautiful Fisher cherry wood upright piano arrived. I was thrilled and overjoyed.

Every Saturday morning, Sam drove me to my lessons. In a few short months, I was already able to play a simple child's piece. However, even from earlier on it was evident I had the talent to become a more accomplished pianist.

My petite hands had nimble fingers and being so blessed, I was great with the quick *staccato* notes. Elastic and agile, I was able to gracefully play within a two-octave range. This gave me the ability to execute some introductory pieces and the will to study, practice and learn how to eventually master the keyboard.

My days were spent between piano lessons, my friends and school. Mr. Cash was my mentor, a caring man with whom I had a great relationship.

Whenever I went to him crying, "They were mean to me at home," he would look into my eyes and respond, smiling, "Mary, play the piano. When you get angry, instead of using harsh words like they do—just play the piano. Absorb your sadness in your music." I followed his advice and released my anxiety and frustration on the keyboard.

Music was a magic potion. It healed my sorrow, filled the icy hollowness with happiness and allowed me to express my feelings in a positive way. I was in high spirits when I was playing—it was as if the notes and melodies carried me off to another world. As soon as my fingers felt the refreshing coolness of the ivory keys, they made music—lifting me from my melancholy.

One evening around Christmas time, Bob and Helen invited me to *The Nutcracker Ballet* at the Shrine Auditorium in Los Angeles. I was thrilled!

Although I was immediately captivated by the colorful costumes, at only ten years of age I lacked the ability to understand the plot and appreciate the extraordinary talent of the performers, as I do today. However, thanks to the kindness of Helen and Bob who lived in such close proximity, I was blessed to be introduced to the cultural world of opera and ballet.

After the Nutcracker experience, they took me to see *La Traviata*. Once again, although incapable of following the intricate story line, the flourishing fanfare and elaborate costumes delighted my lively childish imagination.

It was 1969, a crucial year that left behind a great historical, political and social legacy. In a sense it was a year of revolutionary changes and events—from Richard Nixon's election as the thirty-seventh president of the USA to Neil Armstrong's pioneering lunar walk and famous words, *"That's one step for man, and one giant leap for mankind."*

Forced to grow up in a hurry for my own survival, I, too, was taking giant leaps for a child my age. I was already independent and self-sufficient while still an elementary school student.

Curious and interested in what was happening, I browsed the newspapers Sam left on the table, reading the headlines about the political situation occurring in *Việt Nam*. Wanting to know more, I paid attention to the daily newscasts which Sam listened to religiously.

When the images of war-torn *Sài Gòn* flashed on the screen, I saw young children running naked and barefoot, their slender faces and frail bodies covered with a splattering of mud. In the background I could hear people speaking Vietnamese—my native language. Yet, I was no longer able to understand what they were saying. All that remained of my heritage was the memory of my name, *Nguyễn Thị Thanh Hiền,* my mom's name, *Nguyễn Thị Thanh*, the first ten numbers and the song "Jesus Loves Me."

Although incapable of fully understanding the evening broadcasts, they represented the only link to my roots. Often, I was confused by the jumble of words I heard and not quite sure what it all meant. However, despite the inner confusion even the tiniest glimpse of a *Việt Nam* I no longer recognized gave rise to stirrings of nostalgia.

It was more than evident from the TV broadcasts that Vietnam was in deep turmoil. One evening I heard an interview on CBS. Lt. Willaim Calley was being questioned about the *thảm sát Mỹ Lai*, *Mỹ Lai* Massacre. It was November 20, 1969 and although the massacre happened in March of 1968, the Americans had not received any official word until almost two years after the fact.

Although I was far too young to judge, I later learned that war and conflicts have a tendency to bring out the "best" and "worst" in people. There are many unknowns in battle and often a situation presents circumstances only those who are living in the moment can understand. Hundreds of Vietnamese civilians including women and children lost their lives as a result of the *Mỹ Lai* Massacre. And, although the atrocious incident created outbursts around the world, we will never truly know the thought process behind the decision taken that tragic day.

However, gruesome images were flashed every evening, accompanied by frightening accounts of bombings and deaths. As I drew closer to the TV I heard Brinkley report on the three hundred unarmed Vietnamese civilians who had lost their lives as others were forced into a ditch, scared by the threats of an unrelenting fury of machine gun bullets. The pictures and sound effects were distressing. And as an impressionable young girl I was disturbed by the media coverage. It increased my sadness and made me think of my mom who had been killed during the bombing of her village.

Sickened and upset, I always promised myself I would not watch, but seldom maintained my word. Whenever Margaret was present during a broadcast she not hesitate to remind me, "Mary if it wasn't for Sam and me you would be either a victim of war or living on the streets as a whore!"

To avoid getting into it with her, I would merely nod my head and walk away. It was a far better solution than listening to her yell insults at me. However, on one particular evening Margaret apparently was having one of her "bad days." She shouted at me, then turned her attention to Sam, once again accusing him of having an affair with my mom during the time we all lived in *Sài Gòn.*

"Shut the 'f' up—Jesus Christ, stop it!" Sam yelled in response.

Although vulgar words were common parlance and the Mustards' vocabulary was heavily laced not only with the abominable 'f' word, but with the sacrilegious G—D—expletive I always found so offensive and disrespectful, I always cringed during her outbursts.

Enraged by Sam's arrogant behavior, Margaret ran out of the condo. The door slammed with such force, it caused the room to vibrate. I heard the thud of her heavy footsteps as she walked down the steps. Where she was going was a mystery. At the time I had no idea about the nature of the cruel deed she was contemplating.

Once outside, Margaret headed for the storage area. Our luggage was kept there because we did not have sufficient closets to accommodate more than our clothing. When she reached her destination, she grabbed my yellow suitcase and with willful intent to cause emotional pain, she threw it into the dumpster! All the remaining photos of my mom as well as her precious letters and gifts were trashed. It was the eradicating of the last traces of my Vietnamese heritage. That day Margaret suffocated *Hiền.* She destroyed what little had remained of the tiny girl from *Sài Gòn.* It was a cruel act—a deed beyond forgiving.

I was still inside the house and unaware of what she had done. Several weeks later, when feeling lonely for my mother,

I went out to the storage to read her letters and play with the little dolls I had packed so diligently to guarantee they would be preserved forever.

I noticed the yellow bag was not in its place. Frantic, I looked around to see if perhaps one of the Mustards had moved it to another spot. I didn't trust Margaret and since we shared a room, I thought it best to hide my treasures in the suitcase. At least they would be safe. Children have such pure intentions.

I couldn't find my suitcase anywhere. Tears rolled down my cheeks even though in the initial moments I was in shock, not realizing what had actually happened.

"My yellow suitcase is gone!" I screamed through the sobs as I came into the house. "Sam—it's missing. It has all my mom's stuff in it." I repeated it over and over—"it has all my mom's stuff in it." I was crying so hard I barely made any sense. Sam had to calm my hysteria in order to understand what was wrong. No greater tragedy could have happened to me.

Without saying a word, Sam rose from the chair, staring in shock. Feeling my grief, his eyes welled up. The once placid man was visibly angry.

Sam smashed his cigarette in the ash tray, spilling ashes on the table. I noticed his fists were clenched and his jaw tense. Breathing heavily, he ran outside to look for it. It didn't take long for him to understand what had happened.

Sam returned to the house. Beads of sweat had formed along his forehead. His complexion was flushed. There was no doubt in my mind—Sam was upset.

Margaret, hearing my cries realized Sam had uncovered her vindictive misdeed. He was enraged. Cursing mercilessly, he boldly approached her raising his arm to hit her. I was standing in the entry way, trembling, petrified something awful would happen and they would cause physical harm to each other. It was a feeling I often felt especially since Sam and Margaret fought all the time.

Anticipating his intention to strike her, Margaret left the room before he could carry out his "sentence."

Sometimes I questioned if perhaps my mom had survived the drastic bombing only to realize it was unlikely since I no longer received any letters from her. I also realized I had to 'bury' her in my heart, painful as it was and move on, feeling grateful for the beautiful memories she left me with. And although I did accept her passing, I was incapable of dealing with the heavy grief. I continued to cry all the time. Eventually, I turned to my diary and released my sadness on the blank white pages.

I found an entry in one of my journals, dated January 11, 1967 in which I had written:

> *"With my mom gone in Việt Nam and who I loved so much, I wish I could die sometimes. God please help! Please let me be with them all the time. Oh, Mom, I love you so very much. I'll always love you all my life."*

One day while trying to overhear the Mustards' conversation, I discovered that Margaret was accused of physically abusing a child in school. She had hit a boy during a disciplinary confrontation. Although there was no condemning evidence, she was forced to deliver her resignation and leave the school.

Years later when I discussed the incident with my brother Bob, he told me that Margaret's problem with the Newhall

Public School was indeed an altercation. However, in the late sixties, such 'disputes' were handled with a pink slip dismissal or forced resignation. Nothing more was ever said about the incident.

Margaret was no longer employed. "We have to leave the area," I heard Sam say. "We can move to Thousand Oaks and either buy or rent a house. In addition, I have the opportunity to buy a McDonald's franchise."

Interested in the final outcome, I leaned forward to get a better view of what was happening. Margaret was seated at the dining room table leaning on both elbows. Her chin sat snugly between her joined wrists.

"Who would want to pay money for hamburgers and French fries?" she said, convinced her question was legitimate. "Sam," she continued, "McDonald's would be the worst investment you could get involved in. You'll have employees stealing from you—maybe even unsatisfied customers complaining about the food. It'll be just like a greasy, noisy hamburger joint!"

It was obvious Margaret was not in favor of Sam's business proposition. After all, in her mind how could a 'meat and potato' operation ever be successful—all that chaos and greasy food. What made me smile was her convenient memory loss. She seemed clueless, almost in denial of the fact that I grew up on that kind of fast food!

Margaret was sure they would exhaust themselves and end up penniless! "McDonald's," she said scoffing, "what an awful idea!" I guess it is more than evident she lacked foresight and a business vision.

Absurd as it all seemed, Margaret won that round. Sam dropped any idea of becoming a McDonald's franchisee, opting to purchase a home instead. Once again, it was time to pack up and move. And once again I found myself leaving behind a school and the many people I cared for, especially my close friends and my doting sister-in-law Helen who, living just a few blocks away, was a constant presence in my life, giving me so much love and attention.

With what remained of my life crammed into a suitcase, I waved goodbye. And once again I faced the adventure of acclimating myself to a new city. As always, I questioned the unknown—what would it bring me this time?

CHAPTER 7

The Path to Maturity: A Legacy of Torment Part II

*"The supreme happiness in life is
the conviction that we are loved."*
—Victor Hugo

We were now in our new home in Thousand Oaks. It was a nice size house, larger than the condo, and had enough space to allow individual sleeping quarters. Not having to share a room with Margaret was both a relief and a thrill. I now had privacy and a place where I could go to be alone with my thoughts.

Once settled in I resumed my life as a junior high school student. At twelve years of age, I was beginning to blossom into an attractive adolescent; a young girl who started to resemble my mother in a striking way. As a result Margaret's jealousy intensified, becoming more pronounced.

My presence was a constant and painful reminder of Sam's affection for my mom. Perhaps that was why Margaret was always on edge, nervous and irritable. Sam no longer looked at me like an adult gazes at a child. It was apparent he was transferring his desire for his beloved Yvonne to me although he never acted upon it. Limiting his actions to gawking and staring, he made me feel rather uneasy.

Sam's penetrating stares produced an uncomfortable, somewhat anxious feeling. To ease my fears I would shut the door and quickly shove a chair under the doorknob before I went to sleep every evening. I knew that if someone tried to come in they would have to struggle to gain entry. For, the noise of the chair hitting the floor would surely awaken me. It was my way of protecting myself from suddenly finding either Margaret or Sam at the foot of my bed.

Once again, I sought a life outside the home with my new friends in Thousand Oaks.

Not long after, Karen Eiswald entered my life. Like a special guardian angel, she soon became a 'sister' to me. At the time, I was unaware that our relationship would grow so deeply and continue indefinitely.

Karen had spirited hazel eyes and long, blonde waist-length hair. At five feet eight inches tall, she was and still is a beautiful, classy lady. Together, we were quite a striking contrast since I was dark-haired and a petite four feet eleven. However, Karen's assets were not limited to her extraordinary physical beauty. An equally exceptional intelligence gave her the edge both in school and in the social arena. Karen had it all.

Our meeting occurred at a bus stop en route to Colina Junior High School. Two eye-catching soon to be teens, we discovered much to our amusement that we had similar tastes in hat-wear. Plopped on our heads was the same Yoko Ono-John Lennon seventies era soft suede hippy 'rasta cap' with a cord circling along the brim and dangling down the back. Pointing to each other's hats we exploded in giggles, covering our mouths with the palm of one hand as if we had slipped and spoken a naughty word. Immediately, I knew she would be my new best friend.

Karen and I were in Core together; a class that merged History with English. We sat side by side and often whispered to each other during the lesson. Our relationship developed and soon I was invited to meet her parents. This was a new experience, a wonderful occurrence I soon became attached to.

Karen's family was a remarkable copy of the Cleavers. Her mother, Bettie was a trim, attractive woman with a creamy ivory complexion. A mass of short sandy curls framed her bright blue eyes. Dressed *a la* June Cleaver in crisp, pastel-colored shirtwaist dresses, she was a statement of the times.

Unlike Margaret, Bettie was a stable presence in a home that welcomed guests with warm smiles and the delicious aroma of fresh-baked goods. Food was plentiful and a place was set at the table immediately for any last minute and/or unexpected arrival. When I visited, we sat around the table enjoying Bettie's mouth-watering meals and the loving company of Fred, Karen and Greg, her husband and children.

Fred was a delightful man with a quick-witted sense of humor, smooth olive skin and a jovial, round face. The general manager of a car dealership, he was a hard worker and good provider for his family. When Karen's father crossed the threshold every evening, he was greeted with a piping hot home cooked meal and loving company. As a result of Fred's talent for delivering jokes with his son and worthy sidekick, Greg, the dinner table was filled with lively conversation and hearty laughter.

Greg was tall and athletic, a football player two years older than Karen and me. As a team, father and son were hilarious, bouncing punchlines between each other while the rest of us enjoyed the 'evening comedy routine.'

Once in their delightful company, I never wanted to leave. I respected and was drawn to the special bond the family shared, a bond they soon widened to include me. Bettie would always take my face in her hands, lean over and kiss me on the cheek. "Mary," she'd say, smiling widely, "you're our little China doll. You're our special Twinkie—yellow on the outside and all white inside."

This was the Eiswalds' lighthearted way to tease me about looking so typically Asian, yet living and thinking with the mindset of an American. We would laugh and giggle until our sides ached. Yet, the startling truth about my scarcity of knowledge regarding my culture and heritage both surprised and amazed each one of them.

Unlike Sam and Margaret, the Eiswalds were committed Christians who carried their faith from church to their home. It was not uncommon to see them join hands to say grace before meals, asking God to bless everyone—those present around their table and those in need.

On the other hand, the Mustards were concerned with making an impression on the community by attending church services on a regular basis, which was twice on Sundays. However, once the hymns quieted and the preacher said his final Amen, they left the congregation and lived as Christian imposters.

Margaret became more ruthless in her aggression towards me. The emotional abuse and badgering continued. After awhile, I began to stand up to her. I guess I was starting to think for myself. Maybe it was the onset of puberty and a resulting adolescent rebellion. Whatever the motive, I no longer took her nasty, demeaning comments in silence, but answered her back. Of course, my snappy rebuttals infuriated her even more.

Consumed with jealousy, she picked on me mercilessly. Most of the time, my wardrobe selections would trigger a nasty screaming match. A typical teenager, I dressed in miniskirts and hot pants following whatever the current fashion trend dictated. Ironically, it was Margaret who chose and purchased my clothes. This fact enhanced the absurdity and evil nature of her tantrums.

"Mary," she'd say when she caught a glimpse of me leaving for school, "your skirt is too short. You look like a tramp! I can see you're growing up to be a whore like your mother!"

"Well, Margaret," I blurted, quickly defending myself against her unjust accusations, "why would you buy clothes for me, then criticize me for wearing them? You tell me one thing and expect me to do something different. I just don't get it. I'm trying to understand what I'm supposed to wear."

"Mary," she growled through clenched teeth, "you're sassing back to me now and being a little bitch."

Flushed and breathless, she walked over to her desk, grabbed the wooden yardstick, raised her arm and swatted me across the thighs several times. Of course, she made certain to hit me below the hemline. Aiming for my bare skin, she knew I would feel the burning sting more intensely. This time she was right!

Although these abusive and demeaning accusations were repeated almost daily throughout my junior high and high school years, they always hit with the same intensity.

Regardless of the frequency, the screams and insults were hard to digest.

As I released my anger and frustrations making rebellious comments that had to ring true even to Margaret, she would whip out her hand and whack me several times across the face to silence my tongue.

In 1971 I was a high school freshman. I signed up for physical ed. and met Nancy Agulia, another dear friend who, like Karen, was destined to be part of my life forever. Nancy had a magnetic sense of humor, a set of hazel, penetrating eyes and thick brown hair which ended midway down her back. Undoubtedly, her looks were fabulous and her wit and personality simply extraordinary.

We met during a PE class. I heard a contagious laugh, glanced over my shoulder and there she was. We hit it off immediately. I introduced Karen to Nancy, and the three of us became an inseparable trio.

Nancy's family was typically Italian. That meant lots of laughter, hugs and excellent food. I tasted menus I had never known existed. Both Karen's and Nancy's families invited me often, and I happily divided my time between the Eiswalds and the Agulias.

In school I was doing well and together with Nancy was nominated for Freshman Homecoming Princess. Excited, I told Margaret. "Oh, Mary," she said, frowning, "you're not going to get it. Who's going to vote for you? You don't know anyone."

After the votes were counted, it was announced that Nancy was elected Homecoming Princess. I was thrilled for her. Naturally, from Margaret I received a sneering, gloating, "See, I told you …I told you, you wouldn't get it."

I was livid. "You are the meanest person I know," I shot back at her. "OK, so I didn't get it. But, why would you gloat over that—why do you always get such pleasure when I lose? Why do you continue to tell me I'm not good for anything? You crush my self-esteem and try to make me feel as if I'm not able to accomplish anything. If I get any pleasure out of life, you try to spoil it with malicious comments."

Upset, I continued, "You don't have to love me—but why can't you just like me even a little bit? I clean and scrub your house. You won't let me go out on Friday nights unless the house is spotless. I study hard. I get good grades. I spend hours practicing the piano. Most parents would be proud to have a child like that. But, all you have are malicious comments and accusations for me—never a word of praise."

I was all wound up and going a mile a minute—just letting her have it. Of course, uninterested in hearing the truth, Margaret's sole intent was to shut me up. And the only way to do this was through violence. She lunged forward and gave me a swift double palm and back of the hand slap across the face, once with her right hand and once with her left. The swats echoed in the silence. Pleased, she stepped back. On her face she wore a grin of self-satisfaction. Margaret had accomplished her mission to quiet me—at least for the moment.

My cheeks swelled and stung. I must have been beet red. Although I didn't sleep very well that evening from the pain and tears, I later found out that because of the repeated blows to my face and ears she had ruptured my right eardrum.

It was as if Margaret's goal and purpose in life was to purge me of any self-confidence and convince me I was a total zero. Thankfully, she failed to achieve her objective. I took several psychology classes later on and realized how important the first six years of life are in the development of an individual. Looking back, I felt reassured that despite my humble beginnings, I received the love and nurturing necessary for healthy psychological growth. These are the most vital years, and they influence the basic foundation of the future adult.

Furthermore, I learned that my mother, Yvonne had instilled in me all the good qualities I possess today. She cared for me with devotion, tending to my emotional and physical needs in the best manner possible during that early period of our life together. Therefore, much as she tried, Margaret had little if any success in destroying all that my mother had built.

Eventually, I realized my only refuge from Margaret's rage was to enroll in different activities that would keep me away from home as much as possible. Following this survival strategy, I added church functions to my extracurricular activities. I have fond memories of exciting outdoor sporting events and nightly devotions around the campfire during the many summer vacations I spent at church-sponsored camps in Big Bear.

One breezy evening huddled around a crackling campfire with the other kids, I opened my heart to the minister, revealing parts of my life with the Mustards held in secret until now. Feeling my sadness, he encouraged everyone to join hands in prayer. I felt uplifted and empowered by the support from my friends and minister who seemed empathetic to my unhappy family situation.

Shortly thereafter, the minister approached me one day, handing me a hymnal open to "Angry Words," a song we had sung during Sunday services:

> *"Angry words! O let them never*
> *From the tongue unbridled slip.*
> *May the heart's best impulse ever,*
> *Check them ere they soil the lip."*

"Love one another thus saith the Savior,
Children obey the Father's blest command,
Love each other, love each other,
'Tis the Father's blest command."

—Horatio Palmer

I learned the words and music by heart, and whenever the Mustards fought or Margaret shouted and hit me, I ran to the piano, pounded out the notes on the keyboard and sang, "Angry Words."

It didn't take Margaret long to figure out my behavior pattern. She'd storm over to the piano and angrily slam the keyboard cover down on my fingers. The pain was instantaneous and piercing. Eventually, my knuckles painfully swelled and bled from the torn skin, forcing me to ease up on my playing.

However, whenever she retaliated with such annoyance and violence, I seemed to be 'inspired' to croon even louder. At this point, aggravated beyond reason, just as I wanted, she'd slap me across the face in a desperate attempt to silence me. But, the angrier she became the more I sang. Yet, the more I sang the more she struck me. And the more she hit me the harder I persisted, shouting "Angry Words." I just wanted to exasperate her. Had it not been so malicious, it probably would have qualified as an amusing slapstick comedy routine.

Through it all Sam sat stiffly at the dining room table, staring into space, puffing on his Marlboros. He never supported or defended me. Instead, he behaved as if I wasn't even present in the room.

Infuriated by his exaggerated detachment and indifference, I took a confrontational approach. "Sam," I shouted, "why do you just sit there? I thought you loved me! Why don't you help me? Why don't you say something?"

I was on a roll. All the painful, angry feelings locked within for so long spilled over. My hormones were raging and I was relentless. Never getting either a reaction or response from Sam, I ran out the door and headed for Nancy's house. It was my escape. It was a matter of survival.

Margaret's annoying heckling was incessant. One day she called out to me as I was going out the front door, "Mary, where are you going dressed like that—you look like a slut!"

Margaret labeled me and anyone else who dressed in short skirts or hot pants, a slut. I had heard the insult over and over, but it never ceased to distress me. After all, it was her mission to ruin my day. And she certainly had a knack for accomplishing her goal. But I promised myself I would not let her get away with it.

"Why do you always try to destroy my day?" I shouted at her. "Just shut up—let me go to school, otherwise I'll be late. I want to get out of here—let me go in peace. You're such a witch!"

Unable to digest the truth, she ran after me trying her best to whack me across the face. Fearing the worst, I clenched my fist and raised it up to my head just in time to block her arriving palm. My defense tactic was not easily accepted. Margaret became increasingly enraged. She grabbed my hair, pulled it until I screamed and dragged me towards her with the strength of an adrenaline-fueled mad woman. The pull was unexpected and its force threw me off balance. I fell to my knees. Instinctively, she tugged harder!

My scalp burned from her ferocious yanking. Actually, the throbbing sensation scared me even more than the intense pain. Without thinking, I lifted my leg and gave her a swift, hard kick in the shin. Although it felt so good, I could never have anticipated the sheer nastiness of her reaction. I was willing to suffer insults and a few painful slaps, but Margaret used another weapon this time. Running to her drawer, she pulled out a shiny pair of scissors, grabbed my hair, briskly twisted it and snipped off about seven inches!

When I turned, I saw her gloating face. Enclosed in her clenched hand was my hair. I had to admit Margaret was a master in the art of getting back at me. She knew how to 'hit hard.' My long, shiny hair was special to me. Clever in an evil way, she had found my Achilles tendon.

Surprisingly, Sam who had witnessed the "battle" ran over and pulled us apart before she scalped me or I had time to retaliate, angering her further.

Once freed from her reach, I ran to my bedroom, wailing, "I would have been better off dying in *Việt Nam* with a mother who loved me."

Margaret, in turn, stormed out of the room. Sam trailed behind her into the bedroom. He snatched the portable alarm clock near her bed and hurled it at her. Dramatic as it may have appeared, it was a scene I had viewed many times before.

The clock grazed the lamp on the nightstand, creating a shower of shattered glass. Hitting the floor, the broken pieces crackled loudly in the momentary silence. However, Sam had missed his target. His usually placid face was crimson and contorted in anger, his breathing heavy, almost labored. In a raspy voice he yelled, "You mother f___ bitch!"

I was shocked! This was an absolute first—not the vile swearing, but his willingness to come to my rescue. From this point on, the bickering intensified and escalated. It was now a daily part of life.

During another moment of heightened conflict, Margaret continued her accusations against my mom. She made certain I was well aware that the only reason Sam adopted me was because he was in love with my mom, knew he could not have her and took me instead.

This was a litany I would hear over and over again throughout my teen years. It was a part of life at the Mustards' and another painful secret I concealed from my best friends.

Early on I had learned that if I wanted to incorporate happiness in my life, I would have to make the right decisions to create it. In fact, I planned my time around after-school extracurricular activities and the company of people I was certain would not only bring joy to an otherwise miserable existence, but would stimulate and allow me to better myself and eventually mature into the woman I am today.

Although high school was an enjoyable experience, the situation at home kept deteriorating. In the evenings, exhausted from a busy, productive and eventful day, I would return home just in time to crawl into bed and lay my head on the pillow. This strategy served as a means of limiting my confrontations with Margaret. Her violent outbursts and often unexplained temper tantrums frightened me. I never knew just how far she would go.

On January 24, 1973, I turned sixteen. Nine months older than Karen and Nancy, I was the first to have reached the legal driving age. By now, it was known among my friends that the Mustards rarely celebrated birthdays. Fully aware even this milestone event would go unobserved unless they stepped in, Karen and Nancy organized a surprise party for me at a Pizzeria in town. I was thrilled by their thoughtfulness and loved them more for being such great friends. Even though I tried my best to conceal my sadness, my classmates were now old enough to understand something was not quite right.

The following day hearing the piercing ring of the phone, I ran from the shower to grab the receiver before the caller would hang up. "Mary," I heard Karen say, excited, "can you come over—my parents would like to talk to you."

"OK, Karen," I replied, always happy for an opportunity to visit with Bettie and Fred.

When I arrived, the Eiswalds welcomed me in the living room with hugs and a cool refreshment.

"Mary," Fred said, smiling, "I heard you just passed your driver's licensing exam. You and Karen are good girls; you study hard and earn high grades. Mary, you have been so conscientious that we're going to let you drive Karen's car until she turns sixteen. She's not old enough to get a license and it's just sitting in the driveway collecting dust. We'll get the insurance and you can pay for the gas. All you have to do is get behind the wheel and drive carefully, following the rules you were taught in driver's ed."

Overcome with emotion, I remained speechless. Fred handed me the keys to the large brown station wagon. I was so excited. I couldn't believe I had a car to drive! That afternoon Karen, Nancy and another friend, Becky, piled in and we went for a ride.

Cruising down Thousand Oaks Boulevard, I was driving in the right lane. Still unsure of myself, I was traveling at a moderate pace. I wanted to make a left turn and immediately without thinking, flashed my turning lights and cut straight across four lanes. Within less than sixty seconds I heard Karen's voice, "Mary, I think there is a police car with a flashing red light in back of us."

Gazing into the rearview mirror, I noticed the officer was pulling up next to me. Honking his horn to get my attention, he rolled down the window and gestured for me to stop. Realizing what was happening, I broke into tears.

"Do you know what you just did?" the tall, ruddy-complexioned policeman asked, looking me straight in the eyes. "Let me see your license," he said, before I could respond.

I grabbed my purse, fumbled a bit through the useless junk I toted around, then pulled out my brand new license. "Officer," I said with a crackling voice, "I know what I did." He looked at my license.

"Mary," he asked, how long should you drive in a lane before crossing into the next one?" Of course, having just taken my written exam I knew the correct answer.

"Well," he continued, "you know what to do—but did you do it?" At this point, teary-eyed and scared, I decided the best thing to do would be to confess my crime and accept the consequences. Dramatic and prone to exaggerating, I announced, "Guilty as charged—OK, take me to jail."

After contemplating my fate behind bars, my fear turned to Margaret. I knew she would be absolutely furious if she found out about my driving altercation. I imagined how many slaps I would get and how piercing her screams would be. Just the thought of her palm on my skin made me shudder.

Obviously, I was not handcuffed, "mugshot-ed" or booked. Instead, the kind officer gave me a warning and sent us on our way. An important lesson was learned that evening!

I got my license and I now had a car. Independence gained, I was prompted to seek part-time employment after school and on weekends. I wanted to be able to handle this part of the expenses myself. I felt it was time I started to earn some money to prove I was a responsible teenager.

My first job was at the Melody movie theater where Nancy worked. Actually, she was a big influence and the reason why I chose to work there. Having a job equated with spending less time at home. It was a great escape and allowed me to distance myself form the Mustards. I enjoyed having my own money and being accountable to myself for my spending.

During my junior year Karen and I became varsity song leaders even though Margaret tried to brainwash me into believing I would never be voted in. With determination to quash my self-esteem, she kept rehashing the old incident of Nancy winning the Homecoming Princess title instead of me in freshman year.

Often she would pick up my yearbook and count how many pictures of me were included as opposed to those of Nancy or Karen. Slapping me across the face because my photo appeared on less pages, she would shout, "Nobody likes you, Mary!" However, proving her wrong was a sweet triumph, even if I had to endure her countless humiliating slaps and insults for no valid reason.

Karen, Nancy, Becky and I spent hours running through our song leading and cheerleading routines either on the school campus or at Karen's house. We took it seriously and felt we had to get it right. Cheering at football and basketball games were important highlights of our high school years.

Music was in my blood and nurtured in my early years through endless visits with my mom, Yvonne to the Vietnamese theater group. Reminiscing about these entertaining outings brought to mind the loss of my yellow suitcase and all my treasured letters, photos and gifts. Among my treasures was the glistening gold treble clef my mom had given me just before my departure from *Việt Nam*.

I envisioned the morning in which she had clasped it around my neck. Now that I was a song leader and played the piano, I couldn't help thinking how appropriate it would have been to wear the treble clef as a symbol of my passion for music and performing.

Another bright spot in my life occurred when our high school song-leading group was selected to entertain and cheer at the football game between the San Francisco Forty-niners and the Denver Broncos in Candlestick Park. Since this was before the NFL engaged professional cheerleaders, it was quite a thrill and an honor to be chosen. In fact, as a tribute to us, a parade was organized in Thousand Oaks.

Although Sam and Margaret did not attend the big event, Bettie and Fred came along to cheer us on and take pictures.

I realized when Karen turned sixteen, I would have to return the car to Fred. Concerned about losing my transportation which had become, in a sense, my lifesaver, I knew I had to find another solution. However, sensing my dilemma, Fred offered to speak to Sam about buying me a car of my own. He told Sam I was a good student and a responsible girl holding a part-time job to help cover my expenses.

Apparently, Fred was both very convincing and an excellent salesman. Shortly thereafter, Sam signed his name on a $1,800 check, and I got the keys to an off-white 1968 Ford Mercury Cougar. With shiny chrome vertical bars in the front and side marker lights, it was beautiful. I was ecstatic and eternally grateful to Karen's father. Sam actually seemed pleased to see me so happy.

Senior year was fast approaching. With the thrill of graduation and prom night not far into the future, we reflected on the fun times we had enjoyed in these four short, but intense years. There were unforgettable football games, parties, close friendships and extracurricular activities. The memories we created were exciting and endearing. Since it was inevitable that our lives would take us in different directions, we knew our recollections of the wonderful times would always keep us united.

High school years were important years—years characterized by much laughter and tears, questioning and coming of age; years of searching and years of finding the happiness lost as a seven-year-old child; years that took us from childhood into early adulthood.

High school was all about making the right choices to become who I wanted to be and who I am today. With determination and persistence I discovered I could flip a miserable life into an enriching experience, attain my goals and maybe even enjoy myself.

Circumstances forced me to grow up more precociously than my friends and to assume sole responsibility early on, not only for my today but more importantly for my tomorrow. Therefore, my maturity level was somewhat accelerated for an eighteen-year-old high school senior.

I listened to Karen, Nancy and Becky whose parents had intervened in their lives, helping them make plans to continue their education. They were encouraged and supported throughout the stressful process of SATs, applications, interviews, visits to the various campuses and the nerve-wracking anticipation of acceptance letters.

Realizing I was alone, I sought advice from the school counselor who, aware of my situation, encouraged me to seriously consider attending college at the local California State University in Northridge. Informed by the Mustards that I was expected to support myself after high school, I did not have many options. Apparently, they were of the opinion that at eighteen years of age I was old enough to be responsible for putting a roof over my head.

I, on the other hand, believed I was uprooted from a poverty-stricken, war-ravaged *Việt Nam*, adopted by American parents and 'blessed' to have a chance at a better life; a life in which I would get an excellent education and the possibility of making something of myself.

The other option would have been to remain with my mom, Yvonne in *Sài Gòn*. Undoubtedly, my fate would have been her fate—death from the bombing attacks that destroyed the village in which we lived.

Eventually, reality set in along with the realization that if I was going to "make it," I was going to do it on my own. I had to come to terms with the truth, and senior year was my moment of truth.

In one of my last battles with the Mustards, Margaret once again attacked me for wearing a miniskirt to church after I had been voted "best dressed" by my peers. Years later looking back, I realized it was never about my wardrobe or how I dressed. It was, instead, about a little Vietnamese girl, *Nguyễn Thị Thanh Hiền*, the first-born child of a beautiful woman for whom Sam felt a 'special fondness.'

The same scenario played out with Sam serving her an f word insult that triggered a fast-paced ping-pong match of flying verbal vulgarities. Once again unable and unwilling to keep my mouth shut, I became defensive and let it all out. "Why are you two still married? There is no love in this family—only hate."

Catching my breath, I swung around on the driveway as Sam was getting into the car to drive to Sunday service. I glared at Sam and shouted, "Why didn't you defend me all these years? I thought you loved me. I thought you took me to America to protect and take care of me. All I ever wanted was for both of you to like me, even if as a friend and not a daughter. I was just an innocent child taken away from my mom. You raised me with so much hatred and jealousy. What a racist and bigot you are, Sam!"

I again turned on my heels, extending my index finger towards Margaret who had her hand on the car door. Enraged by her insult for the last time, I stammered through clenched teeth, "And you—you are the BITCH, not me! Sometimes I wish I was dead! I know I'm not supposed to hate—but I hate you both."

Much as I always tried to remember the hymn, "Angry Words," when faced with trying situations I realized I was pronouncing the very words I would eventually regret.

Sam slammed the car door shut. He walked over to where I stood on the passenger side of the car. Red-faced and breathless he lunged at me, positioning his hands around my neck. Before I knew what was happening, he tightened his grasp and with a clumsy, brusque movement shoved me forward, banging my head against the garage door. I felt a sharp, piercing pain and an immediate wave of nausea. My breath was taken away. I tried to scream, but the least movement intensified the agony and suffocated whatever bit of air I could get into my lungs.

Fighting for my life, I raised my leg and plunged my knee directly into his groin. Stunned and in agony, he released his hold on me. Margaret sat stone-faced. It never entered her mind that Sam could kill me. Immediately, I ran away, never looking back.

I went to Karen's house and unable to conceal my swollen eyes, tear stained face and the huge red welt around my neck, I blurted out what had happened.

"Mary, you have to call Bob and tell him," Fred said with parental concern. "You have to leave. You cannot go back there—call Bob!"

Bettie and Fred advised me to just take a few things and leave while Sam and Margaret were at work to avoid any nasty confrontations. "Mary, leave your bedroom intact," Bettie advised. "Just take some clothes." They both insisted I tell the Mustards I was leaving, but I was fearful of the consequences and chose to leave in silence.

I called Bob and Helen and told them what had happened. Bob was sympathetic, but not surprised and told me horror stories about his own life with the Mustards. And he was their biological son! He related one incident in which both Sam and Margaret had mistreated him beyond endurance. In a fit of rage he grabbed the pan of hot tomato sauce sitting on the stove and dumped the entire contents over the heads of his parents!

"Of course, I ran away and stayed with a family from church for about a week," he said. "Afterwards they hit me—but it was well worth it."

"Well Bob," I said, listening to his colorful tale, "I guess that is why Margaret never cooked another meal."

"Mary," he responded, "after that incident, I vowed that when I turned twenty-one, I would legally change my name. I wanted nothing to do with the Mustards and didn't want to be associated with their family name.

It was as if Bob wanted to erase the Mustard family from the face of the earth and cancel all the horrendous memories of the emotional and physical abuse he was forced to endure during his childhood.

"Mary," he murmured, sighing, "just the sound of their name brings to the surface such painful and horrible memories."

Bob suffered chronic episodes of depression and had several bouts of major depression which in the sixties and seventies were identified as nervous breakdowns. The most serious mental breakdown occurred when he learned the Mustards were planning to return from *Việt Nam*.

He kept his vow. Shortly after his twenty-first birthday, Bob hired an attorney and changed his name, slashing the Mustards out of his life and memory like a surgeon slices through a metastasized cancer, in a last desperate attempt to save a life.

The following Wednesday, Greg and Karen drove over to the Mustards to pick up my car. They returned to pick me up, and as planned we all headed for Northridge. Bob and Helen had made arrangements for me to room with one of his friends, Carol Kindshi, who worked at Cal State and had an apartment right across the street from the college. She had agreed to take me in as a guest, reassuring Bob I would be welcomed, safe and secure. My brother thought rooming with Carol would be a convenient living arrangement since I was going to attend college at Cal State in the fall.

A pleasant woman in her mid-thirties, Carol had short auburn hair which framed an attractive oval face. Although older, her sense of humor and fun-loving personality soon put me at ease. She became a great mentor during my first semester, teaching me how to cook and offering me dating tips. Listening to each other's romantic stories, we shared some good, hearty laughs.

It was now *29 tháng tư*, April 29, 1975, and the media was reporting on *Operation Frequent Wind*. I heard the newscaster mention that American and Vietnamese citizens as well as visiting foreign nationals and diplomats were being evacuated by military helicopters from *Sài Gòn* and transferred to off-shore US Navy ships. The operation began with the airing on Armed Forces Radio of the song "White Christmas." I listened attentively, feeling my heart race.

The following day, *30 tháng tư,* April 30, *Fall of Sài Gòn,* the City was re-named *Hồ Chí Minh City.* At precisely 3:30 pm, General *Dương Văn Minh* in a radio broadcast announced, " I declare the *Sài Gòn* government completely dissolved at all levels."

The *Việt Nam* War was officially ended, and April 30 was proclaimed *Ngày Chiến thắng*—Victory Day.

I was eighteen years old and two months away from graduating from high school. I had the right to vote and was legally an adult. Ironically, the fall of *Sài Gòn* did not signify just the end of the *Việt Nam* War—but also the end of my war with the Mustards. I had finally left the battlefield. It was my own personal *Ngày Chiến thắng!*

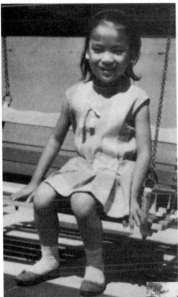

My home, early 1960s.

Me on swing, living
with the Mustards.

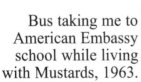

Bus taking me to
American Embassy
school while living
with Mustards, 1963.

The cargo plane on which Sam Mustard flew.

My Baby,
I'm very sad because you are gone. I miss you very much. I had a letter from you one month ago. I'm very happy you have a lot of friends in school.
I've kept your Viet Namese dress and the p
Please write
Be happy.
Mees tand sou are now not a l
I'm happy
girl very p

My first bike.

Me and Margaret Mustard.

Me and Mom.

Saigon 4th November 1964th

Dear Mr and Mrs Sam.

Now, I work all the day so that I can't go to the house at street Hồng-thập-Tự. Please you said to my daughter Hiên write to me and send to this address 376/336 A, Phan Đình Phùng Saigon.

I remember her very much. All the day I always think to her and her letter.

Thank you very much

Yours faithfully
Yvonne

Margaret and Sam
Mustard on cyclos.

Me and a friend.

At the airport, leaving for
America, September 3, 1964.

Mom in 1962 at Pagoda.

he Adoption Agreement made at t
10, 1964;

the fact that SEON MORRIS MUST
ELLEN MUSTARD had agreed to adopt NGUYEN THI TH
sex, born in 1957 at the 3rd District of Saigon;
Orders the publication of this Decree at the
Head Office of Gia-dinh Province;
Orders that the statements thereof shall be
full into the birth registers of Saigon 3rd Dist
in the margin of the Decree doing for birth cert
issued by the First Instance Court of Saigon on
in the records of said District and at the Cler
Court,
Leaves the costs at the charge of the peti
This Decree was thus made and pronounced p
and month and in the year as aforesaid.
Signed : TON THAT HIEP and NGUYEN THI THU
In the margin is written : Recorded in Sai
Judiciary and Extra Judiciary Deeds, on August
Folio 15, N°161/3.Received : VN$240 - The Reco
(signature and seal).

A True
Saigon, Au
The Head
Signed

ERTIFIED TRUE TRANSLATION

VU KHAC HONG
Sworn Translator.
My oath was administered by
the Saigon Justice of the Peace
8h January 2 1962.
Office address : Law Court,
131, Công Lý Street, SAIGON.

Adoption decree

Threads of my past, given to the Red Cross to aid in their search for my mom.

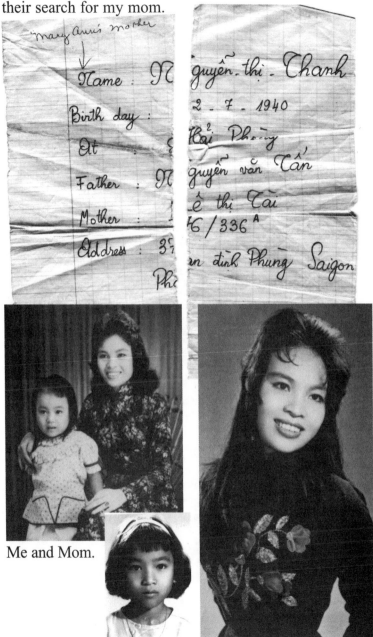

Me and Mom.

My passport photo. Mom.

American Red Cross

July 26, 1993

Ms. Mary Reed
Huntington Beach, CA 92646

Our Case: ISS 16227
Reg: Nguyen Thi Thanh

Dear Ms. Reed,

We are pleased to inform you that
located at the following address:

Dao Thi THanh (Bich Van)
1, Rue de la Noue   *Paris*
Bat 3, Appt 165
93170 Bagnolet
France   011 331
Telephone 48.70.92.30

We are happy to have

Sincerely,

Tung Van Nguyen
Southeast Asian Spec:

My brothers fleeing to
Singapore.

Me, Mom and my three kids,
right after the reunion in 1993.

Family in France.

Five of my seven sibling performers, Paris in the late 1980s.

My kids, left to right, Denny, Jenna and Kevin.

My family, 2007.

The return to Vietnam forty-three years later, December 2006.

Me, Mom and
Phương.

Full circle—the street
where I lived and
where, miraculously,
my mother found
the American Red
Cross flyer.

Upgraded
bathroom.

FALL '93

THE ORANGE COUNTY UPDATE
✛ American Red Cross

VOLUME 13, NUMBER 3

HUNTINGTON BEACH WOMAN'S QUEST HAS HAPPY ENDING

Mary Reed (on left) introduces her daughter Jenna to her grandmother Thanh (in center) as Mary's sister Phuong looks on.

The bright pink sign that said, "Dreams Do Come True! Welcome Thanh" was held aloft by Mary Reed's friends as they surrounded her awaiting the arrival of her mother Dao Thi Thanh at the LAX Airport the evening of September 3. September 3, 1993 marked the end of an incredible journey for Mary and her mother. Their journey spanned

29 years, three separate continents, and three different cultures.

In 1964, 29 years ago to the day, Mary, born Nguyen Thi Thanh Hien, bid a tearful farewell to her mother in the Saigon airport. As the turmoil in Vietnam escalated, Mary was very ill with smallpox and her mother sought the

THE GIFT THAT KEEPS ON GIVING

This year as you are writing your holiday gift list, choose to give Red Cross Holiday Donation Program greetings. These holiday cards are the perfect way to remember all those people you have a hard time choosing a gift for — your children's teachers, the mail carrier, all those friends and acquaintances you want to remember during the holiday season. You might even consider purchasing some in your children's or grandchildren's name to teach them the spirit of giving.

And in the spirit of the holidays, it will make you feel good because your support will help the Orange County Chapter continue to provide essential services to the community's disaster victims. And, those friends, relatives, and business associates who receive the Red Cross greetings will appreciate your thoughtful generosity and the donation was made their name.

The Holiday Donation Program is important to the community so that programs like disaster services, service military families, refugee relocation, Holocaust and War Victims Tracing, services, HIV/AIDS education and prevention, health and safety education can remain available for all.

The good news is that the Red C

B6   WEDNESDAY, AUGUST 18

REUNION: Family Will Meet in Paris

Continued from B1

network in 146 countries, but who found her and how remains a mystery.

Reed had been able to supply only her mother's name and age and the name of a younger sister.

"The only things I remember in Vietnamese are all three of our names," Reed said.

In Little Saigon, the same tracking service frequently finds people separated from family during the Vietnam War. In 1992

WHAT'S INSIDE

MIDWEST FLOOD UPDATE
page 2

KEZY "FLOOD RELIEF"
RICOH HELPS MIDWEST FLOOD VICTIMS
page 3

VOLUNTEERS LINK OUTSIDE WORLD
page 5

DREAMS DO COME TRUE!
WELCOME THANH

September 3, 1993—LAX reunion, twenty-nine years to the date since I had left Vietnam.

RED CROSS CHRONOLOGY FOR ISS 16227

Sought Person:	NGUYEN THI THANH (married name: Dao Thi Thanh).
Inquirer:	MARY MUSTARD (married name: Mary Mustard Reed).
9/20/1990	Tracing Inquiry received by International Social Services (ISS), American Red Cross, from American Red Cross chapter, Orange Co., CA.
10/18/1990	ISS, American Red Cross, sends tracing inquiry to the Red Cross of Vietnam.
10/18/1990	ISS sends acknowledgement of the inquiry to Orange County chapter.
5/14/1991	ISS, American Red Cross, sends follow-up inquiry to the Red Cross of Vietnam.
12/14/1991	ISS receives acknowledgement from the Red Cross of Vietnam that this inquiry is an open case with their society.
10/3/1992	ISS sends a second follow-up inquiry to the Red Cross of Vietnam.

1/17/1993	ISS advises Orange County Chapter that no news has been received on this case, but if and when it does, ISS will notify the chapter.
6/16/1993	Red Cross of Vietnam advises ISS, American Red Cross, that the sought person has been located in France, and provides her address and phone.
7/1/1993	ISS informs the Orange County Chapter of the sought person's address and phone number.
8/9/1993	Orange County chapter informs ISS that inquirer has been able to contact the sought person in France.
8/24/1993	*Los Angeles Times* prints the reunification story. A twenty-nine-year separation of mother and daughter is now successfully resolved.

CHANGING TIDES

CHAPTER 8

Freedom:
The Reprieve

*"Freedom is not a reward or a decoration that is celebrated
with champagne...Oh no! It's a...long distance race,
quite solitary and very exhausting. Freedom is nothing else
but a chance to be better."*
—Albert Camus

A new chapter of my life was beginning and though somewhat apprehensive, I faced it with enthusiasm and a certain sense of relief. Although I was free from the Mustards, I questioned over and over—what now?

The nightly news broadcasts with heart-wrenching reports and deplorable images of Vietnamese citizens shoving their way into the US Embassy for a chance to have a better life weighed heavily on my spirit. Glued to the TV, I watched day after day as desperate women pleaded with unknown soldiers to take their children, handing them over fences whenever they spotted an American in uniform.

It was now considered a crime for the Vietnamese to leave the country. Many defied the 'law,' were caught, imprisoned and tried again—only to be re-sentenced. Life was tyrannical with neighbors forced to tattle on neighbors who broke the Communist rules. Religious freedom was banned, and in some instances practicing Christians were forced to denounce their beliefs in writing. Poverty was widespread and the humiliation over not being able to care for family and children brought desperation. Looking at the wasted, often contorted faces shown on the news was a testament to the cruelty and suffering these people were forced to endure. Many were ousted from their homes and relocated to "re-education camps" in destitute areas. According to French journalist Jean Lacouture, this is "a prefabricated hell and a place one comes to only if the alternative to it would be death!"

In the spring of 1975, one hundred thirty thousand battered and weary refugees seeking a better life crammed themselves into wooden boats sailing for days in the wind and rain, until the fuel ran out and they just drifted through the remaining six hundred often rocky miles to the Malaysian coast. Famished, hungry, exhausted and weakened from the disastrous conditions, the *Boat People* sought freedom and a dignified life. Sadly, many never made it. They perished during the journey and were buried at sea.

Although I was living with Bob's friend, Carol and facing the exciting experience of college and life as a young adult, I could not shake the memory of US helicopters, their propellers in a constant spin, perched on top of the American Embassy. It was a continuous reminder of the atrocious Communist takeover.

Bob informed Carol about the Mustards, and feeling saddened by the nastiness and deprivation I had endured, she treated me like a little sister. Knowing the history made her even more compassionate towards me. In fact, she didn't ask me to help with the rent. When I moved in she said, "Mary, don't worry about it. You don't have to contribute anything. But if you want to get a job and pay for some of the food that's OK."

I was determined to make it. Standing on my own two feet meant getting a job. Soon after I became Carol's roommate, I sought work and was hired by Windsor Fashions. This was a woman's retail clothing store located in the Northridge Fashion Mall. The clothes were beautiful and Windsor sold it all—dresses, purses, shoes and everything in between. For a young girl with a flair for fashion it was a lot more exciting than making popcorn and walking up and down the aisles in a movie theater.

Besides the fun job, working at Windsor's gave me the opportunity to meet another wonderful friend who, today, continues to be a very important person in my life. Like me, she was working her way through college. That morning I went to work anticipating a busy day. I came into the store to begin my shift and was immediately approached by another girl just about my age.

"Hi," she said with a broad smile, "my name is Dara-lee—you know like Sara Lee the cake." She chuckled and her eyes lit up.

"Hi Dara-lee," I responded, not bothering to quiet my own giggles, "my name is Mary Mustard—you know, like the mustard you splash on a hot dog!" We looked at each other, broke into laughter and bonded immediately. I knew I had a friend for life.

Dara-lee Norris was and still is a beautiful blonde with equally impressive brains. She had three sisters, a set of dazzling eyes and a captivating smile. Barefoot, she stood about five feet five inches, which from my four-feet-eleven perspective is classified as tall.

Soon after our meeting, Dara-lee took me home to meet her parents, Mr. and Mrs. Norris, a Norwegian couple with strong Christian principles. Warm and loving people, they were members of the Baptist Church. We hit it off immediately. On many occasions I was invited to family dinners. In a sense they 'filled in' for the Eiswalds who were back in Thousand Oaks and far too distant for daily visits.

Graduating from high school brought many changes to my life. It was a rite of passage that separated me from Karen and Nancy—at least for a few years. Karen applied to and was accepted at Principia College in New Jersey. I was saddened by the news.

'Losing' my best friend and her family were difficult, even if I knew it was not forever. Nancy, on the other hand, decided to postpone her college education and dive into the workforce instead. Choosing to remain in Thousand Oaks, she accepted a full-time position at State Farm Insurance. Eventually, during senior year in college we did room together while she pursued and earned a degree in education.

This temporary interruption did not cool our friendships. Karen, Nancy and I remained soul mates even though at this point in time we journeyed along different paths.

The days and weeks flew by and soon summer came to an abrupt end. However, it was a time of new friendships and experiences. Meeting Dara-lee was the beginning of a lifelong friendship and my introduction to sorority and fraternity life.

Speaking with Dara-lee one afternoon, I learned she was a member of the *Alpha Phi Sorority*. Curious, I asked her what it all meant. In response, she read me their charter. "Mary," she said, *"Alpha Phi* is *a membership organization dedicated to promoting sisterhood, cultivating leadership and encouraging intellectual curiosity and advocating service."*

"It sounds good to me," I said.

At the start of freshman year, I rushed. Rushing is a recruitment process which allows the girls to participate in events, meet their sorority sisters and become acquainted with the *Alpha Phi* way of life before actually joining.

Enjoying rush, the girls I met and the ideals and mission of *Alphi Phi* encouraged me to sign up. It was a decision that opened up a whole new world and experiences.

There were twenty-six new members in my *Delta* Pledge class. Dara, a year older and a sophomore, was in the *Beta* Pledge class. However, despite my active participation in my own pledge class, through my close friendship with Dara I bonded with the *Beta* Pledge sisters, Debbie Srery, Sheri Fox and Nancy Procop all of whom were destined to become lifelong friends.

Dara was also a little sister in the *Sigma Chi*, a male fraternity with similar values involving service, leadership and brotherhood. She invited me to a couple of sorority functions and took me to the *Sigma* parties. "Mary," she said, while we were attending a meeting at the campus sorority house, "you don't know anyone here. This is a great way to meet people, make friends and start a whole new life." Eventually, I also became a Sigma Chi little sister like Dara.

My relationship with Dara blossomed immediately. Looking back, I recall that it was Dara who introduced me to Chinese food, in particular rice. In fact we share fond memories of gorging ourselves on cheap Asian food.

Since Dara was an English-Journalism major, she had the task of proofreading and correcting my English homework. Sometimes she actually rewrote my papers to be certain I got the grade I deserved for good research and content, even if not perfectly expressed. Although I was fluent in English, I still had some difficulties with sentence construction. Perhaps this 'failing' was partly responsible for my comic appeal.

Dara also spent hours interviewing me and incorporating my life story in her class assignments. Since I had emigrated from *Việt Nam* just eleven years earlier, the events and impressions were still somewhat vivid in my mind.

Confiding in Dara, I told her about my treasured yellow suitcase and the sorry fate it suffered at the hands of my mean, vindictive adopted mother, Margaret. Participating in my emotional devastation firsthand, she would cry and sob with me as I relived the painful experiences of my early life with the Mustards.

Before assuming the presidency, Debbie, a close long-term friend with a generous, giving heart was sorority treasurer during my freshman and sophomore years. And thanks to her, I was able to remain in *Alpha Phi.*

Once I joined, I was responsible for the initial fee and monthly dues. Since my job at Windsor's provided a modest earning, and I did not have any family backing, this was a bit of a hardship.

Debbie seemed to understand my dilemma. Realizing I was unable to meet these financial obligations, she did not collect the dues from me. Though she didn't know all the minute details, eventually she discovered I was estranged from my adoptive parents and consequently responsible for my own college tuition and living expenses. Furthermore, she knew I had the moral, ethical and intellectual qualities to be a conscientious sorority sister. The only thing I lacked was the dollars and cents.

Based on this criterion she made the decision to relax the monetary responsibility, believing my presence and contribution to *Alpha Phi* far outweighed her closing an eye on the economic aspect of the organization. After all, it was about service oriented endeavors, building leadership and sisterhood bonding—all of which had nothing to do with dues, unless of course, you had the means to pay.

But Debbie felt that penalizing me for insufficient funds because of my deprived situation was not in keeping with the principles of *Alpha Phi*. And there was absolutely no possibility to solicit Sam's help.

As far as I was concerned, the Mustards were a closed chapter! They had no influence on my life. They couldn't hurt me anymore—or so I thought.

Sorority life was fun. There was a wonderful camaraderie, and for once in my life I felt a reassuring inner peace; a serenity I knew resulted from my separation from the Mustards. The *Alphi Phi* girls were my family. We shared our thoughts, feelings and dreams. We were inseparable.

The weekly chapter meetings brought us closer together as we tearfully opened our hearts, held hands and joined our voices in song. The girls were loving and sweet, and I was encouraged to speak more freely about my past. For me, it was a very new and different feeling.

After rooming with Carol during my first semester, I moved into the sorority house. Grateful for the kindness she demonstrated, I knew it was time to move on, even if supporting myself was difficult on a minimum wage of $1.75 an hour. Though meager, this amount had to cover rent, tuition, books and personal expenses.

Learning how to budget my money, I nourished myself on Kraft Macaroni and cheese which at seventeen cents a box was affordable and substantial enough to satisfy my hunger.

Debbie, Sheri and Nancy often cautioned me about not earning enough money to stay in school. At one point I had to borrow $100 from my brother, Bob. However, accountable for my decisions, I paid him back with interest.

Concerned I would be forced to quit school and seek full-time employment because of my dire financial situation, Debbie spoke up for the others, "Mary," she said, "why don't you apply for a waitress position at Coco's Restaurant?" Since she was working there as a waitress, she knew they were hiring. "Mary," she continued, "in retail you don't make that much money. But as a waitress you get great tips. The pay at Windsor Fashions is hardly enough. You can't support yourself like this—you need to make more money. Why don't you work with me at Coco's?"

I listened and heeded her advice, but kept my sales position at Windsor Fashions because I adored beautiful clothes and loved the discount I was entitled to as an employee. But I needed money and Debbie was right. Ambitious and needy, I was now working two jobs besides going to school.

I majored in Business-Finance; Debbie, Business Management; and her boyfriend, now husband, Scott, Business Accounting. This common interest in various aspects of business brought us closer as we studied together in the library on the third floor. However, I have to confess that my presence on the third floor was not exclusively linked to my studies.

Gregarious and adventuresome, I repeatedly lost my concentration. Once distracted, I gazed around the room to check out the young business majors engrossed in their studies. My objective, which I successfully accomplished, was to date some of the 'guys' from the third floor library!

After classes and dinner I would entertain my sorority sisters with amusing tales of my dates, encouraging them to share their experiences. Laughing and enjoying each other's company, we would stay up well into the wee hours, exchanging dating stories.

Besides the 'frat house,' our nightly encounters at *Alpha Phi* soon became the popular 'social happening place' on campus. Despite the fun and extracurricular activities, we all graduated in four years proving the validity of the old expression—"we studied hard, worked hard and played hard!" I guess the end did justify the means in this particular case.

Although, as many friends told me, I was the life of the party outwardly, secretly I was badly scarred and in need of healing. The consequences of the Mustard reign of terror would live within me for decades if not an entire lifetime. But I was determined to keep my promise. I would overcome my demons. I would find the happiness I knew I deserved—one day.

Conscientious about my responsibilities, I continued working at Windsor Fashions and Coco's. Sticking to my budget plan, I was able to trade in my old Ford Mercury and get a new navy Chevy Monza. In so doing I began to establish credit and began building a credit history.

Karen was now a student at UCSB in Santa Barbara, and one weekend we had set an appointment to meet at her parents' house in Thousand Oaks. Always eager to see Bettie and

Fred, I was now excited to show them my recently acquired Chevy Monza.

My new car was a disappointment, and by the time I arrived at Karen's house I was rather upset. That evening at dinner Fred asked me about my car. "My car doesn't run very well," I responded, "it's such a piece of lemon."

When Karen reacted with a chuckle, I was stunned and upset at the same time. "What's so funny, Karen?" I asked, a bit irritated.

"Oh, Mary," she replied, chuckling, "the car is either a lemon or a piece of shit! Mary, you got a lemon—that's the correct expression. I'm sorry for laughing, but this is too funny. You never get the saying right. It seems as if you have your own interpretation."

The more my friends tried to teach me the proper phrases and idioms, the more I said them wrong. I had to face the truth—I just couldn't master the art of clichés.

Although the Mustards were no longer a part of my life, I did see them at Bob and Helen's holiday party. During that visit, I learned they had just moved to Sutter's Creek, a mining town populated with Victorian style construction. By now they were quite elderly. Sam's chain smoking had taken a toll on his health, and Margaret was not doing too well herself. Some serious health issues had left her weakened and frail.

At the conclusion of the semester, a group of eight *Alphi Phi* sisters decided to spend the summer in Hawaii. Debbie, Nancy and two other girls remained in Waikiki while I, along with three other sorority sisters, enrolled in a summer program sponsored by the University of Hawaii, in Honolulu. We decided to apply for housing in the campus dorm.

It was summer of 1977. The night of our arrival we went the

Foxy Lady Club. Exhausted from the long flight, I sat with the girls trying to get a feel for this beautiful Paradise. The towering oceanfront Nippon style hotels, breathtaking mountainous panoramas, striking evening sunsets and corrugated volcanoes designing part of the skyline were awesome. I already felt as if I was in another world.

"How far I have come from the one-room grass hut," I thought to myself, smiling. Suddenly, like a fast moving cloud my mood turned gloomy as my mind raced to the moment I stepped from the plane onto American soil here in Hawaii for the first time. "It was thirteen years ago," I whispered to myself sadly, "and I lost the pretty gold purse with all the photos my mom gave me."

That Friday night I had no idea my life was about to change, until I met Jon Boyd, a drop-dead gorgeous guy who stood six feet two inches tall. A tanned to perfection complexion highlighted his shinning blond hair and deep blue eyes.

He had the self-confidence of a young man who never had a problem getting a date. His broad smile attracted like a magnet. The atmosphere was electrifying, and I fell for his polished charm immediately. Somehow, he seemed different from all the other guys I had dated in Northridge.

Jon was twenty-two—two years my senior and a college grad with a degree in finance. I noticed he was impeccably dressed. He asked me to dance and we bonded on the dance floor, becoming inseparable. Kind and gallant, he was attentive and looked after us the whole summer.

I told Jon I was taking Marketing and Hula classes at the University of Honolulu, and Monday morning while leaving my first class, I saw him standing outside the door. "Mary," he said, flashing a perfect set of pearl white teeth, "I'll walk you over to your marketing class."

"OK, Jon," I said, happily agreeing. During the walk I realized it was going to be rather difficult to focus on any course I had enrolled in.

And then it happened—I came down with Scarlet Fever. If ever something bad or disturbing had to happen, I always seemed to be the target. Now I was sick with an infectious disease. The dorm was immediately quarantined. I felt miserable, achy and exhausted.

The agonizing ordeal of my bout with smallpox crossed my mind. However, this time I had a comfortable bed, plenty to eat and drink and medical attention. Although almost delirious with a high fever, I recognized how far I had traveled on my journey in such a short period of time.

Highly contagious, the Scarlet Fever spread through the dorm. The place was pulled apart and sanitized in an attempt to halt the outbreak. I was agonizing. My skin first itched, then burned from my nails scratching and digging in. I tried to stop the itching and did not understand that an itch is a lot better than a nasty scrape from repeated scratching.

My throat felt raw—making it painful to swallow.

The doctors arrived and treated us with antibiotics until everyone was cured. As soon as the quarantine was lifted, Jon ran over. He took one look at me and noticed I was weakened by the ordeal.

Caring and incredible as he was, he took me to his apartment and nursed me back to health. I was deeply moved by his devotion. Considering the short time we had known each other, I was deeply touched by the kindness and caring he demonstrated.

Towards the end of summer, my return to Northridge was imminent. "Mary, I'd like you to remain in Hawaii with me,"

Jon said. "Why don't you transfer to the University of Honolulu?" My heart skipped a beat. A part of me wanted to say, "Yes," immediately. I really didn't have to think about it!

"Mary," Jon continued, realizing it was too quick a decision to make at a moment's notice. "We'll talk about it tomorrow night at dinner."

Though I agreed, while on my way back to the dorm I had already decided I would transfer to Hawaii to be with Jon.

That evening I received a phone call from Sam Mustard. "Mary" he said, in his standard aloof monotone, "Margaret was diagnosed with pancreatic cancer."

I was devastated—my world had just shattered into pieces. Finally, I had found happiness. But was I delusional in thinking I had finally met someone who would love, protect and care for me?

"Mary," he continued, "I'd like you to come home!"

That evening, unable to control my tears and barely able to speak, I told Jon that Sam called and asked me to come back to California because Margaret was dying. "What are you going to do? You're not going back—are you?" Jon asked, excited.

"I have no choice," I sobbed. "I have to go back."

"But Mary," he responded, visibly irritated, "why would you go back to see her when she was so mean and cruel to you? She never loved or treated you like a daughter. Why this deathbed loyalty and devotion?"

"Jon," I said, sighing, "I have to follow my conscience— I have to do the right thing."

"Mary," he said, gently taking my trembling hand, "I'm afraid that once you leave Hawaii, you'll never come back. If you stay, I'll help you with school—Mary, I'll be here for you."

Although Jon's words were comforting and encouraging, I knew there was no way I could stay, much as I so desperately wanted to. I had to visit Margaret knowing full well that my decision was motivated by obligation, not love.

A couple of days later, Jon accompanied me to Honolulu International Airport. It was a short ride from downtown. Holding onto my ticket, I was wiping the tears with the back of my hand.

When he pulled into the departure area I felt a sinking feeling in the pit of my stomach. People were pulling luggage from their cars—people were chatting and scurrying about. We went inside. I had to quicken my steps to keep pace with Jon's long stride.

"Mary," he said, "let's get you checked in." As I brought my luggage over to the counter and handed my ticket to the clerk, I saw Jon standing at attention. I knew he would be with me until the flight was called.

Another airport—another painful goodbye to someone I loved. Once again, I had to turn my back on a person who cared for me, board the plane and trade a smile for tears.

I checked in. "OK, Mary," he said, "let's go over to the departure gate and wait until it's time for you to board."

We sat and talked while hordes of travelers scurried in front of us. Suddenly, my flight number was called—I felt my pulse quicken—I knew it was time to board.

Jon handed me my boarding pass and took me in his arms. When our lips met for the last time, I regretted my decision to sacrifice my happiness. Jon was nurturing and kind. Jon was there for me.

Reluctantly, we pulled apart. "Goodbye, Mary," Jon said.

As I turned to enter the plane I whispered ever so softly, "Goodbye Jon."

I shoved my purse under the seat, sat down, and buckled my seat belt. "How many more goodbyes will I have to say?" I questioned, tightening my grip around the packet of Kleenex in my hand.

CHAPTER 9

A Nod of Forgiveness: Heart or Conscience?

"The weak can never forgive.
Forgiveness is the attribute of the strong."
—Mahatma Gandhi

Jon's influence in my life was a blessing. He was like a knight in shining armor, a gallant cavalier—always ready to come to my assistance whether it was to nurse me back to health or just care enough to be there for me.

Although I had never before felt as strongly for any man, I realized I had to walk away from someone who cared for me to be with a woman who caused me grief and humiliation; a woman I scorned and disrespected for her heartless cruelty. Despite the mixed emotions, I did what I thought was right. I left Hawaii.

My return flight to L.A. seemed endless. Saddened by the unexpected conclusion of my Hawaiian adventure, I tussled with all the 'what ifs' that sprang to my mind. What if I would have decided differently? What if I would have stayed with

Jon? What if Margaret would have passed away without seeing me one more time?

Feelings of fear and abandonment, like unlawful trespassers, continued to intrude in my thoughts. But despite the painful memories, I knew what I had to do.

I went to visit Margaret, and although the diagnosis was rather grim, she was not yet in the terminal phase of the illness. She had maintained her weight and didn't show any visible signs of the cancer. As a result she was able to go about her daily routine without much difficulty. Sam seemed happy to have me by his side, though true to his distant nature he was unable to express any emotions either for Margaret's illness or my arrival.

Several months later, just a week short of Thanksgiving, he called to invite me over for the long weekend. I had not seen the Mustards since September and was quite surprised to see how she had deteriorated in just two months. Rather frail and unsteady, she had dropped about fifty pounds. Her face was ashen and drawn and the look in her eyes was one of impending death. The chemo had resulted in severe hair loss; in fact, she was totally bald. She no longer walked with a steady gait, but dragged herself with wavering steps. It was a sad scenario, and despite the mistreatment and negligence in my regard, I felt sorry for her. It was obvious she was fighting a painful, but losing battle for her life.

With Margaret near death I thought maybe Sam would open up to me and talk about his experiences in *Việt Nam*. However, he sat shut in silence, smoking one cigarette after another. Apart from every consideration, it was cruel to submit a dying woman to his toxic secondhand smoke. Even if there was no hope for Margaret, the nicotine infested environment made it more difficult for her to breathe.

After the Thanksgiving visit, I had made the trip to Sutter Creek several times in the following four months before I received Sam's last phone call.

"Mary," he said, "Margaret is dying. It could happen any day now. I think you should come and say goodbye to Mom."

I hung up the receiver. A shiver ran through me. In my heart I didn't want to go. As far as I was concerned, I had already said my goodbye to her when she stood by listlessly as her enraged husband tightened his grip around my neck.

That evening I told my friends about Sam's phone call and my plans to see Margaret.

"Mary," Dara-lee said, "I can't believe you're doing this. After the awful way the Mustards treated you—how can you go back?"

I asked myself over and over, "How can you go back? How can you visit her on her deathbed after all the abuse?"

Torn and tormented, I had no answer. However, I felt I should just do it. I flew up to Sutter Creek, realizing this would probably be the last time I would see Margaret.

Sam drove us over to the hospital. During the ride, four whispered words cut through the tense silence. "Mary, Mom is dying." I remained silent.

"How strange," I thought to myself, "now that Margaret is dying Sam refers to her as Mom. Yet, throughout the years whenever he spoke to me about her, he always called her Margaret.

When we reached the hospital, Sam dropped me off at the entry and went to park the car. He didn't even ask me to wait for him, but sped off. I guess he felt he had said enough.

I waited in the lobby and as soon as he returned, we walked toward Margaret's room. The sights and sounds were distressing. I could hear some distant moans and groans echoing from behind closed or partially opened doors. People were suffering—people were dying. It would be almost impossible to describe my thoughts and feelings during that somber journey to her room.

The pungent aroma of disinfectant did little to ease the queasy feeling in the pit of my stomach. I did not want to be here. I did not want to see Margaret. But, I knew I had to. I prayed for the strength to survive this torturous moment.

"Mary," Sam said, pointing his finger in the direction of a shut door, "that's her room."

I was not prepared for the devastating image of death! Margaret's face was ashen—the portrait of a fatal disease that had conquered its victim. Her wasted body sprawled limp under the covers showed little if any sign of movement. Once round cheeks were now hollow pits etched with deep furrows. Every vein and artery was visible in her shriveled neck. She was visibly jaundiced and looked ghastly. I could see that despite the heavy sedation and medication, she was riddled with pain.

I walked over to her bed really not wanting to look into her droopy eyes: the same eyes that once glared at me with envy. Her breathing was labored, but shallow. Life was seeping right out of her, willingly or otherwise. It was a despondent scenario; one I knew would remain forever vibrant in my mind.

Margaret seemed so tiny lying there. She was helpless, defenseless and so docile. Yet, this was the same lady who had swatted me so hard across the face over and over again both with the palm and back of her hand. This was the same woman who, unconcerned about my feelings, shouted offensive obscenities at me, leaving me in tears, angry, and humiliated. The tide had turned. Margaret was now the needy, vulnerable 'child' in pain, and I the strong, powerful adult.

There was only one difference—whereas Margaret was never there for me—I was here for Margaret.

As I neared the bed, I noticed her withered, bony hands were snuggled one on top of the other across her heaving chest. Beneath the gnarled fingers was a black Bible.

"Mary," she said, "come here and put your hand on my Bible." I stepped closer. Slowly she lifted her hand and placed it on top of mine. I noticed how weak she was and how difficult it was for her to move. Her fingers felt icy cold against mine. I shuddered, but resisted the urge to pull away. For the first time Margaret Mustard became emotional as her eyes filled with tears. I looked at her frail, sixty-pound body and knew I was not going to be able to do this without crying.

"Mary," Margaret whispered, "can you ever find it in your heart to forgive me for the way I mistreated you all these years? I want to go to heaven, Mary. But I have to have your forgiveness before I leave. Mary," she continued, through gasps, "can you ever forgive me?"

She turned her head slightly and raised her eyes to meet my gaze. We were both in tears. "Mary," she said, "was I really that mean to you?"

Her question caught me off-guard. I felt my insides tighten. Unable to breathe, I tried to muffle my sobs. I lowered my head without saying a word—though I'm certain Margaret knew the answer to her question even before she asked it.

"Mary," she murmured, "can you try to forgive me? Can you find it in your heart to forgive me for what I have done to you? I want to go to heaven and I need your forgiveness to get there. I have to know that you and God will forgive me."

Her hand went limp. I nodded my head, granting her a non-vocalized forgiveness. There was no doubting it—she knew I had forgiven her.

The deep furrows in her forehead seemed less severe. Her tight-lipped grimace relaxed. She closed her eyes. In an echoless sighher final breath was silenced...Margaret Mustard had gone to meet her Creator. The curtain had lowered on a very sad part of my life—it was over. However, even forgiveness could not ease the anguish of trying to forget.

Nodding my head yes when Margaret asked for forgiveness was the hardest thing I had ever had to do. I realized that in my heart I was unable to give her the pardon she wanted. Decades later, I struggled with my inability to forgive. I just couldn't let it go.

After saying goodbye to Margaret, I flew home to continue the second semester of my junior year. Needless to say, I had a difficult time concentrating on my studies and was unable to shake the devastating memories of my twelve years with Sam and Margaret. Even though all the abuse was in the past, I kept reliving the agonizing scenes in my mind over and over. The pain was far too hurtful and lingering.

I was angry, distraught and depressed. As a result I did rather poorly in my classes. Most of my days were spent in tears. My sorority sisters were wonderful, paying extra attention to my needs and trying to take my mind off the disturbing thoughts I was plagued with.

Despite the emotional roller coaster I was trapped in, I completed all my course work and graduated from college, in four years—just as I said I would. In fact, my friends always described me as a tenacious person, I guess because I was so persevering, determined and driven. Since I inherited these traits from my mom, Yvonne, I considered them as part of my genetic make-up. There was no doubt—my mom and I were survivors from early on. We survived and we overcame all the curveballs life pitched in our direction.

It was 1979—just four months short of fifteen years since my departure from *Sài Gòn's Tân Sơn Nhất* Airport. I was twenty-two years old. When the Dean of Cal State called my name, I proudly walked up to the podium to collect my diploma. En route I thought of my mom, Yvonne and how proud she would have been had she lived long enough to see me graduate from college. I also thought about little *Hiền* who ran about barefoot and naked laughing and skipping, so carefree and innocent. How far she had come! *Hiền* was a college graduate with a degree in business administration and a finance option!

Several months after graduation, I packed my bags and headed south to Newport Beach. Worried I would be alone and without anyone to turn to for advice and support, I listened to my friends' encouragement and advice to remain in the "Valley." However, sure of my decision to move on, I rented an apartment in Newport Beach.

A year later, my sorority sister, Nancy Procop joined me. Two struggling young women looking for a suitable place to live, we now had to find a way to support ourselves. Browsing through the classifieds, we found an apartment on Seashore Drive, just fifteen steps from the Ocean. It seemed ideal—and the view was amazing.

With my business-finance degree tucked securely under my arm, I was ready to step into the professional world.

I started the interveiw process at the British based Royal Globe Insurance Company. Tiny at four feet eleven inches, and with extremely long dark hair, I looked even younger than my twenty-two years. I presented myself professionally dressed, with my resume and the enthusiasm of embarking on a new adventure.

After the introduction and a firm handshake, the manager, James Aust, looked me directly in the eyes. "Mary," he said, "why should I hire you? Why would you be good for this position?"

I kept my eyes focused on his gaze. "I'm tenacious and don't give up," I replied, convinced of my words. "I've been financially independent since graduating fom high school and worked my way through college, holding down two jobs."

He apparently liked what I said and hired me as a claim's adjuster. The starting salary was $12,000 a year. It was 1979, and at that time I was the only woman in a male dominated corporate environment.

After a short career with Royal Globe Insurance Company, I felt I was not moving in the right direction fast enough. Somewhat disappointed, I set my goal on entering the pharmaceutical industry; a goal I could not achieve at the time because of my lack of sales experience. Told I had to have a proven track record, I applied for and obtained a position with Presto Products, certain this would be a great opportunity to get the experience I needed.

I was now involved in outside sales with a company whose competitors were Hefty, Zip Lock and Glad Bags. Presto Products handled private label plastic products, disposable plastic trash bags, and food storage 'sacs' and wraps.

My territory extended from Tijuana, Mexico, up to Santa Maria, California, and out to Palm Springs. I was practically living behind the wheel of my car, covering thousands of miles.

One amusing episode remains in my mind, repeatedly provoking a chuckle whenever I think of it. I was covering the

Watts district in L.A., a low income neighborhood which the seventies sitcom *Stanford & Son* put in the spotlight.

There was a little boy not more than eight years old who liked to play in the entry of one of the grocery stores I frequently visited. Greeting him one afternoon, I said, 'hi' and asked him how he was. Looking up to meet my gaze, he flashed me a half-moon, toothless grin. "Here comes the trash bag lady—here comes the trash bag lady," he sang over and over, giggling and lisping through his missing front teeth.

His playful teasing expanded my smile into a deep belly laugh. Unknowingly, he had brightened my day with a bit of old-fashioned, slapstick Rowan and Martin humor. It was a *Laugh-In* "*here come de judge*" moment. Only this time the subject of the quick, one-line catch phrase was, yours truly, "*de trash bag lady.*"

CHAPTER 10

Mary Mustard Reed aka *Hiền*: Wife, Mother, Career Woman

*"I know God will not give me anything I can't handle.
I just wish that He didn't trust me so much."*
—Mother Teresa

In October of 1980, right around Halloween, as the air was turning crisper and the evening sky dimming earlier, I met Gordon Reed. A lieutenant lifeguard in Newport Beach, he was an extremely handsome man with sandy hair, expressive light eyes and a rock-solid athletic build. Without a doubt at six foot two inches, Gordon was a head turner ten years my senior who found me as attractive as I found him. I guess every girl daydreamed about drowning and being carried to shore nestled in his strong arms.

The courtship was short and intense. We just adored each other. Unafraid to demonstrate his feelings, it was obvious to everyone that I had captured his heart.

I knew I had found in this wonderful man everything I was looking for. Emotionally starved by the Mustards, my need for affection and attention was fulfilled by Gordon.

One evening Gordon phoned. "Mary" he said, "I'm coming over in a little while. Maybe we can go a movie and get a quick bite to eat." Excited, I didn't care what he had in mind. I was just interested in being with him.

When Gordon arrived he seemed a bit distracted. After a kiss 'hello' he sat down on the sofa and patted the pillow several times, signaling for me to join him.

Gordon gently lifted my hand, without changing the direction of his eyes, firmly fixed on mine. My heart raced.

"Mary," he said, his lips slanting upward in a very charming smile, "will you marry me?" Before I could respond he slipped a shiny diamond on my finger.

"Yes, Gordon," I said, my eyes glowing, "I'd love to marry you."

That was by far the easiest part of saying, "I do."

Anxious and frustrated, I agonized for months before deciding who would accompany me down the aisle to meet my waiting groom. In my heart I preferred to ask Fred since together with his wife Bettie, the Eiswalds' were always there for me. Loving, attentive and nurturing, they were more like parents than anyone, let alone the Mustards.

Always motivated to do the right thing, and riddled with guilt knowing Sam brought me to America to have the opportunity to live a better life, I made the phone call asking him to escort me down the aisle.

Apart from his role as "father of the bride," Sam neither intervened in any wedding plans, nor assumed any financial responsibility. His only task was to present himself on time to accompany me to the altar. Yet, despite the uncomplicated demand, Sam was late for the photo shoot. My sister-in-law, Helen had to teasingly phone him. "Sam, have you forgotten today is your daughter's wedding day?" Just in case he didn't show, she inquired if there was a backup tux for Fred!

Needless to say, Sam's lackadaisical attitude, though consistent with his personality, did not inspire the love and affection a daughter feels during her life-altering stroll down the aisle on her father's arm. Absent also was the teary-eyed glance of a doting dad as he entrusts his 'little girl' to another man. Mine was truly not exactly a moving "Father of the Bride" movie moment.

Gordon and I became husband and wife on March 6, 1982—*Hiền* now answered to the name of Mary Mustard Reed. Despite Sam's cool demeanor, we had a beautiful church wedding followed by an elegant reception at the waterfront Balboa Bay Club & Resort in Newport Beach.

The setting was spectacular with views overlooking the harbor. It was the perfect backdrop for a romantic celebration of two young people celebrating the start of a new journey.

After the reception we departed for a Cancun honeymoon, not planning for the nasty bout of *Montezuma's Revenge* that would keep my groom in bed for a few days. However, once he was back on his feet we had a delightful time snorkeling, touring and just behaving like a newlywed couple in love.

As a newly married woman settled into a new home and lifestyle, I missed my music—especially the opportunity to play the piano. It had always given me such joy and comfort. Luckily, Sam did not sell my Fisher upright after Margaret's death, and it was able to survive through all the various address changes.

Finally, just as I was about to announce my pregnancy, the piano returned to my living room. Happily expecting my first baby, I awaited the new arrival, delighted to play my favorite classical pieces. Music was always so uplifting and my own personal way of expressing all the joy and excitement I was feeling.

Both Gordon and I were excited about starting a family. The Doctor had calculated my due date around August 6. However, just a month earlier, the night before my baby shower, I suffered intense pain and cramping accompanied by fever, severe weakness and bouts of nausea and vomiting.

Concerned, Gordon took me to the emergency room at Hoag memorial Hospital in Newport Beach. After a series of tests, I was diagnosed with severe pancreatitis. All food and drinks were prohibited.

My throat felt raw and dry. Unable to swallow, I was hydrated with an IV drip and chips of ice pressed against my cracked lips to quench my thirst. The cold of the ice burned my feverish skin. Fearful the debilitating and life-threatening nature of my condition would result in shock, I was ordered to remain in the hospital confined to strict bed rest.

The pancreatitis was aggravated by my pregnancy. In agony from the excruciating pain that traveled from my stomach to my chest and back, I was barely able to lift my head from the pillow. The fetal monitor strapped to my distended belly and the catheter inserted to drain my bladder intensified the agony. Speaking in barely audible raspy whispers, I told Gordon I was terrified for myself and my unborn child. Slipping in and out of delirium, I couldn't help thinking I was on my deathbed.

Twelve days later my water broke. After a long and agonizing nine-hour labor, the obstetrician scheduled a

C-section, realizing I was having a difficult time. The pancreatitis ordeal had drained my energy.

When my friends came over to visit, they were shocked to see how frail, heavily sedated and wasted I was. Most of my pregnancy weight had been lost.

On July 13, 1984 at 8:53 pm, my first-born, Jenna Lee Reed came into the world. I was beyond ecstatic when my beautiful baby girl was placed in my arms. Gordon was present for the entire birthing process. A proud new Dad, he was immediately enchanted by his beautiful daughter with her full head of dark, shiny hair.

The joy of giving the gift of life erased all the pain and agony I had experienced during the previous weeks. Gordon and I were in another world—we had just experienced the thrill of becoming parents.

Bettie, Fred and Karen drove down to visit and 'meet' Jenna. They walked into my hospital room as I was cradling my newborn in my arms. "This is my own flesh and blood," I whispered, smiling at the tiny little face looking up at me.

Overcome with joy, tears streamed down my cheeks, I could see that the Eiswalds were moved by the emotionally touching scene between a new mother and her first-born daughter.

Gazing into Jenna's innocent eyes, I vowed to myself that she and all the other children I would eventually bring into the world would never have to experience the painful loneliness and fear of negligence and abandonment. They would always be my number one priority and would have all the love and nurturing they deserved.

"Mary," Bettie said, bending over to kiss me and caress Jenna's face,"you do everything the hard way, but you always get through it—and you always come out smelling like a rose."

Bettie and Fred stayed with me awhile, until I regained my strength. Always supportive and demonstrating so much love and concern, they became as the Germans say, *Oma* and *Opa*—Grandma and Grandpa.

Once back on my feet, Gordon decided I should quit my job at Presto Products and dedicate my time to caring for Jenna. Although I realized we would have to make sacrifices, I was in full agreement. However, we both felt it was well worth it.

But, after a year as a stay-at-home mom, I decided to go back to work on a part-time basis. Calm and easy to raise, Jenna presented little if any of the challenges new parents face. Furthermore, I had the support of loving friends.

Recently I had met Maxine Augusta, a trim, vivacious woman in her late twenties with golden blonde hair that hugged her shoulders. A kind, caring friend, she was quick with the one-liners, often making me laugh, especially when the chips were down.

Actually Maxine, who I 'acquired' through marriage, was more like a sister than a friend. Together with Gordon's mother, Lucy, they were a great help in my busy day.

Since my sorority sisters and high school friends lived far away, Maxine and I spent much time together—we chatted for hours on the phone. In later years my children teased me. "Mom," they'd say, giggling, "how could anyone spend two or three hours on the phone talking about nothing!"

The children and I spent many holidays together in each other's homes. Unlike the Mustards, the Augustas loved to remember the joyful occasions and capture Jenna, Kevin and Denny's growing years in photos.

Besides being there for me, Maxine was instrumental in shaping my professional career. Employed in the pharmaceutical industry, she was aware I was interested in getting back to work even if part-time. Excited, she ran over one morning.

"Mary," she blurted, walking through the door, "I saw an ad in the *Los Angeles Times* for a part-time sales rep at Whitehall Laboratories. Why don't you give it a try?"

Whitehall Laboratories, in 1985, a division of Wyeth-Ayerst, was an over-the-counter pharmaceutical company responsible for Advil. This was a whole new concept at the time and in competition with McNeil Pharmaceutical for a share of the Tylenol market.

I applied and was hired for the position. My job description involved calling on family physicians in the Huntington Beach area. Thrilled to be back in the work force, I enjoyed the challenge of a new career, even if not full-time.

Soon after I began working, I discovered I was pregnant again. Despite the awful time I had with Jenna, I was excited about bringing another child into the world. However, in keeping with my challenging life, during my last trimester, I was once again diagnosed with *placenta previa,* a condition characterized by a low-lying placenta that covers the cervix.

I was at risk of suffering a life-threatening hemorrhage and prescribed strict bed rest. That evening I told Bettie. "Mary," she said, "everything in your life has been a struggle. You always have to overcome obstacles—nothing is ever easy for you. But in the end you always get there. That's the bottom line, Mary. You always have to take extra steps, but you always arrive." I had to admit that Bettie was right.

As soon as my high school friends learned of my diagnosis, Karen came immediately from Thousand Oaks and took Jenna back with her, fearful I would lose the baby. Karen and Nancy, together with *Oma* and *Opa* took excellent care of my baby daughter. Considered as my extended family, we all have such wonderful endearing memories of beautiful holiday celebrations in each other's homes.

On Thanksgiving Day, November 26, 1986, at 2:45 am, Kevin Bruce Reed breathed his first breath. Unlike Jenna with her full head of dark hair, Kevin was practically bald except for a light covering of sandy blonde fuzz. Tinier than Jenna, he was just as adorable.

Once again, Gordon was by my side—this time to greet his son. We were thrilled to have given our daughter a baby brother.

Soon after the holidays, I was surprised to receive a phone call from Bob.

"Mary," he said, "Sam has some serious health issues. You know they had to amputate his leg several years ago because of his circulation problems. Mary, Sam is dying—it looks like this is the end."

I did not visit Sam on his deathbed, and he passed away without ever seeing me again. He never participated in my life. True to his distant, aloof personality, he had only visited his granddaughter Jenna once in two and a half years.

With two small children and a part-time career, life became a bit of a challenge. Then to top it all off, I discovered I was pregnant again. When my water broke on Sunday evening April 10, Gordon drove me to the hospital. A little less than two hours later, at 1:26 am on April 11, Dennis (Denny) Tyler Reed made his debut with loud piercing cries. Gordon and I were blessed once again. We had another darling baby with less hair than Jenna, but significantly more than Kevin.

With three children my days were full from morning to evening. We were totally dedicated to our family and planned activities and outings that would involve the children. Close in age, Jenna, Kevin and Denny enjoyed the same things and played nicely together.

Bath times were a fun event, and although tired from a hectic day working part-time and caring for the family, it was both relaxing and distracting to watch our 'three little bears' giggle and splash each other with fluffy soapsuds. All three seemed to love the water.

Afterwards, they always smelled so fresh and clean—a scent that remains in my memory along with their darling, smiling faces and high-pitched, excited voices all talking at the same time.

Like all proud parents, Gordon and I tried to capture every moment on video. We delighted in our children's antics and watching them grow up each day was beyond all thrills.

One incident remains so vivid in my mind it almost seems as if it happened yesterday. Jenna was four, Kevin two and Denny had just about reached six months. Hungry and tired, we were about to sit down for dinner. Returning from dance class, Jenna came prancing in on her toes, dressed in her leotard, proud to give the family a preview of her dance routine.

In a split second Kevin was on his feet trying to mimic his sister's steps. He twirled unsteadily on his tiny bare feet. Glancing up at Jenna, he lisped through his missing front teeth, "Sissy, sissy, I wuv you!"

Overcome with emotion, I felt the tears run down my cheeks. I walked over to Jenna to join her in dance, raising my arms above my head, improvising my own choreography. Perhaps feeling the beat of the moment, Denny, seated in his highchair slapped his hand in the plate repeatedly. In just a few short seconds there were more Gerber peas and carrots on the baby, floor and walls than in the entire bowl!

Quick to recognize a priceless moment, Gordon grabbed the camera and taped the scene. By now, Kevin was feeling like he was losing the spotlight. No one could hear his endearing, "I wuv you," declaration to his sister, since we were all singing, dancing, clapping our hands and laughing.

Suddenly, an ear-piercing—"Siii-syyyyyy, I wuv you," cut through the uproar, demanding attention. Stretching his tiny lungs, Kevin had succeeded in capturing the spotlight and in giving us one of the many precious moments enjoyed as a family.

This was a cheerful time and I wanted my "happily ever after" life to continue. However, Gordon and I had some problems to work out. No longer in agreement about many different issues and points of view, we seemed to have grown in different directions. Young and vulnerable, my judgment was somewhat clouded by my need to be loved and adored.

My husband, on the other hand, seemed to have a very different definition of daily moderate social drinking than did I, which I could not accept. There were too many differences; differences which left us unbalanced and with little if anything in common. As a result of the irreconcilable conflicts we argued most of the time, becoming visibly incompatible. Our relationship became strained, and fearing for the serenity of our children, we thought it best to part ways.

The divorce was painful—another tragic pulling apart of two people who once loved each other. However, the pain and anguish of a failed marriage taught me another life lesson. Painful as they were, I always learned from the trials in my life; trials which in the end gave me the strength to move forward.

Empowered by the new hardship, I stepped into my role as a single parent feeling less self-confident, but responsible and ready to 'bear another cross.' After all, I was a survivor; therefore there was never a doubt in my mind. I knew I would overcome this obstacle, also.

Ironically, many of Jenna, Kevin and Denny's classmates' parents were unaware of our divorce in 1991, since we always attended Little League, soccer matches, basketball games and other school activities together for the sake of the children.

Gordon and I agreed our daughter and sons were the number one priority in our lives. Therefore, we rarely dated others and did not consider finding new mates during the schoolage years, realizing this was the only way to create a serene, familiar, stable and uncomplicated environment for the children to grow up in.

Consequently, with little remorse or bitterness we maintained a friendly relationship, dedicating our lives to the welfare of the children.

As a struggling single mom with a three, four, and six-year-old, I now had to work full-time. I needed a car, medical and dental insurance plus a more substantial salary to maintain my home payments and support my three precious angels.

With the prayers and encouragement of my friends, I dusted off my resume and applied to several pharmaceutical companies. After careful consideration I chose Ciba-Geigy (Novartis Pharmaceuticals). The territory I would be assigned to was less extensive and in the Huntington Beach and Fountain Valley area.

I was sent to Basel Pharmaceuticals, a division of Ciba-Geigy, and given the job to launch Habitrol, a new prescription drug. A nicotine transdermal patch, Habitrol was applied to skin to help smokers kick the habit. I was thrilled! I thought I had died and gone to heaven!

My salary was increased from the $18,000 I received as a part-time sales rep. In addition, I was given a new company car, health and dental insurance and a $10,000 sign-on bonus. I was the first person hired in Southern California and chose Huntington Beach, Mountain Valley and Westminster as my territories because they were close to home.

I tried my best to juggle parenting, a full time position, as well as feelings of loneliness. Often overwhelmed, I cried myself to sleep exhausted and wondering if I was going to make it this time.

Sadly, I have to admit I had quite a few "pity parties" for myself. However, always pulling myself together I moved forward. Gaining full custody of the children, I had little time off—they were always with me. Often exhausted, I was emotionally and physically drained.

Although my dear friend, Maxine had her own family she was always available to intervene if I needed her. The number of times she dropped whatever she was doing to be by my side are countless. I cried so often it was well known that I had my own Niagara Falls. But loyal and faithful, Maxine was always there. A remarkable woman, she had and will always have my respect, love and gratitude.

I was also blessed with another wonderful 'guardian angel,' Beth Kimble. Affectionately known as 'Nanny Beth' she lived just three blocks away from me. A *petite* five-foot-two-inch phenomenal, multi-task woman, she had sandy blond hair and a creamy, fair-skinned complexion. Fabulous in the kitchen, Nanny Beth prepared every meal from scratch, including desserts.

With her sweet accommodating personality and many talents she took care of two generations of children, building quite a commendable reputation as the Huntington Beach Nanny—loyal, efficient, warm and nurturing. Thankfully, she was a constant presence in my life, tending to my children during their pre-school, elementary and early junior high school years while I worked.

After my family came my career. And I was just as diligent, conscientious and interested in succeeding as I was in rearing my children.

When I introduced myself to business colleagues and clients, I always used my maiden name, Mary Mustard, since I was sure it was a great way to make a memorable and lasting impression and assure myself I would never be forgotten. After all, the name Mary Mustard is rather unique, catchy and certainly unforgettable.

Unlike my brother, Bob who cancelled his family name, I wanted to use it to my best advantage. Mary Mustard was my claim to fame more or less because of the 'clue' game. Creating amusing and catchy stories and phrases centered on my name assured that people would always remember me.

At the time I did not know that my decision to accept the position at Ciba-Geigy would alter the entire course of my life. As a starter, my new career path led me directly to Orange County's "Little Saigon." Located in Westminster and Garden Grove, it is the oldest, biggest and most prominent Vietnamese community in the United States, second in population only to

Sài Gòn, known as *Hồ Chí Minh* City after the May 1, 1975 reunification of North and South *Việt Nam.*

In Little Saigon I met many Vietnamese doctors, many of whom spoke their native language fluently and with ease. This was my first connection with Vietnamese people since my departure from *Sài Gòn* in 1964.

I was excited by the cultural opportunity to finally sever the Mustard taboo and learn about my country. I had my drugs to launch, but I was attentive to their discussions, eager for any information about *Việt Nam* I could possible catch.

Sharing lunches and dinners together with this Vietnamese community, I began to build interesting relationships which encouraged me to delve deeper into the history and culture of *Việt Nam.* Most of the doctors had immigrated to the United States in the mid seventies and eighties after the *Việt Nam* War. They were surprised to discover I couldn't speak a word of my native language, but insisted I greet them with a *"chào Bác sĩ,"* which translates to—hi doctor!

I shared my personal story with two physicians in particular, Dr. Henry *Nguyễn* and Dr. *Hùng Hữu Nguyễn.* Both men were captivated by the events of my life, from my adoption to my life with the Mustards and the death of my mom during the war.

At dinner one evening, after we had discussed business, Dr. *Hùng Hữu Nguyễn* leaned over and gently took my hand in his.

"Hiền," he said, gazing deep into my eyes, "as I hold your hand and talk to you, I get an uncanny feeling."

He paused, took a deep breath and continued. "I feel your mother's presence. *Hiền,* I can't pin-point it, but I have an inkling your mom is alive somewhere!"

I felt a shudder run down my back. My pulse quickened. "You think my mom is alive?" I questioned to be certain I heard correctly. "Yes, *Hiền,*" he said, confirming his initial statement. "But Dr. *Nguyễn,*" I interrupted, trying unsuccessfully to control my tears, "we were informed that my mom was killed in 1966. That was so many years ago."

"*Hiền,* were her remains found?" I shook my head, no. "*Hiền,* how can you live your whole life without proof? You were a young child. You didn't know the whole story—only what you were told. How can you live with that? You need evidence of her death before you can accept it as true. If it takes you the rest of your life, you have to search for your mother!

"In the Vietnamese community our roots and our families are a vital part of our culture. They are who and what we are. You cannot accept the explanation of your American parents. *Hiền,* it's time to discover the truth. You must search for your mother and I will help you! If you give me a picture of you and your mom, I will run an ad in the Vietnamese language *Người Việt Daily News.*"

The ad ran only once and did not bring any news. Dr. *Hùng Hữu Nguyễn* held firm to his belief. He was unyielding.

"*Hiền,*" he said, "I'm going to take you to the American Red Cross."

"The Red Cross—why?" I asked, puzzled by his suggestions. "Well," he replied, "the American Red Cross works with international organizations around the world to locate family members who are dispersed as a result of war, natural calamities or civil strife."

The Doctor's news caught me off-guard. I was under the obviously mistaken impression that the Red Cross focused exclusively on natural disasters or blood donations.

"*Hiền,*" he said, "I will go to the Red Cross with you. Let me know when you are ready."

I was overwhelmed by this unexpected turn of events. I wanted so desperately to believe Dr. *Nguyễn.* I really never did have any proof of my mother's death. Even Sam had to take Bill Neil's word.

Could Dr. *Hùng Hữu Nguyễn* be right? Could I trust his intuition? Or was I setting myself up for a painful disappointment and the agonizing heartbreak of re-opening old wounds?

CHAPTER 11

HOPE: THE RED CROSS

*"We must accept finite disappointment,
but we must never lose infinite hope."*
—Martin Luther King

Meeting Dr. *Hùng Hữu Nguyễn* was both an emotional and inspiring experience; an event that changed my life forever. I never would have expected his decidedly uncanny reaction when we shook hands. His penetrating glance and eerie words about my mother's presence around me were thoughts I could not shake from my mind. Could he possibly be right, I asked myself over and over? I was afraid to believe there could be a morsel of truth in his bizarre gut feeling.

On one hand I was excited about this tiny even if absurd possibility, yet on the other so very scared to think I might be in for another painful disappointment. I did not want to build up my hopes only to be forced to grieve all over again after clinging to a false hope.

Meeting the Vietnamese doctors and coming into contact with various people from the Little Saigon Community gave me a very different perspective about the horrific post-war South Vietnamese condition and the desperate fight for asylum in a free world. I could see their eyes swell with tears and the anguish reflected on their faces as they related stories of these tragedies, either lived and personally experienced or lived through surviving family members.

On September 20, 1991, Dr. *Nguyễn* accompanied me to the Orange County Chapter headquarters of the American Red Cross at 610 N Golden Circle Drive in Santa Ana.

The twenty minute drive from 'Little Saigon' to Santa Ana was reflective. I sat in silence, staring down at the envelope holding the few treasured memories of my past.

The car came to a halt, interrupting my thoughts. We went inside and headed over to the Holocaust & War Victims Tracing & Information Center and walked over to the International Tracing desk.

With the assistance of *Tùng Nguyễn*, the Asian Refugee Specialist for the Santa Ana Chapter, I initiated proceedings for a tracing inquiry on my family. The only documentation I had was a piece of wrinkled paper reporting my mom's name, birth date, birthplace and address at 376 *Phan Đình Phùng*, in addition to three photos of myself and a few faded letters.

I also had my old passport photo as a seven-year-old child wearing the shiny gold treble clef my mom gave me when I left *Việt Nam*. It was rather flimsy information to work with, but since Margaret had discarded my yellow suitcase filled with all my treasured mementos, it was all I could provide. Of course, I couldn't help doubting it would be sufficient. Was I reaching for the stars?

I completed the *Red Cross Tracing Inquiry Form 1609* and the tracing coordinator forwarded it to the ISS, International Social Services division of the Office of International Services in Washington, DC. The ISS in turn transferred my information to the *Chữ thập đỏ Việt Nam,* the *Việt Nam* Red Cross. I was told that as information came in, I would be contacted and updated periodically. It all seemed so easy—but I wondered if anything would come of it.

I had absolutely no idea of the global dimensions of the Red Cross. I believed the organization was focused on blood donations and disaster relief in the instance of natural calamities. Learning how widespread and far-reaching their scope was to include locating holocaust survivors, war victims and missing persons and uniting them with family members was amazing.

Although the Red Cross does not engage in tracing requests on the part of adopted children seeking biological parents, it makes an exception for Vietnamese-Americans and US fathers. This made my case acceptable. Once I had begun the necessary proceedings, I was both nervous and eager about moving forward.

On the return drive, I thought of my mom and the war. It had really escalated in the late sixties, causing so much devastation and destruction. After the fall of *Sài Gòn* in 1975, the Communists sent the American allied South Vietnamese people, government personnel, and intellectuals to "re-education camps" in "new-economic zones."

I shuddered at the very thought, but did nothing to change the overwhelming images flashing across my mind. If people lived it—I could think about it—or better, I should think about it.

Those postwar years were a daily nightmare for South
Vietnamese survivors. The Communists' idea was to repro-
gram their minds and ultimately utilize them to develop
barren wastelands into productive agricultural land.

Citizens were forced to work long hours with their hands
and legs bound in shackles. They were whipped with thorn
incrusted bamboo canes until their flesh was raw and bleeding.

I remember reading about these atrocities and listening to
the human rights activists protest the degradation and new
wave of slavery with slogans, political protests, demonstra-
tions, books, articles and songs.

It saddened me to see the evening news broadcasts day
after day, filled with distraught images of *les réfugiés de la
mer,* the "boat-people;" refugees from these post-holocaust
concentration camps desperately seeking a safe haven.

To escape physical, psychological and emotional
maltreatment and humiliation, refugees piled into poorly
crafted vessels and un-sturdy boats, like sardines in a can.
Crossing over into the USA and Canada, they braced against
storms and raging tidal surges for the right to freedom.

Many perished along the way due to starvation, pirating
and or drowning at sea, and still others were labeled clandes-
tine and illegal immigrants and deported upon arrival.

This was why I couldn't imagine how with one crinkled
and faded piece of paper with a name, address and birth info,
the Red Cross could possibly locate my mother—assuming of
course that she was still living in South *Việt Nam* and actually
alive as Dr. *Hùng Hữu Nguyễn* felt.

As agreed, I kept in contact with *Tùng Nguyễn,* the Asian
Refugee Specialist, phoning him on a monthly basis to check
for updates.

Time after time he would reply, "Mary, I'm sorry but as of today, I have no news for you regarding your mother." This scenario was repeated for almost three years. I was told from day one that the process was often slow and could take endless time. I had put in the inquiry on September 20, 1991—I wondered just how long I would have to wait and more importantly, what would be the final outcome.

In the spring of 1992, I received a call from *Tùng Nguyễn*.

"Mary," he said, "I jut got word that the ISS has final received an acknowledgment that the *Việt Nam* Red Cross has opened your case."

"Mr. *Nguyễn*," I said, excited to hear a different response, "how long do you think it will take to find my mom?"

"Oh, we can't give a time frame," he replied, taking a deep breath, "you just have to be patient." He followed up his phone call with a letter confirming the fact that the *Việt Nam* Red Cross had opened my case. It was out of my hands. All I could do was pray and wait. I did, and soon after I received a second communication stating there was no news to report. I continued to pray and put my faith and fate in the Lord's Hand.

The weeks and months seemed to evaporate in time as seasons spun from Easter to Thanksgiving to Christmas and another New Year. It was now 1993, and I still had not received any news regarding the whereabouts of my mom.

I tried not to let the anticipation and anxiety of a great unknown interrupt my daily routine. With three growing children to nurture and a profession at Ciby-Geigy to develop, I had to keep going.

Tired and drained when I tucked Jenna, Kevin and Denny into bed each evening, I thought of myself at their age—a lonely little girl sent to a new country with strangers—no goodnight kisses or hugs—no falling asleep with a smile on my face and never a bed-time story. Just tears, sobs, silence and sadness.

The thought disturbed me. But I had to be patient, believe in the Red Cross and continue living my life without any great expectations.

It was now the summer of 1993. The sorority sisters, Debbie, Dara and I together with out families were invited to a Fourth of July barbeque at Sheri's house. The night before, *20/20* on TV had featured the story of a Vietnamese woman who after many years of estrangement returned to *Sài Gòn* to be reunited with her mother.

Since we had all followed the program, and the girls were fully aware of my persisting quest to locate my mom, it was the main 'barbeque topic of conversation' that Independence Day. Intent on sharing some treasured memories of my past, I had taken with me some of the few precious mementos I was able to preserve.

Unfolding one of my favorite letters, I read it aloud:

"My baby, I very sad because you gone. I very much miss you."

We were all huddled together crying as I sobbed to my sorority sisters, "When is it going to be my turn? When will I be able to hug my mom? Will I ever see her again?" I was inconsolable.

I folded the letters one by one, careful not to drench the already delicate pages with my tears. I had read them so many times they had become quite worn and frail.

Through tear-filled eyes we glanced at our precious children, clutching on to each other's hands, and breaking into sobs at the thought of being in a position in which we would have to entrust our beloved little ones to strangers. I knew there was no way I could ever wave goodbye to Jenna, Kevin and Denny. They were my life!

Impassioned by the desire to locate my mother, the feeling accompanied me every day and haunted me every evening— I was unable to shake it off.

I had considered flying to *Việt Nam,* but realized that with three little children and the exorbitant cost of such a trip, it would not be feasible. However, although the obstacles seemed insurmountable, my friends encouraged me to keep believing that one day soon I would be returning 'home.'

Several hours later after we had dried off the children and enjoyed a sumptuous barbeque, we went our separate ways. The kisses and hugs shared that evening were many and so much more intense. It was a beautiful bonding of hearts, spirits and minds.

Three weeks later, on Sunday morning, July 25, 1993 at precisely 9:00 am, I stepped out from the shower just in time to catch what was probably one of the last of a long series of telephone rings.

The voice on the other end of the receiver was unfamiliar—strange because Sunday callers were always my dear friends. Puzzled and somewhat anxious about the 'unknown,' I felt my muscles tighten. Holding my breath I listened. Apparently, the caller had something to either tell or ask me.

A mysterious voice identified himself as a coordinator for the American Red Cross in Washington, DC. I felt my heart accelerate.

"Mrs. Reed," he announced in a clear, steady voice, "we've located your mother, *Đào Thị Thanh!* She is living in Paris."

"No, no," I blurted, "my mother's name is *Nguyễn Thị Thanh*—this is not *the right* person!"

"Mrs. Reed," he insisted, "we have the name as *Đào Thị Thanh*. This is the only information I have at this time. I will have more for you at a later date."

Uncertain of the validity of the telephone call, my mind wandered along different paths. Was this a prank, or an honest mistake? I didn't want to abandon hope—but I was not willing to set myself up for a painful disappointment.

The gentleman from the Red Cross had no answers for my questions. Instead, I was instructed to contact *Tùng Nguyễn* at the Orange County Chapter of the Red Cross.

I sat Indian style on the floor, grasping the receiver long after the voice on the other end was silenced. Stunned, rigid and confused, I didn't give in to tears. It was as if the stranger's news was part of a dream. I couldn't bring the event into reality and didn't really know if I should keep refusing to accept the truth that my mother had been found—but what if? What if *Đào Thị Thanh* was my mother?

On one hand I wanted to believe, yet my joy and optimism were soiled by what I feared could be a case of mistaken identity. I lived through Sunday like a zombie unable to feel and unwilling to think.

On Monday, after a restless night turning and tossing in my bed, I phoned *Tùng Nguyễn*. He was unavailable and I was transferred to Mike Canon. My dubious reaction to the news was surprising to Mike, since most phone calls announcing a lost loved one had been found were received with elation and repeated words of thanks. However, here I was, recently told my mom had been located after decades of silence, and I responded with skepticism and pessimism, if not total mistrust. Their excitement was met with resistance. I was almost afraid to believe.

"Mrs. Reed," Mike said, after absenting himself for a few moments to check the files, "according to the information you gave us, we are certain *Đào Thị Thanh* is your lost mother. The Red Cross reports only positive findings to the initiators of tracing requests. Therefore, we would not have contacted you if we were not a hundred percent sure we had found your mother."

Nothing he could have said would have convinced me. I remained doubtful, much to Mike's surprise. He tried to impress upon me that the Red Cross does not engage in false reportage and questioned why I was so adamantly resistant to the "good news."

When Mike told me, "Mrs. Reed, I know this is a scary moment for you," I realized that all my protestations, doubts and resistance were nothing more than fear. Mike was correct—the news terrified me.

He tried to reassure me, telling me my reaction was understandable considering the circumstances. I reflected on his words and thought back to Margaret Mustard's attempts to impress upon me that my mother did not want me. Also, I did not want to suffer any disappointment—maybe my mother would not welcome me in her life. Perhaps she did not share my feelings for a reunion. I wasn't sure, though I was certain I did not care to subject myself to the pain of an *encore* rejection.

Several days following our conversation I received a letter from *Tùng Nguyễn* in which he included my mother's address and phone number in *Bagnolet* Paris. Once again in a trance-like state, I held the letter, staring at the few typed written lines. My mother was just a phone call away. After so many sad and painful years, could it really be that easy?

Still apprehensive, I confided in my friends, sharing the 'good news.' Overjoyed, they wanted to be with me when I made the important call. However, this time I preferred to be alone.

Still hesitant to believe, I struggled with bouts of fear. Since I had forgotten how to speak Vietnamese, I might not be able to communicate with my mom. And I was still not certain the woman who gave me up for adoption almost thirty years ago would actually want to hear my voice!

Putting aside my fears and doubts, on Friday, July 30, 1993 at approximately 10:45 pm Pacific Time, I summoned my forces and walked over to the telephone. In Paris it was 8:45 Saturday morning.

Running my hands up and down the sides of my legs did little to dry my clammy plams. I felt as if I was in a sauna, sweating profusely while trying to catch a breath of air. Knowing that deep, slow breathing can be calming, I tried to focus my attention on getting into a more relaxing tempo. However, the sudden queasy feeling in my stomach distracted my concentration. It seemed as if a handful of butterflies were trapped inside and struggling to get out.

I pulled myself together, lifted the receiver and dialed my mother's number. With each ring my pulse accelerated. Suddenly, the ring was silenced—in its place I heard the smooth, soft, almost whispered, *"allô"* of a seemingly young girl. I blurted out, "Hi, I'm *Thanh Hiền—Thanh Hiền—Thanh Hiền!"* I kept repeating my name because I was certain they might not understand since I probably did not pronounce it correctly.

I heard a gasp then a shout—"It's our sister!" In the background the pitter-patter of shuffling footsteps filled the pause. It was more than evident her loud piercing cry had awakened the entire household.

I knew the Red Cross had found my mother!

"*Hiền*," she said between the sobs, "I'm your sister, *Phương*. I'm your sister! There are pictures of you everywhere. I'm looking at you as we speak."

I completely lost it. Tears ran down my cheeks. I was overwhelmed by the realization that my doubts no longer had validity. I clutched the receiver unwilling to lose a connection almost thirty years in the making.

I caught my breath. "*Hiền*," she said once again in her soft voice, "Mom has told all of us about you."

"All of you," I blurted. "How many are you?"

Amused by my startled reaction, *Phương* chuckled— "Are you ready for what I'm about to tell you?" she asked. Without waiting for a response she continued, "You have four sisters and three brothers!" To say I was startled was actually minimizing how I truly felt in that moment!

I was excited to learn *Phương* spoke English, because on the *20/20* segment I had seen several weeks earlier, the woman was unable to communicate with anyone in her family. It was sad to find a loved one and not be able to express your feelings.

"*Hiền*," she said, Mom missed you! She never stopped loving you—never wanted to give up looking for you. One day she hoped to find you."

"Where is Mom?" I asked, longing to hear her voice after decades of silence. It was the voice that put me to sleep in the evenings. It was the voice that awakened me to a new day every morning. It was that very special voice that lived safe and protected in my mind and heart!

"Mom is not here at the moment," *Phương* responded. "She went to *Biarritz* to visit our sister. Unfortunately, you'll have to wait to talk to her because they don't have a telephone."

"When will she back in Paris?" I asked, somewhat disappointed I had to wait a bit longer to talk to my mom.

"*Hiền,* Mom will be back in three days," she replied. "Oh, *Hiền,* she will be so excited to talk to you!"

I could hardly control my enthusiasm—the following days were a big blur. All I could think about was hearing my mom's voice. Three day later my dream came true. Once again I dialed my mom's number.

Phương answered and immediately called Mom.

"*Hiền, Hiền,*" I heard through the sobs—"*Hiền, ma petite Hiền.*" Her sweet voice reached deep down into the core of my being. It warmed my heart. I closed my eyes praying the echo of her cherished words would never again leave me.

My sister had told me that Mom did not speak English—just French and Vietnamese. I did not predict this shortcoming, but *Phương* was there to translate. One thing was certain—we were both in tears and overcome with joy!

"You cry—Mom cry," she whispered. "We stop crying—OK, we talk now! *Hiền, Je t'aime beaucoup-beaucoup-beaucoup,*" I love you very-very-very much, she blurted into the phone.

"*Moi aussi Má ,*" Me also, Mom, I said in my extremely limited French—"*moi, je t'aime beaucoup!*"

Soon after taking a breath she asked, "How is Sam? How is Bob?" No mention was made of Margaret!

I told her with *Phương's* help as a translator that the Mustards had passed away but Bob was fine. Not feeling the need to say more, I dropped the train of thought.

I phoned my mom almost daily and through my sister was able to express, even if superficially, some of my feelings. Although she was able to understand basic English, *Phương* did not have a command of the language to warrant more detailed conversations.

After many *Je t'aime* dialogues and medleys of sobs, we decided it was time to meet. We exchanged photos and letters while waiting to be able to wrap our arms around each other. It was a way of getting to know our extended families.

In the meantime, Judy Iannaccone, the Red Cross Director of Public Affairs called me for permission to contact the L.A. Times and news media with my story. She recognized the empowering human interest appeal and the awesome success of the Red Cross in being able to locate a person who had been lost for decades in a war-torn country. It was time to share it with others as a source of inspiration and encouragement. I was excited and more than willing to give my consent.

Dara also had taken the initiative to alert the media of the pending reunion. She sent out a press release to a friend who worked for the Los Angeles independent stations KCAL 9 TV and KCOP 13.

Shortly thereafter, *Phương* phoned late on evening. "*Hiền*," she said, excited, "Mom's flying out to L.A. on September 3!"

September 3, September 3—I repeated over and over to myself. How eerie! September 3, 1964 was the day I left *Việt Nam*—the day in tears I hugged my mom goodbye at *Sài Gòn's Tân Sơn Nhất* Airport. Now exactly twenty-nine years later, on September 3, 1993, at LAX Airport, I would once again hug my mom in tears. But this time I would shed tears of joy.

CHAPTER 12

LAX AIRPORT: SEPTEMBER 3, 1993

"A mother understands what a child does not say."
—Jewish Proverb

It was a balmy evening, a bit warm and muggy. However, seated in the back of the car I opened the window for a brief moment, just long enough to capture the freshness of the evening breeze. The sun had begun its gradual decent beyond the horizon. Despite the blast of red and orange that colored the darkening sky, I could see a flimsy trace of the dense fog that would eventually settle over Los Angeles.

Aggressive drivers wove in and out of lanes sometimes straddling the white and yellow lines to move forward through the congestion, even though we were driving against the rush-hour traffic. Several speeding cars cut right in front of us. It was more than obvious that L.A. drivers were neither patient nor overly cautious.

My sister, *Phương* had preceded my mom's visit by
three days. Since she spoke English I felt relieved she was
accompanying me and secure just in case I failed to recognize
my mom after the twenty-nine-year absence. We had commu-
nicated extensively and exchanged photos during the past two
months, but sometimes a printed image does not do justice.
Therefore, I looked upon my sister as a reassuring handrail,
offering support and encouragement.

Carrying less than a hundred pounds on a petite five-foot-
two-inch frame, *Phương* at twenty-three was a rather slim,
stylish young woman who shared my love of fashion. And
although her English was somewhat uncertain and fragmented,
we were beginning to develop a strong sibling bond. I was
delighted to have a younger sister—and discovering it was a lot
of fun.

After watching the *20/20* special in which a woman had
found her Vietnamese mother living in poverty in the rice
paddies, I was relieved to see my seven brothers and sisters
were all well-educated and lived, together with my mom, a
dignified middle-class life in a suburb of Paris.

Like me, all my siblings seemed to have a thirst for
learning, a passion for music and a flair for fashion and
style. Amid the many differences attributed to upbringing
and environment, we shared some very distinct similarities
which would make our reunion more joyful and meaningful.

Since Dara-lee mentioned she had contacted the media, I
realized the press would be at the airport to capture this momen-
tous event. All the rest was a deep, dark unknown and a tangled
mass of questions for which I would eventually find answers.

The car did not seem to travel fast enough, though I was
certain we were racing above the accepted speed limit. I read
each exit sign to myself realizing I was getting closer and closer

to LAX. Was this really happening? After all the lonely years, could I actually believe I would hug my mom again? My mind drifted for a moment, interrupting my concentration.

It was September 3, 1993, the twenty-ninth anniversary of my September 3, 1964 departure from *Sài Gòn's Tân Sơn Nhất* Airport. The events of the past six weeks were exciting, but not without repercussions. Since learning my mother was alive, a feeling of apprehension overshadowed my days leaving me restless and often unable to sleep.

After years of mourning her death, I had to come to terms with the idea that my mom was alive. Although many decades had passed, I still felt her presence in my heart. Even as a grown woman with three children of my own, I continued to miss her special love; the love only a mother could give to a child. Something was always missing from my life—there was a big dark hole that nothing could fill.

"*Hiền*, I think we are almost at the Tom Bradley arrival gate," *Phương* said, quickening her step. Thirteen years my junior, she was bursting with energy and excitement. I, on the other hand, was fueled by nerves and apprehension. I wondered if my mother would really accept me as her daughter.

Gordon, *Phương* and the children were at first unusually quiet. Jenna was nine, Kevin seven and Denny a precocious six-year-old who soon began chatting almost non-stop. Puzzled and too young to understand the meaning behind all the commotion, he pursued a why line of questioning that continued without pause.

"Mommy, why are they taking pictures of us—you are just going to see your mommy? Why are all these people looking at us?" he asked over and over. The impact of the emotional event seemed to have left both adults and children unsure of their expectations.

To reach the arrival gate we shouldered our way through throngs of Asian people conversing in languages foreign to me.

"This must be the gate," I said, pointing to a sign that said Paris-Los Angeles. *Phương* rummaged through her bag and checked the flight number she had scribbled on a crumpled piece of paper to be certain we had the right gate.

"Yes, *Hiền*," she said. "Mom will come out from here. Let's get closer so we won't miss her when she comes through."

Although I had anticipated media coverage, I was not fully prepared for the barrage of cameras and journalists congregating on the sidelines. As we neared I was able to read their badges and noticed they were from *KCAL TV, KCOPN* and *KFWB-AM* radio news.

Dara-lee had kept her word. We had full news coverage. From the corner of my eye I spotted Judy Iannaccone who was present to write a follow-up report of the reunion for the Newsletter of the American Red Cross.

I also noticed journalists from the *L.A. Times* and *Daily News* as well as the *Orange County Register* with their shiny badges, microphones and tape machines sprawled near the gate ready to cover the reunion. The media spectacle was a mixture of TV, print and radio media personnel.

Their presence along with the cameras and microphones was drawing an exaggerated swarm of onlookers, curious to learn what all the excitement was about. In a few moments the crowd had doubled with inquisitive onlookers anxious to see 'the main attraction.' There were whispers of, "Who's coming?" and "It must be some big star, VIP politician, or something!"

A month earlier, Wilson Cummer of the *L.A. Times* had photographed and interviewed me and the children for the first part of the story—the Red Cross's successful efforts in the search to locate my mother, a presumed casualty of the *Việt Nam*War for nearly three decades. His feature provided an interesting introduction and equally fascinating background to the main event—*Thanh's* arrival and walk across the threshold into LAX and her adopted daughter's life. He was now eager to write the amazing follow-up—the airport reunion story.

My sorority sister and friends had come out to the airport as well as a handful of individuals from the Red Cross. The girls toted a huge white banner and were able to get through the masses without undue difficulty. In super-sized block lettering was the message:

'DREAMS DO COME TRUE!'

The mood was electrifying. Mounted TV cameras were positioned near the entry and the cameramen stood side by side speaking among themselves; their camcorders ready to record, capture and immortalize the image of a middle-aged Vietnamese woman, after years of painful separation, hugging her daughter for the first time as an adult.

Over the loud speaker we heard an announcement that the flight from Paris was delayed several hours because of compromising weather conditions. The children were getting restless, but Gordon was helpful in calming them down. Finally, we heard the words we were waiting for—the flight from Paris was in.

After collecting her luggage and passing through customs, at around 9:00 pm an elegant *Thanh* passed the jet's cockpit, thanked the flight attendants for their wonderful service, walked down the ramp and stepped into the airport!

A petite, slender woman dressed in a flowing blue silk *áo dài* emerged. I immediately noticed how graceful and gorgeous she looked, even after an eleven-hour flight. She was truly an amazing woman.

My mother's gait was somewhat slow, but steady and her beauty unmarred by the passage of time. The long, shiny hair did not show even a faint trace of grey. Her pain and suffering left no footprints. *Thanh* was simply captivating.

The spell was interrupted only by the flashes of light and clicks of the cameramen's cameras.

I lowered my head into my open palms, unable to control my tears. My heart was racing and I could feel my stomach twist in knots.

"My mom is even more beautiful than I remembered," I whispered to myself. I wanted to break ranks and just run into her arms, but the press, eager to capture her first comments, thoughts and feelings, got to her before I could.

I waited twenty-nine years for this moment; a moment that was a repeated scenario in my daydreams and thoughts before retiring in the evenings. I knew I couldn't be patient. And I knew I couldn't delay it any longer.

Sobbing, I ran straight up to my mother, past the journalists, curious onlookers and cameramen and threw my arms around her. When our tear-stained cheeks touched, I noticed the still soft smoothness of her skin. "*Má,*" I whispered, struggling to catch my breath, "*Má* it's your *Hiền!*"

"*Hiền,*" she murmured through the sobs, "*Hiền, ma petite fille, Je t'aime beaucoup!*" I wrapped my arms around her. I didn't want to let her go—not ever again!

After the first initial greeting, Gordon, Jenna, Kevin and Denny came running. We stood embraced in a huddle, crying and clinging to each other. Newscasters were shoving micro-phones in front of our mouths, asking us endless questions.

Roaming around the tightly knit huddle in circles, they tried to get responses and comments. It was an incredible moment, and although I appreciated the press's attempt to document every emotional word and hug, a part of me just wanted to be alone with my mom. There was so much to say, so many questions to ask—and so much lost time to make up for.

Phương fought the tears, trying to remain composed to answer the journalists' questions. She had to translate my mother's words and mine so that we could express our feelings to each other. The moment was far too emotional for her to retain her composure and within minutes, she also was sobbing.

Jenna extended her tiny hands, offering my mom an aromatic bouquet of flowers. Dropping her arms from around my waist, my mom approached her grandchildren and embraced each one, softly whispering, "I love you," in their ears.

Our eyes were red and puffy from crying, our cheeks streaked with tears—but our hearts were filled with a joy beyond description. It was a magnetic moment...as Dara-lee, Karen and Sheri stood waving the **'Dreams do come true'** banner. There was no doubt—I was certainly living my dream!

"Is this your mommy?" Jenna asked, immediately imitated by Kevin and Denny. "Is she—is she—is she our grand-mother?" the boys repeated in unison, tugging at my pants.

Once again, Gordon intervened and calmed the boys down, but not before I smiled and said, "Yes, this is my mommy!"

During the three days *Phương* stayed with us, she had taught my children a few Vietnamese words with which to greet their grandmother.

"*Bà ngoạ,i*" hello grandma, the children giggled, looking up at my mother with wide open eyes. Their faces were flushed and their full-tooth smiles told of the joyous moment.

"*Bà khoe không*" How are you? They questioned in a garbled Vietnamese laced with a thick American accent that made them even more endearing, if not hilariously comical. A radiant grandmother patted them on their heads, bent over and gave each one a kiss.

"*Je t'aime*," she whispered, "I love you."

Much as I had dreamed and fantasized about seeing my mother again during my childhood, as an adult I was unprepared for the overwhelming emotional explosion the realization of this dream would trigger. It was all I had imagined and certainly a great deal more empowering than anything I had ever designed in my mind.

There were so many unknowns to clarify and the one decades-old question burning on the tip of my tongue from dawn to dusk. However, I had been advised not to bombard my mother with questions right away.

That evening I refrained from inquiring why she had given me up for adoption. One more time, I buried it in the back of mind and opted to let her settle in. After such a grueling voyage across continents and having to deal with the overwhelming emotion of being reunited with her daughter after twenty-nine years of longing, she needed a moment of tranquility to gather her thoughts and feelings.

The ride home was smooth. And the happiness was evident as we continued to reach out to each other, hugging and kissing.

When we arrived at the house, Gordon helped unload the luggage from the trunk and unbuckle the children from their safety seats. *Phương*, my mom and I went inside and I accompanied them to the master suite.

They were happy to be roommates sharing a queen size bed. How different it was from the way mom nestled me under her arm as a small child in *Việt Nam*, and settled herself on a tiny mat for the evening's rest.

I knew Mom and *Phương* would have privacy since the master suite was on the upper level and distant from the hullabaloo usually occurring in the children's rooms.

With the time change, my mother had been up on her feet for more than twenty-four hours without pausing to rest. However, this sleep-deprived state seemed to have little effect on her exuberance. She arrived with luggage that weighed more than she did and was intent on opening the bags before calling it a day.

Gordon lifted the bags, placing them on the bed. *Phương* and I helped her unpack. It was amazing to note how much she had taken with her and how much stuff you could squash into one bag.

"*Phương*," I blurted excitedly, "it looks like Mom brought a whole gift shop with her!"

"*Hiền*," she replied, smiling, "*Má* wanted to bring something for everyone."

"OK," I said, laughing, "but she didn't have to buy out the entire store."

We enjoyed a chuckle and continued to unpack. Mom brought gifts, chocolates, and cosmetics for me, the children, my sorority sisters and friends. It was Christmas in September! The children were delighted and kept coming up to their grandmother touching her silky *áo dài* and repeating the Vietnamese greeting—*Bà ngoại,* giggling and encircling her chair.

"Jenna, Kevin, Denny," I said, "Grandma is tired. Give her a kiss and go to bed. You will see her in the morning."

Reluctantly and with repeated prompting, they obeyed, scuffling their feet as they left.

The room quieted down except for a surprising pop and the unexpected swish of bubbles too long imprisoned in a bottle, finally escaping.

It was unbelievable. Her energy was boundless and certainly not in need of replenishment. At almost 11:00 pm—8:00 am Paris time, my mother opened the bottle of champagne she carried across the ocean. She had something to celebrate—and it just could not wait!

"Well," I thought to myself recognizing my love for the bubbly, "there's no doubting whose daughter I am. Mom is a woman after my own heart—chocolate and champagne!"

I excused myself and went to get the glasses. A mist of champagne sprayed my mother's face enhancing an already glowing complexion. She accepted the tiny drops without making even a minimal effort to wipe them away.

We sat up talking and toasting our reunion. I spoke in English with a smattering of French. *Phương* responded in Vietnamese laced with broken English, acting as the translator, and my mother added a little French, Vietnamese and a sprinkling of English words all in one sentence.

Yet, despite the confusing *Babel* of jumbled languages, tears and laughter, hugs and encore facial caresses, despite the exhaustion and intense emotion of such an extraordinary day, my mother understood exactly what I was thinking just as I knew her own thoughts.

But more importantly, we knew in our hearts how we both felt in that precious, life-altering moment in time. There is a very special complicity between a mother and her child—and nothing—not even decades of separation can sever certain bonds.

However, time and circumstance have left a mark. Our reunion after twenty-nine years was and is a bittersweet experience. Yes, I'm joyful for having found her, but the decades lost can never be returned.

Though emotionally close as a mother and daughter, the language barrier divides us as two strangers. But I have learned not only to be grateful for the wonderful miracle I have received, but to graciously accept the blessing of my today and tomorrow without dwelling on what can never be—the impossible.

CHAPTER 13

Assembling the Puzzle

"You cannot gain back the time lost with a parent.
You have to accept the relationship for what it can be—
not for what it could have been.
—Mary Mustard Reed

After the initial reunion at LAX, My mother and I tried to settle down and begin the process of getting reacquainted as two adult women. Although we knew what was in each other's hearts, there were many unanswered questions and endless blank pages in my memory which needed to be filled. Once the excitement of the reunion had calmed, the sad reality of our language differences became a frustrating barrier, straining our relationship.

Turning to my Vietnamese connections in Little Saigon, I immediately hired an interpreter. Certain this would eliminate the language obstacle, I felt secure it would give us the opportunity to dig deeper than the *"Je t'aime,"* which we already shared. Having lost twenty-nine years, I was determined to discover who I was by learning who my mother was and what kind of life she had led until now. But, I questioned, would I have all the pieces I needed? Would I be able to assemble the puzzle?

It was understandably surprising to find out that my mom had visited California's Little Saigon in Westminster several times. In fact, she had made some friends among the Vietnamese immigrants. Ironically, it was a rather sad reality, since I lived barely seven miles from there—yet we never connected. Estranged since 1966, she never imagined I could be so close.

Another coincidence included the fact that my sister, *Bich Nga's* uncle through marriage was a cardiologist in Westminster. This was uncanny because I was dealing with the Vietnamese physicians for my work at Ciba-Geigy, found myself in the same office in which he was practicing medicine, yet by some twist of fate was never able to have a discussion with him. So near, but still so far. It seemed as if fate pushed me in the right direction, then pulled me back before I could enter into my past. Perhaps the time was not right!

Breaching the cultural and language barriers was even more intricate than I had anticipated, and the intervention of interpreters sometimes made me uneasy. I was frustrated and although I often felt awkward, I tried not to focus on the presence of a third party. After all, my purpose was to become reacquainted with my mother and learn all about this phenomenal woman who had given me life.

Information starved, I was eager to urgently know it all. But little did I realize how much patience I would have to acquire, and that it would take over thirteen years before I would have all the pieces of the puzzle.

In just a few short days, my house underwent a pronounced cultural makeover, setting the stage for a distinctive Vietnamese ambience. Mom went into the kitchen and assumed the role of master chef. In the blink of an eye, all traces of my California culinary heritage evaporated into thin air. In its place I noticed the strong whiff of a peculiar aroma. It traveled from the kitchen, eventually invading the entire house, one room at a time.

"*Má*, what is that odor?" I said one afternoon, unaccustomed to anything even remotely similar to it.

"*Hiền*," she said smiling, "don't you remember—it's *nuớc mắm*."

I was always puzzled how something so weird smelling could possibly be so appetizing. My children had neither tasted the sauce nor come in contact with the pungent aroma, since the only time I ate Vietnamese food was when I dined in Westminster's Little Saigon restaurants with the doctors.

I rarely prepared rice and when I did, it was in the typically American way. Selecting a box of Uncle Ben's, I'd boil it in the pre-measured pouch or pour one cup of rice into two cups of water, then add a slab of butter. It was not necessary to speak a common language to understand the surprised glances my mother and *Phương* exchanged. Two rather stunned faces revealed their intense feelings of shock and disbelief. I was ashamed to admit I was an Asian woman totally clueless about preparing one of the main staples of the Vietnamese diet.

This was a period of transition—a time of questioning, exploring and new beginnings. I felt as if I was crammed into a roller coaster careening at full speed. The emotional highs and lows left me drained and exhausted. Working my way through the confusion, sadness and uncertainty, I knew I had to come to terms with the realization that I would never be able to recapture the lost time.

My siblings, *Bích Nga, Phú, Tuấn, Thúy, Tuyền and Phương* were born one year after the other, and six years later my brother *Việt* arrived. All seven were loved and well cared for by an ever-present, doting mother. Most probably, they were unable to comprehend the anxiety and frustrations of growing up without such a nurturing and caring mother.

Therefore, observing my mother with *Phương* was sometimes a bittersweet experience. On one hand I felt happy witnessing the special bond between mother and daughter and on the other, I was saddened, realizing I did not share the same feeling regardless of how much love there was between my mom and me. Somehow, love was not sufficient—it could not fill the twenty-nine-year void.

It is impossible to recapture the time lost between a parent and child. And I knew in my heart I had to accept my relationship with my mother for what it is today and resist the foolish temptation to dwell on what it could have been. The past was gone, but I had a future to look forward to.

Through interpreters and a splattering of jumbled words from the three different languages, we were able to answer some of each other's questions.

"*Hiền*," my mother said one evening after dinner, "why did you stop writing to me? I waited for your letters, but none came."

"*Má*," I responded, "the Mustards told me you were killed during the war in 1966. Sam said there were terrible bombings after which you were missing and presumed dead. I was devastated when I found out I had lost you forever."

As we spoke clinging to each other, we broke into violent tears, reliving the moment while reminiscing about the intense feelings we experienced both then and now.

"What happened to you, *Má*?" I continued, searching for an explanation. "Bill Neal went to *Việt Nam* to look for you and told us you were gone. All he found were piles of rubble where the house once stood. Where were you? As a child I cried myself to sleep every night because I missed you so much. I held onto a few of your letters like a security blanket. They gave me comfort during the long sleepless nights. I felt so alone."

I realized it was difficult for my mom to talk about such a deplorable period of her life. But between French, Vietnamese and the interpreter's ability to translate her thoughts and feelings, I was able to understand what had occurred.

In 1966 the village of *Vĩnh -Viễn* on the outskirts of *Sài Gòn* where my mom lived had been bombed, raided and totally destroyed by the *Việt Cộng*. However, an unplanned trip to the market with her husband, *Nam Nguyễn* and the children proved to be a life-saving twist of fate.

Although unharmed, my mother lost all her possessions among which were my letters, some photos and the Mustards' address in California. Therefore, the line of communication was severed making it impossible for her to contact me with the news that she had survived the attack.

Ironically, my letters reaching the wreckage that was once her home were cast into the trash and obviously never read. This lack of communication led to the mistaken conclusion that she had been killed. Thankfully, my mother carried my photos in an oversized purse which she took to the market with her that day.

After she explained the mystery of the broken communications, she took my hand, smiled and said, *"Hiền,* how was your life with the Mustards? Were they good to you? You know Sam, he promised me he pay your education."

Much as I anticipated this question, it was still very painful for me to go back in time and describe my growing years filled with parental neglect, loneliness and abuse. I realized the truth would cause misery, but I felt my mom had to be aware of some of the events of my early life. Careful not to make her feel sad and guilty regarding her decision to give me up for adoption, I omitted some of the awful experiences. Her frequent bouts of tears confirmed she was in agonizing pain.

My mother put her arms around me, gave me a hug then gently cradled my face in the palms of her hands. *"Hiền—Má* so very sorry," she whispered.

"Má," I responded, my voice crackling with emotion, "I had a good life. I was fed, lived in nice homes, had beautiful clothes and a good education. But more importantly, I had and have wonderful friends, like Bettie and Fred who acted as surrogate parents. They were always there for me. *Má,* the Mustards were just not able to love."

Our conversation was difficult though in a sense necessary even if it opened up old wounds. The truth, agonizing as it may be, offers a certain release. It liberates.

And hearing the truth left my mother devastated. She lowered her head into the palm of her right hand and sobbed. I knelt in front of her and gently put my arm around her tiny body to comfort her.

Losing my own composure, I buried my head in her lap and cried uncontrollably. We both knew there would be recurrent bouts of tears and a persistent sadness that would be a part of who we were for many years.

What I didn't know until a future conversation was that, ironically, once again there was a strong correlation woven into our lives. While I suffered the consequences of maltreatment and parental negligence at the hands of the Mustards, coincidently, my mom was dealing with her own difficult marital issues and conflicts.

After I left *Sài Gòn* in 1964 my mom went to live with *Nam Nguyễn's* parents. As a famous entertainer, he traveled often with the theater company, leaving her alone and lonely. She took care of all the domestic chores. Cleaning the house, preparing meals for the family and traveling great distances in the rain and heat to fetch water for the family was daily routine. Tired, she toted a cumbersome pole with two buckets across her shoulders back and forth from the house to the water fount.

The family home was roofless, and in the evenings leaves were strewn on top of the open structure to insure some measure of protection from the elements.

Not very kind, her in-laws would demand money, hitting her when she mentioned her husband had not sent her any. Believing their son, *Nam Nguyễn,* was a much sought after entertainer, they were of the mistaken opinion he regularly sent her funds from his singing engagements. Refusing to accept her denial of any money received, they continued to mistreat her.

It was more than obvious that my mother's life was one of suffering and grueling hardship. *Nam Nguyễn* returned from time to time, leaving her pregnant every year for six years before their last child.

With the end of the war in 1975, and the Communist takeover, rich Vietnamese citizens were deprived of their wealth and property. Often the male heads of households were seized and arrested. In their absence, homes were easily ransacked, and robbed of possessions.

By this time, my mother had seven children to tend to. Food, especially meat products was rationed. My mother was allotted two kilos of rice and a half kilo of meat every other week—with eight mouths to feed!

In order to purchase the provisions she had to arise at 3:00 am, walk in the dark to the food station and stand in line with hordes of others. Many times even this sacrifice would not suffice. But optimistic, she believed tomorrow was another day and would present another chance to receive her appropriate allotment.

However, sometimes cupboards would remain empty as the food was far from abundant to take care of the family's needs. The supply either fell short of the demand, or the produce was not of the best quality.

But my mom soon learned and would pack a paring knife in her purse. When handed the potatoes, she quickly turned them over and cut away the rot. Since the produce was distributed by weight, she did not wish to pay for waste—plus the portions would be smaller for everyone. How clever and ingenious she was!

Frustrated and exhausted both physically and emotionally, she was forced many times to return empty-handed, to her hungry, crying children.

When luck would be on her side and she would bring home a chicken, the skin and carcass would have to be discretely discarded after consumption to prohibit the neighbors or Communists from finding the remnants and arresting her. Life was a daily battle as she struggled to survive and provide food and nourishment for her seven children.

It was more than apparent both my mother and I were survivors. Our hardships may have differed, but our strength and instincts for self-preservation were the same. My mom and I cried together for the suffering we shared even if in diverse parts of the world. Today, our tears were a selfless reflection of our sympathy towards each other. I cried for my mom's pain and suffering and she for mine.

But while I eventually grew up and away from my miserable childhood, the hardships had continued for my mother. During the later part of the seventies she made four failed attempts to escape from Communist dominated *Sài Gòn* with her husband and children. Finally in 1979, *Nam Nguyễn* and two of his eldest sons, *Tuyền* and *Tuấn*, along with twenty other passengers, completed a successful escape crammed into a small a fishing boat twenty-five feet long and seven feet wide, headed for *Cần Thơ,* the largest city in the Mekong Delta. The plan was to eventually board a larger vessel and reach a far away destination where they would be free from Communist rule.

That evening the Communists knocked on my mother's door questioning her about the whereabouts of her husband and sons. Scared and concerned about her five children standing behind her, she held firm when they tried to force her into admitting *Nam Nguyễn* and his sons had made an attempt to escape. Quickly, she thought of an explanation that would seem credible. "No," she said, "he did not escape—he ran off with another woman. I don't know where he is."

Grabbing her brusquely without any concern for her crying children, the police escorted her to jail where they held her for three days before releasing her.

Meanwhile, *Nam Nguyễn* and my half brothers sailed for three days from *Sài Gòn* to *Cần Thơ,* terrified of being spotted and captured by the *Việt Cộngs.* Once on land, they traveled by foot to the fishing province of *Cà Mau,* guided only by their instincts. Boarding a small wooden boat not larger than twenty-five feet long and seven feet wide along with twenty other people, they set sail for the South East China Sea.

Just minutes after the early morning sunrise, the craft reached the open seas. It seemed as if the escape would run smoothly. Then suddenly, the boat tipped to one side. There was a crackling sound like something splitting, followed by a splash—something had fallen from the boat. It didn't take long to realize the rudder was gone. It had broken loose from the stern and fallen into the water, leaving the boat without a steering device.

Several hours later the motor was silenced, forcing the craft jam-packed full of women and children to stay afloat for five days without food, fuel or water. Fearful, the children huddled under their terrified mothers' arms, crying.

My brother told me they were fortunate to be traveling in December, the rainy month. Utilizing the pelting raindrops as drinking water, the refugees were able to stay alive. Weak and exhausted from the ordeal, the few men took turns remaining vigilant to guard against a very common and dangerous pirating.

With sturdy iron boats these ruthless pirates would approach, steal, snatch and rape the women and girls. After massacring the passengers they would ram their iron boats into the small wooden crafts of the fleeing Vietnamese people. Once the boats had sunk, all traces of the crime were destroyed.

On the fifth day *Nam, Tuyền* and *Tuấn* , lucky to have survived this far, noticed clouds of smoke spreading along the horizon. Lighting cigarettes, they tried to send distress signals. However, at first their efforts were useless until three hours later when an oil tanker appeared traveling towards the barely floating boat.

The weight of the approaching tanker rippled the sea, causing the waves to swell, unnaturally. The boat rocked and swayed as the people shouted and cried. Some were leaning over vomiting, but since they had not eaten in days, the violent heaving brought up nothing but digestive juices.

Once the Captain understood the 'evading' nature of the mission, he wired various Embassies in Thailand, Hong Kong, Indonesia, and Malaysia to seek refuge: all to no avail. The response was the same over and over—"no." No one was willing to accept a boat-wrecked load of fleeing Vietnamese citizens. Eventually, the captain received an OK from Singapore, and the passengers were allowed to board the tanker, spending twenty days at sea en-route to their destination.

With his weary feet finally planted on dry land, *Nam Nguyễn* began to work at odd jobs, from serving coffee in cafes to eventually accepting a position in a garage as an auto mechanic. Once he had accumulated sufficient funds to immigrate to Europe, he decided to settle in Paris, France. Soon after his arrival, *Nam* started to send my mother a small amount of funds to help sustain the family. The money was transferred *via* China using a secret code, "Yvonne."

Meanwhile from 1979 until 1984 my mother earned her livelihood as a street vendor, selling wallets to maintain herself and her children.

Although exhausted from family responsibilities and house-hold tasks, she carried her merchandise on her shoulders, often walking in the heat and humidity for lengthy periods of time.

Since this type of 'commerce' was illegal, she had to pay strict attention not to get caught. Many times spotting a police officer, she would hurriedly pack up her wares in blankets and run home before they noticed her street corner peddling 'business.'

However, luck has a short-life span and a sly way of running out. One day, tired and distracted, she was not quick enough to throw the wallets into blankets. Consequently, she was caught red-handed, arrested and removed of her merchandise. Thankfully, she was given just a two day sentence.

Five years later, coincidentally, on the day my first child, Jenna was born, July 13 1984, my mother and her five remaining children departed for Paris. *Nam Nguyễn* had made the arrangements and was waiting to greet his family at the airport.

Many things had occurred during the lengthy period of separation. And it was more than evident my mother and I had much to discover and uncover about each other. After all, we had been apart for almost three decades, and with the language difficulty it was not easy. Although words kept us apart—feelings entwined and linked us together.

Dara-lee was present to record our conversations, especially since I had planned very early on to write a book. Listening to the agonizing events of our respective lives, she as well as the interpreter was in tears. It was a distressing scenario repeated throughout the weeks, months and years.

The more we spoke and opened our hearts to each other, the more I realized just how parallel our lives had been—and still at this point I did not yet truly know the exceptional woman who gave me the gift of life.

Several weeks later, during a quiet moment, I sat beside my mother while she was going through some papers in her purse. "*Má*," I said, "why did you give me up for adoption?" Her dark expressive eyes filled with tears. For a moment her gaze took on a distant look as if she was returning to the time of her life-altering decision. She cleared her throat.

"My baby," she said, turning to meet my gaze, "I loved you very much—you have to understand." She looked deep into my eyes, and fell silent.

Thinking back, I remembered sometimes overhearing bits and pieces of conversations between Sam and Margaret, and often there were innuendos which at the time I was too young to comprehend. But I recall Sam mentioning that I was an illegitimate child, and when my mother remarried, her new husband refused to accept me as part of the family.

This explains why I was entrusted to an American couple who made promises of a better, more secure life away from *Việt Nam*. Therefore, when I became ill with smallpox, Sam took me home after the hospital stay. Living in his big house with *Hai* and *Cô Cúc* to cook and take care of me was undoubtedly a blessing. I was well dressed, had good food and nice toys to play with.

Previously living in sheer poverty in an unfurnished one-room hut and left naked most of the time, of course I was happy with the Mustards in *Việt Nam*. However, little did we all know the 'privileged' lifestyle was destined to be merely a brief interval.

When my mother understood that Sam had broken his promise to her regarding paying for my college education, she became reflective; saddened by the reality unveiled before her. I reassured her it didn't matter at this point in time, since I was able to work and put my self through college. The end result was the same—just the means to obtaining my goal were not as she had hoped or planned.

"My sweet *Hiền,*" she continued, sighing, "I so sorry for everything—so deep sorry. I hope you forgive me."

There was never any doubt—of course, I did not fault her for the decisions she made as a poor, desperate young girl barely out of her teens and alone in the world. Therefore, I certainly did not want her to spend her days consumed with guilt.

I tried my best to reassure her that despite it all I did have a better life. I was well-educated, had a good paying job, a nice home and three healthy, beautiful children.   Observing life from a philosophical perspective, I used my challenging experiences to grow and mature into a stronger adult. Like my mom, I turned adversity and hardship into virtue. I became a survivor with an indomitable will to overcome.

Amazingly, another parallel linked us. Both our lives were dependent on life-changing decisions, each based on the answer to one difficult question—would I be better off in America with the Mustards and would my mom have a better life marrying a man who would rescue her from the hardships of working numerous jobs, father seven children with her, and provide for the family? Answering 'yes' to both questions was the determining factor in the unraveling of our destinies. And thanks to *Phương's* translating, my mother and I learned about the numerous, almost uncanny similarities in our lives.

Two years after the reunion, in the spring of 1995, I traveled to Paris and was finally able to meet my siblings as well as embrace my sister, *Bích Nga.* Discovering they all inherited a flair and distinctive talent for music was a delightful surprise. They are in a sense like the Jackson Five, performing, taking their bows and winning the applause of their enthusiastic fans. I was fortunate, also. I inherited my love and ability to sing and play various instruments from my mom, consequently musical skill was a common trait we all shared. Numerous impressive photos of my brothers and sisters situated around the house documented their performances in clubs and theaters.

But she never forgot me. In fact, I was quite moved to see my photos displayed throughout the Paris apartment like precious works of art. Unprepared, I cried, imagining how painful it must have been to have this reminder of her 'lost daughter' as a constant presence in her life.

Although initially discouraged by the language barrier, I was thrilled to learn that my two youngest siblings, *Phương* and *Việt* both spoke English, having studied the language in the Parisian school they attended.

They were so gracious, and our common bond of music made me feel truly welcome. Selecting the instrument we felt most comfortable playing, we ran through a medley of Beatles songs singing with full voices all in perfect harmony. No one would or could dispute the worldwide appeal of this phenomenal British group, which had boomed in all seven Continents. Even my English-challenged siblings knew every word of every song!

As I glanced around the room between songs, I couldn't help seeing and feeling the extraordinary devotion my siblings had for our mother. There was such an abundant outpouring of love and warmth, and yes, perhaps I'd be remiss in not expressing my envy during that very special moment. After all, they had what I so painfully missed and longed for all my life.

I was happy to learn my sisters and brothers all received excellent educations. The boys pursued engineering degrees and *Phương* was an accountant—all without the horrendous Mustard experience!

I could see my mom had much to tell about her life, before and after I came into her world. Hungry for more, I couldn't take my mind off the Red Cross and their phenomenal initiative. Grateful, but rather curious, I wanted to unravel the riddle and discover how they were able to find her on such flimsy evidence after so much time had passed.

There were still many important segments missing from the puzzle, and I was certain beyond any measure of doubt that unless I had these key pieces in my hand, I would not be able to solve and assemble the puzzle. And without the completed puzzle I would never understand who I am and why I am the way I am.

CHAPTER 14

BUILDING A DREAM: THE RED CROSS EXPEDITION

"The Red Cross in its nature, its aims and purposes, and consequently, its methods, is unlike any other organization in the country. It is an organization of physical action, of instantaneous action, at the spur of the moment; it cannot await the ordinary deliberation of organized bodies if it would be of use to suffering humanity...it has by its nature a field of its own."
—Clara Barton

In all fairness I cannot speak of the merits of the Red Cross without giving a special mention to the two pioneering individuals responsible for starting and developing this humanitarian organization, Henri Dunant and Clara Barton.

Swiss entrepreneur, social activist and Noble Peace Prize winner, Henri Dunant, was influenced by the bloodshed during the 1859 Battle of Solferino.

Touched by casualties of combat, Henri began his career as a social activist promoting his idea of developing an organization of neutral affiliation to tend to and shelter wounded servicemen, civilians, prisoners and refugees. He helped organize 'national relief societies' to offer aid and assistance to those afflicted by war casualties.

The International Red Cross and The Red Crescent Movement were established in Geneva, Switzerland, and born politically and socially neutral. Their mission was to extend nonpartisan help to the war's ailing and injured.

On February 17, 1863, the ICRC, International Committee of the Red Cross was founded, and through its compassionate endeavors it was awarded three Nobel Prizes between 1917 and 1963.

Meanwhile, across the Atlantic, an *avant-guard* 'feminist,' Clara Barton was building a reputation as a teacher in an exclusively male-dominated profession. Like Henri Dunant, she was greatly influenced by the consequences of battle—in particular the bloodshed and suffering of the Civil War.

Jeopardizing her own life to preserve that of others, she positioned herself right at the front, to care for the wounded and dying. Two decades later in 1881, Clara, known as "the Angel of the battlefield," founded the American Red Cross, supervising and heading its endeavors until well in her eighties.

Basically, it is thanks to these two revolutionary individuals and the phenomenal American and International Vietnamese branch of the Red Cross Organization that my mother and I were reunited after twenty-nine years. It wasn't an easy task as war-torn South *Việt Nam* had to rebuilt after the destructive fall of *Sài Gòn*—and many streets had been destroyed, rebuilt and re-named.

In 1984 after endless years of hardship and struggle tying to leave *Sài Gòn,* my mother, together with her husband and children successfully immigrated to Paris. However, nostalgic for her native land, once a year she returned to *Việt Nam* and visited 376 *Phan Đình Phùng* where I had lived for awhile with her. Although she had started a new life in Paris, she had few friends and missed her familiar *Sài Gòn* neighborhood.

In the spring of 1993, leaving behind the still chilly Parisian climate, she boarded the plane for the long tedious journey that would take her to *Sài Gòn*, now known as *Hồ Chí Minh City*. However, this time she had no idea she was flying off to a dream come true destiny; a fate that would alter her life and mine, forever.

The scents, sounds and images of her native land encouraged her to reminisce about her yesterday as a young girl struggling to support herself and her tiny daughter. She allowed her mind to take her back in time to a less than serene 'fight for survival' period. Although not a pleasant memory, at least mother and daughter were still together.

Nearing her old *Phan Đình Phùng* neighborhood, the middle-aged *Thanh* was shocked when she spotted the passport photo taken almost three decades earlier of her beloved long-lost first born plastered on the side of the building. "Could it really be *Hiền?*" she questioned, not daring to believe, yet so desperately refusing to disbelieve.

Running towards the picture, she felt her pulse quicken— the image of the young child was indeed *Hiền*. It was an exact copy of the famous passport photo she had kept beside her bed for twenty-nine years—perhaps never losing hope that one day she might be able to embrace her daughter. In *Thanh's* heart, *Hiền* was never lost.

The sweet, innocent face of her first-born child greeted her every morning when she opened her eyes and was there every evening when she closed them to rest.

In the flyer, the little girl, dressed in the pretty pink dress she herself at slipped over the child's head on September 3,

1964 was wearing the shiny treble clef around her neck. There was no margin of error—she was standing in front of the photo of her beloved *Hiền*.

Questioning the meaning of this strange event, *Thanh* turned her head and noticed the same little girl appeared wherever there was an area large enough to accommodate the striking photo-flyer. Apparently, the Red Cross had made a sizeable poster from the time-worn photo I had given them when I engaged the tracing services.

Digging into her purse, *Thanh* pulled out the crumpled photo she carried with her whenever she left the house, since the tearful goodbye at *Tân Sơn Nhất* Airport.

"*Ma petite Hiền,*" she whispered, looking into the expressive almond eyes that seemed so alive in the picture, "where are you, my darling?"

Unknown to my mother, the Red Cross had designed an eight by ten flyer with an enlarged photo and the caption: *Missing Person.* In addition to the enlarged image, it listed my name, date of birth, and the last time I had been together with my mother prior to my departure with the Mustards. Also, the flyer invited anyone with knowledge or information regarding the whereabouts of *Nguyễn Thị Thanh Hiền* or her mother, *Nguyễn Thị Thanh* to kindly notify the American Red Cross.

This extraordinary organization had compiled the flyers and used a mass distribution strategy to gain attention and achieve their objective. The Red Cross was the hot-line—both giving and receiving information in their quest to unite mother and daughter.

Excited about seeing my photo, my mom snatched as many as she could find, digging her nails into the flyers.

These mere pieces of paper, many damaged by the elements were the promise of hope.

Jumping into a taxi with her little treasure tightly secured in her hand, she ordered the driver to take her to the Red Cross.

Speeding toward the organization's representative office situated at 201 *Nguyễn Thị Minh Khai, Quận* 1, *Tp. Hồ Chí Minh, Thanh* once again reconstructed in her mind all the events of her last day with *Hiền*. She cried softly as she countered ten seconds to her arrival.

When the taxi pulled up to the entrance of the Red Cross, my mother felt somewhat 'woozy' from the emotional impact of finding her daughter's face splashed along the streets of *Sài Gòn*. She felt light-headed. Her legs seemed heavy and unsteady and her hands trembled as the reached for the door handle to exit the taxi before the driver could run over to help her out.

Pausing a moment, she waited for the butterflies' clumsy game of tag in the pit of her stomach to draw to an end before moving farther. But calling on the inner strength that made and makes her a survivor, my mother took a deep breath, stepped out of the taxi and walked through the main entry door, still clutching the handful of photos nestled in her clammy hand.

Once inside, *Thanh* felt lost among the crowds of people. Searching for someone to offer assistance, she noticed a gentleman standing not too distant from the entryway. Walking over, she opened her hand carefully as if shielding a precious treasure and showed him the photo. "This is my daughter," she said, pointing towards the little girl's face.

Smiling at the visibly emotional woman asking for directions, he accompanied her over to the International War

Victims Tracing Desk and reassured her someone would be with her in just a few moments; moments that to a mother who had not hugged her daughter since 1964, seemed like an eternity. But courageous and tenacious, she persisted until a tracing coordinator addressed her. Once again opening her hand, she placed my photo on the counter. "This is my daughter," she said, pausing then clearing her throat. "I am *Hiền's* mother!"

Thanh was asked to sit until the individual in charge of tracing missing persons was available. Grabbing her clump of photos, she turned and positioned herself in a vacant seat in anticipation. Several minutes later she was summoned.

Eager to talk to someone, she blurted, "I am *Hiền's* mother," pointing to the photo. Calming her down, the representative was able to understand that although my mother was anxious to get in touch with me, she was unaware of how she should proceed from here.

"*Madame*, we have been searching for you. We do not have all the details about your daughter. There is no contact info—neither an address nor telephone number. We will have to notify the National Capital Chapter of the American Red Cross in Washington DC."

Of course, my mother did not have any documents to prove she was *Nguyễn Thị Thanh*. However, she was able to show her passport to verify her place and date of birth. The document identified her as *Đào Thị Thanh* —her married name. She also showed my irreplaceable, somewhat faded and worn passport photo that she always carried in her purse.

However, perhaps the defining aspect of the issue was not only her mention of Sam and Margaret Mustard, but the photos she had of this American couple who had adopted her daughter. At that point it was certain she was telling the truth. The beautiful *petite* woman with the glowing tear-filled eyes and nervous hand tremor was indeed the long lost mother of Mary Mustard Reed born *Nguyễn Thị Thanh Hiền!*

Thinking back, I cannot help feeling the extraordinary role of the Red Cross in collaboration with an uncanny twist of fate that brought my mother to her old *Phan Đình Phùng* neighborhood at the precise moment in which my photos were still intact. Had she postponed her trip or gone at a later date, *Sài Gòn*'s tropical climate with a propensity for destructive seasonal monsoons and elevated humidity would have reduced the image and information on the flyers, most likely beyond recognition. Thankfully, she had chosen April that year—just one month before the onset of the rainy season.

The probability of my mother being in the right place at the right time was undoubtedly part of a Divine Master Plan, just as my career change, the territory I was assigned, and the chance encounter with the Vietnamese doctors, in particular Dr. *Hùng Hữu Nguyễn had been.*

With his uncanny intuition about my mom being alive, Dr. *Nguyễn* exercised a major role in redesigning my fate. It almost seemed like the unraveling of a dramatic scene from a Greek classic in which destiny played a dominant and influential role in people's lives.

In another sense it was a testimonial to the merits of faith and the power of prayer as well as an unwavering trust in a Superior Force that rewards persistence, tenacity and suffering with not only a reprieve, but a blessing. And guided by this almost forgiving Divine Intervention, the Red Cross worked its own special miracle.

I will always be indebted to this phenomenal organization

for their global humanitarian endeavors in restoring dignity to a troubled mankind. Furthermore, I will always be grateful for the joy they bring to broken families when lost or missing loved ones are reunited.

The Red Cross is a light in the darkness—a hand for the needy, and an empowering inspiration to every human being. But more importantly, The Red Cross is the thrill of hope, and the substance of dreams.

The Journey Home: December 24, 2006 Jenna's Reflections

*"My mom is a phenomenal woman.
Undeniably, I have some huge shoes to fill."*
—Jenna Reed

On our trip to *Việt Nam,* thirteen years after my mother found her family, she was reacquainted with the past she was torn apart from twenty-nine years ago. Together with her mother *Thanh,* sister *Phương*, brother-in-law *Cam,* and their daughter *Alysé*, we journeyed back to her home in *Sài Gòn* where her last memories as a Vietnamese girl remained faint.

This epilogue recounts our tour of *Việt Nam* as well as my observations of a family ripped apart and reunited. I dedicate this to you mom, for being a source of strength to all adopted children searching for answers to their past, and for being an exceptional mother who has given her three children all that she never had growing up; undying love, affection and support. I will never feel prouder of anyone—you have truly inspired me.

Almost thirteen years after my mother was reunited with *Thanh*, she decided she was finally ready to return to her native *Việt Nam*. This decision marked the beginning of an emotional roller-coaster ride filled with memories sheltered from my mom since childhood.

As my mom and I stepped foot into a country that was once plagued by war, death, poverty, and disease, somehow I felt a strong connection. Lugging our bags through the airport, we felt as if we were walking the red carpet. Tons of smiling faces, laughter, and families were gathered together as they waited for their loved ones to return home.

In a crowd of unfamiliar faces, we spotted my grandmother, *Thanh* who had flown in from her home in Paris, as well as Aunt *Phương* and her family from Southern California. As the distance between us narrowed, it finally hit me that this was it; this was where my mother was born. I knew almost immediately that the few memories she had of *Việt Nam* would soon re-emerge.

Although clouds obscured the sun, it was so hot and humid. The streets were crowded with people on mopeds. The chaos and energy were all a new experience to me. My mom and I felt a little nervous during the car ride to the hotel. Traffic lights and street signs were nonexistent; it was a wild free-for-all. At one point we closed our eyes, held on tightly to our seat belts, and hoped for the best.

Although I was riding in a taxi in a different country, dodging mopeds and crowds of people, I experienced a feeling of calmness. Calmness! You would think in all that hustle and bustle I would feel anything but calm! Yet, a feeling of serenity came over me.

Driving through *Thành phố Hồ Chí Minh*, *Hồ Chí Minh* City, I was amazed to see the beauty of both the people and the city itself. And although it does not fit the American standard, I loved that very special type of beauty. The French influence in architecture and the colorful streets made the city vibrant and full of life. Walking through the marketplace near our hotel, I was fascinated by the vendors on every corner selling everything from fruit, magazines, clothing, bags, jewelry, and anything else you could possibly ever think of.

Forty-three years had passed since my mom had seen her birthplace. While growing up, my mom told me stories of her early years in *Việt Nam*, but her childhood memories had grown dimmer with time. We planned to meet *Thanh* and *Phương* on the street where my mom grew up. It was the only street she remembered because she had fond memories of playing there with her best friend, *Nhàn*. While my grandmother, *Thanh* was at work, *Nhàn's* mom, *Ri* watched over them while they played.

Ri was like a second mom, constantly caring and providing for my mother. Unfortunately, after my mom left *Việt Nam*, she lost her Vietnamese identity. After being told her mother was dead, and after the subsequent loss of her precious yellow suitcase, she had only a few photos and her memories.

My mom's broken childhood and separation from her homeland faded her memories of her life in *Việt Nam*. Seeing *Phan Đình Phùng* brought back many memories, not only of her experiences as a young girl, but more importantly of who she was.

We drove around in what seemed like circles. All the streets and alleyways looked exactly the same. Since the street names had all been changed after the war, finding *Phan Đình Phùng* Street felt out of reach and somewhat impossible.

Finally, after what seemed like hours, *Thanh* pointed to a narrow dirt road with rundown brick apartments on either side. Down the alley clotheslines and houses with their front yards filled with gadgets and knickknacks waiting to be sold surrounded us on both sides.

As my grandmother, *Thanh* led us down the end of the alley, she paused and turned to my mom. They exchanged glances, and I was told we were standing in front of *Nhàn's* house. Before we entered, I felt anxious and nervous for my mom. After being separated from the people who loved and supported her, she would finally be able to be reunited with the lost family kin who had cared for her.

I shyly followed my mom through the entry door. Once inside, I noticed everyone's eyes immediately filled with tears. Watching them come together, I couldn't stop my own tears—nor did I try. *Ri's* family was so loving, and although the house was small, they welcomed us, revitalizing the wonderful memories of my mom's childhood. We all gathered around a table while *Nhàn* and my mom reminisced about the times they ran through the streets playing naked in the rain. Afterwards, *Ri* took us next door to my mom's old house.

When we finally stepped foot into the painful past and long lost memories of my mother's old house, I quietly held in tears of joy and sorrow: joy for my mother's ability to re-connect to her birthplace, home, and almost forgotten memories, and sorrow for the conditions of her childhood. Furthermore, I felt a deep sadness for all those who are forced to live the same unfair, impoverished lifestyle.

The house was a single, unfurnished room with bare walls projecting an empty, lifeless feeling of solitude. The unpainted, plastered walls and cement flooring had no warmth, no color, and no personality. I don't even recall ever seeing a bathroom in the house. The stairs that my mom had told me about were just to the right of me. These were the stairs that haunted my mom as a child. The sharp creaking noise my mom had remembered so vividly created a discomforting knot in my stomach.

As I was recording my mother's first steps of childhood and lost time in a house she had been separated from, I realized that she had been robbed of a place to call home. Though these four walls with no amenities, bathroom, or beds were hardly what most people in America would consider home, to my mom it was where she spent the first years of her life.

Being stripped away from her Vietnamese family and surroundings, she lost that sense of home, love, and family which children need, to grow. Until embarking on this journey with my mom, I never really understood how much she still suffered, even today, from the painful wounds of her childhood. Although it was in *Thanh's* best interest to send her daughter to America with the Mustards to live a better life, she did not know just how abandoned her little *Hiên* would feel in a strange new world.

She will never be able to regain her lost childhood, but seeing that house again with her mother brought back emotional and dramatic memories of love, family, pain, and a sense of belonging.

Mother and daughter relationships can be complicated at times, especially when language barriers stand in the way of communicating. This trip was meant to bring the family together, and while it did so on many levels there were still many missing pieces. It was painful to see that my mother's relationship with her biological mother was strained due to the language obstacle that forced them to speak nonverbally, diminishing their ability to become close as a mother and daughter should be.

Yes, they could send messages of love, happiness, pain, and other emotions through body language, gestures, and facial expressions, or thanks to *Phương's* translations. However, mother daughter bonds are made strong through self-disclosure, reciprocation, and sharing experiences and memories through words.

During the two weeks of our journey in which we tried to piece together my mom's past, I noticed something crucial; time is the most valuable essence of relationships. As my mom says, "You cannot gain back the time lost with a parent. You have to accept the relationship for what it can be, not for what it could have been."

The gray sky, polluted air, and chaos of *Hồ Chí Minh City* surprisingly grew on me, and I enjoyed the hustle and never ending entertainment that filled the streets. After being in the city for five days, we wanted to see the countryside of *Việt Nam* and took an eight-hour bus ride to the coastal city of *Nha Trang* to see the famous beaches, catch a glimpse of sunlight and get a breath of fresh air.

During our bus ride, I had to experience life without toilets or sanitation systems—a new experience for me. After a long, bumpy and questionable bus ride, I can vividly remember stopping in a small village outside *Nha Trang* for a restroom stop. Walking the dirt road to the brown wooden shacks that wreaked of urine and foul waste, I was a little skeptical about what lay ahead of me. I figured there would be port-a-potties similar to what we have in America. How wrong I was!

I hesitantly stepped inside the outhouse, plugging my nose. At first I was confused. There was a bucket to my right which gave off a strong stench of urine, and a hole in the ground to my left that was filled with waste. I turned to my mom with a slight smile and realized that this was truly an experience few Americans have or will ever have.

We hopped back onto the bus and arrived in *Nha Trang* a few hours later. My mom had booked a hotel with panoramic views, overlooking the ocean. It was beautiful, peaceful, and refreshing to see a different part of the country and its gorgeous landscape that I had heard so much about.

We arrived late at night and wanted an early start in the morning, so we opted for a good night's sleep and a fresh start. When we arrived at the hotel, we discovered it was standard, but perfect for a quick two-day trip. On the outside, the hotel was deceivingly beautiful and the architecture was very similar to that of American hotel chains; however, on the inside, it was cold and stark, resembling a hospital facility.

The halls were white and bare with bright lighting that flickered as we walked past. The doors to each room had small glass windows that reminded me of a psychiatric facility. The eerie tone and feeling of this hotel left an uncomfortable reaction in the bottom of my stomach. As we finally got to our room, I closely checked the perimeters and noticed that though it was not exactly a Hilton, it did have the panoramic ocean views they promised.

Despite our ocean views, I asked my mom if we could stay with *Phương, Cam and Alysé* since they also went to *Nha Trang* and were staying just blocks away from the hotel. With her nod of approval, we packed up our things and went to stay with them.

Their room had a much softer, comfortable feel than the hospital rooms had. Although there was only one bed, the five of us, *Phương, Alysé, Thanh,* my mom, and I all slept together that night cuddled up close to one another. It was the first time that we had all been in such close quarters, so intimate and vulnerable. Still being unable to express our true feelings verbally, my mom and I used our body language and closeness as a form of communicating our love to one another. This was one of the first times we all had spent the night together, as a family; I cherished this moment for I knew it might never happen again.

I often felt sorrow and guilt when crossing the streets of *Hồ Chí Minh City, Nha Trang,* and *Hà Nội.* The people came from nothing, begging for us to buy fruit, magazines, or whatever they were selling. I wanted to give whatever money I had. I wanted to take everyone under my wing and shelter them from the harsh cruelty and poverty that was brought upon them. Once in *Hà Nội,* the northern capital of *Việt Nam,* my mom and I toured *Vịnh Hạ Long, Halong Bay* where beautiful rock formations stand tall, jutting from the crystalline water.

The sights remain vivid in my imagination; the physical beauty and the children struggling to make ends meet reflect the country's double standard; the stunning views of the coast and formations, and the sadness of people starving, barely surviving without homes or proper care.

A young girl rowing her boat with fresh fruit surrounding her and a brave smile came close to our tour group, begging for someone to acknowledge her. I saw tears falling from her dark brown, sad eyes.

What would she do if her fruits did not sell? How would she make money to survive? I couldn't help but wonder how her life would be, if she did not have support from compassionate tourists like us. I knew I had to buy something. My mom and I went over to her boat. She wiped the tears from her cheek. "Won't you buy—won't you buy from me?" My heart sank. I was entrapped by her distressing, yet captivating gaze. My mom took out her wallet and handed her a few American dollars. In exchange, I opened the palm of my hand and reached for the bright colors of orange and pink fruit, ripe with sweetness that stood vibrant in the sunlight. Finally, the young girl gave a slight grin and rowed away.

We ran into these encounters everywhere, and my mom especially, could not help but give in to her motherly instincts. Her compassionate and nurturing spirit made it difficult to see the devastating conditions and poor health of these children. It made it almost impossible for my mom to control both her feelings and the emotional baggage that weighed heavily on her throughout our trip.

We spent our final few days in *Việt Nam* visiting *Hồ Chí Minh City*, taking in the last breadths of culture and history available to us. Though it would bring back faint memories of a terrible past and unforgettable experience, my mom's last stop would be the *Việt Nam* War Museum. After taking in the culture and being surrounded by such warm and friendly people, in contrast, the museum painted an ugly and horrific picture of the country's history.

The images decorating the walls of the museum did not hang in silence. Just by gazing into these picturesque figures, I saw the complete destruction of innocent Vietnamese civilians, children, and soldiers leaving nothing to the imagination.

Bloodshed, mutilations, destroyed villages and remnants of dead bodies were all painted clearly, sending chills from head to toe throughout my frozen body. The remaining war destruction is an ongoing battle for the people in *Việt Nam*.

The mass amounts of Agent Orange, herbicides, and Napalm bombs dropped over their land left villages and crops destroyed and people either disfigured or burned to death. The atrocious scars of the war still remain. Seeing pictures of innocent children and civilians affected from the aftermath of the war was truly devastating and left us heartbroken and emotionally drained.

As our trip came to an end, I felt there was so much more to learn about my mom's history and the Vietnamese culture. I wasn't ready to leave. In just a short time I bonded to my mom's native land and struggled with my departure.

I feel blessed and so fortunate that I was able to accompany my mom on her first trip back to *Việt Nam* since her childhood.

What would her life have been like if she would have remained *Hiên,* the little Vietnamese girl? Would she have survived the war? Would she have grown up with the love and support that she lacked and yearned for while living with the Mustards? All these questions were troubling, leaving me pondering "what ifs" all during the plane ride home.

Undoubtedly, it took tremendous courage for my mother to relive her painful past and her separation from her mother at *Tân Sơn Nhất* Airport as a young girl. Left with so many questions and no means to find answers, she truly took steps few would be willing to do in order to find the truth. Although my mother experienced abuse and neglect and was emotionally scarred, she has overcome these obstacles by finally facing her demons and moving forward to start a new chapter. She has become more involved in the Vietnamese community and will soon be returning to *Việt Nam* to help orphaned children.

My mother possesses some extraordinary characteristics that no other person I know has. She has an indomitable will to succeed in everything she strives for. With age, I have noticed she gives off a presence that captivates her friends, family, colleagues, and even strangers.

It is no wonder that I someday hope to encompass the traits and characteristics my mom possess. My mom is a phenomenal woman. Undeniably, I have some huge shoes to fill.

—Jenna Reed

AFTERWORD

In reading my daughter, Jenna's reflections of our trip to *Việt Nam*, I discovered that our journey answered many unanswered questions, offering me the closure I needed to move on with my life. It was a journey that involved three continents and many interviews and translations, as well as endless days and nights of trying to piece together all the information I gathered.

Forty-three years later, on December 24, 2006, I returned 'home' with my mother, daughter, Jenna and sister, *Phương* and her family. Jenna's presence by my side was especially moving as I was able to share all my emotional feelings, which she so adequately described in the Epilogue.

This book was indeed a journey; a journey to find myself; a journey to unite *Nguyễn Thị Thanh Hiên* and Mary Mustard

Reed. It was a journey to fill in the missing pages of who I am. Although it did not end with the "lived happily ever after" fairly tale conclusion I always fantasized about, it has given me great inner peace.

I spent many years trying to come to terms with all the emotional feelings and doubts that have bothered me since childhood. After a slow, lengthy, often painful process, I learned about acceptance, forgiveness, healing and how to deal with the past. This part of the journey involved reliving a lot of agonizing memories and forced me to look at my life through the eyes of an adopted child. Yet, despite all the tears and heartaches, it has been very cathartic in allowing me to release many of the pent-up feelings associated with a child's feelings of being 'abandoned' and adopted. Today, I am able to understand what I was unable to years ago

You can live your whole life thinking of all the "what ifs." However, in the end you should accept and enjoy the life you have in the present moment. I am particularly grateful for the wonderful relationships I have developed with two of my siblings—*Phương*, her husband and daughter as well as my English speaking brother, *Việt* from Paris.

Much good has resulted from this book. I have become more involved in the Vietnamese community and have re-connected with the Vietnamese culture, thus rekindling a pride in my own heritage. And at the end of October I will be returning to *Việt Nam* to help orphaned children through a non-profit humanitarian initiative called Project Vietnam, www.projectvietnam.net.

My siblings have also been grateful, because through our lengthy conversations as well as my endless questions, they, too, were able to uncover so much more information about our mom's early life.

I am also thankful that my mom is still young enough to help me uncover the truth and to know that with this book, I will be able to leave behind the history of our Vietnamese family and many childhood memories for my own children and future generations.

Although the Mustards did not give me many pleasant memories or a worthwhile legacy, they did leave behind several slides. However, I had neither the strength nor courage to actually preview them until I wrote the final words to this book. Fear of rekindling negative memories forced me to deny their existence. But having experienced healing, I decided to conquer my apprehension and incorporate the photos in my book as part of my memoir.

My story is about adoption and how early on, I was taught to reject my culture, therefore causing me to be embarrassed about who I was and where I came from. Had my adopted parents allowed me to embrace and be proud of my heritage and culture, maybe I wouldn't have lost my identity and lived my life as a child without a country. To have finally been able to re-connect with my family and roots has been a life-changing experience that can be relative to anyone's life today. This is the underlying purpose of my journey—to prevent other adopted children from feeling lost and alone. Although I suffered hardships, I have to say that I never lived my life as a victim. I was and am a survivor!

—*Nguyễn Thị Thanh Hiên* aka Mary Mustard Reed

PHƯƠNG'S LETTER

H^{i *Hiên*,}

I called Mom this morning and talked a lot with her regarding your "final pieces" for the book. I also told her about your next trip to *Việt Nam* in October to help the orphans, and she is so happy. She told me very emotionally, "*Phương,* I would like to share every moment with *Hiên*, since she left. I want to tell her how much I missed her."

Hiên, Mom also said, "If it wasn't for the Red Cross and *Hiên*, I would have never seen her again." Although happy, she is also sad because she can't share these feelings with you. Mom still has the image of you when you left *Việt Nam*—you were never forgotten.

During the journey back to the USA last year, after our trip to *Việt Nam*, she said in tears, "I still have so much to tell *Hiên,* but I'm afraid I can't share these thoughts and feelings since she doesn't understand Vietnamese."

Mom has a lot to tell you—much more than all of us, because you are the eldest. *Hiên,* you are her first child and your father was the first man she ever loved. I think Mom still has many things to talk to you about—things she never told any of us.

She knows your book is almost done, and she is really happy and excited. She is also sad that because of the language problem she will not be able to read it. However, she knows you always wanted to write this book to share with your children and grand-children and is pleased to know that after ten years of planning it has be born.

Last night *Bích Nga* said, "*Phương, please* tell *Hiên* that all her siblings in France support her the maximum for her book." But, she said, giggling, "Just tell *Hiên* to please cover my picture!"

She also said, "I know my name, *Bích Nga* means a lot to *Hiên*." She says you need to put all your feelings in the book. *Bích Nga* will be happy you mentioned her. But she wants you to learn Vietnamese!

OK, *Hiên,* I hope this will help you to finish the book!

—*Phương*